Forrester Square

LEGACIES . LIES . LOVE .

SANDRA MARTON
RING OF DECEPTION

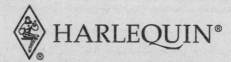

D0288414

HARLEQUIN®

TORONTO • NEW YORK • LONDON
AMSTERDAM • PARIS • SYDNEY • HAMBURG
STOCKHOLM • ATHENS • TOKYO • MILAN • MADRID
PRAGUE • WARSAW • BUDAPEST • AUCKLAND

HARLEQUIN BOOKS
225 Duncan Mill Road, Don Mills,
Ontario, Canada M3B 3K9

ISBN-13: 978-0-373-61271-0
ISBN-10:   0-373-61271-0

RING OF DECEPTION

Sandra Marton is acknowledged as the author of this work.

Copyright © 2003 by Harlequin Books S.A.

This edition published by arrangement with Harlequin Books S.A.

® and TM are trademarks of the publisher. Trademarks indicated with ® are registered in the United States Patent and Trademark Office, the Canadian Trade Marks Office and in other countries.

Visit us at www.eHarlequin.com

Printed in U.S.A.

Dear Reader,

I am bubbling with excitement over my newest book, *Ring of Deception*. When you meet my hero, Luke Sloan, you'll know why. Luke is sexy, gorgeous, tough on the outside and vulnerable on the inside. What more could a woman ask for?

Well, if she's my heroine, Abby Douglas, she might ask to be left alone. Abby's tried love. It doesn't work. Now she has a child to raise, a job to keep, and there's no room in her life for any man, especially one who's liable to ask too many questions.

But asking questions is what Luke does. He's a Seattle police detective, street-smart and accustomed to dealing with hardened criminals. His newest assignment sounds impossible. Luke's going to do surveillance on a jewelry store by going undercover…in a day-care center! He expects the job to be boring, but he's in for a surprise. It's going to be his greatest challenge. Can he handle a brave woman with a secret and a bright little girl who'll steal his heart? And what of his vows as a cop? Will they stand up to his terrible suspicions that Abby is somehow mixed up in a ring of jewel thieves?

Now you can see why I'm excited about this book. I hope you enjoy reading *Ring of Deception* as much as I enjoyed writing it!

With love,

Sandra Marton

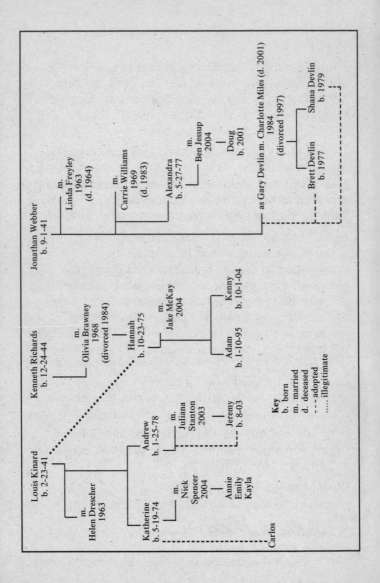

Jonathan Webber
b. 9-1-41

m.
Linda Freyley
1963
(d. 1964)

m.
Carrie Williams
1969
(d. 1983)

Alexandra
b. 5-27-77

m.
Ben Jessup
2004

Doug
b. 2001

as Gary Devlin m. Charlotte Miles (d. 2001)
1984
(divorced 1997)

Brett Devlin
b. 1977

Shana Devlin
b. 1979

Kenneth Richards
b. 12-24-44

m.
Olivia Brawney
1968
(divorced 1984)

Hannah
b. 10-23-75

m.
Jake McKay
2004

Adam
b. 1-10-95

Kenny
b. 10-1-04

Louis Kinard
b. 2-23-41

m.
Helen Drescher
1963

Katherine
b. 5-19-74

m.
Nick Spencer
2004

Annie
Emily
Kayla

Andrew
b. 1-25-78

m.
Juliana Stanton
2003

Jeremy
b. 8-03

Carlos

Key
b. born
m. married
d. deceased
– – – adopted
.... illegitimate

CHAPTER ONE

THE ALARM ON LUKE SLOAN'S clock radio went off at 6:00 a.m.

Luke rolled over on his belly, reached out and slapped it to silence with a perfect aim born of familiarity.

Five minutes later, the alarm screamed again. This time, he let it ring long enough for the unholy shrieking to pierce his sleep-fogged brain. Then he opened one eye, reached out and flipped the switch from Alarm to Radio.

"Cloudy this morning…" a voice said with effusive good cheer, "with showers this afternoon and evening. Heavier cloudbursts possible overnight and tomorrow…"

Luke grunted. Rain and more rain. What a surprise. The guy doing the weather sounded as if he'd just discovered he was living in Seattle.

Rolling onto his back, he stacked his hands beneath his head as the weatherman finally shut up and an old Doors tune came on. Jim Morrison still wanted somebody to light his fire. Luke listened for a couple of minutes, then decided the only thing that would get his fire lit was a pair of extra-strength aspirin.

He sat up, silenced the radio and headed for the bathroom. His head hurt, his mouth was dry and his sinuses felt like they'd been stuffed with quick-hardening cement. It would have been nice to blame it all on last night's celebratory stop at the Nine-Thirty-One Tavern with Dan, but he couldn't.

Dan had ordered a beer; Luke had ordered a shot of rock and rye.

"Cold coming on," he'd said when Dan looked at him as if he'd just sprouted horns.

"Ah." Dan had nodded as he scooped up a handful of peanuts and popped a couple in his mouth. "I was wondering why you looked like day-old crap."

"Thank you," Luke replied. "I really needed to hear that."

"Why don't you come home with me? Molly made chicken soup yesterday. A couple of bowls, you'll feel like a new man."

"Thanks, but I think what I need is a good night's sleep."

Lacey, a stacked brunette barmaid with a way of looking at Luke as if he had a big red *S* on his chest, leaned over the bar.

"How about coming home with me? I'll open a can of Campbell's Chicken Noodle. It's not homemade, but there are other things I can do to make you feel like a new man."

"Oh, to be thirty-five and single again," Dan joked.

Luke had grinned and exchanged the expected male-female banter with Lacey, but he'd gone home without either Lacey or a cup of Molly's soup. He loved Molly like a sister. As for Lacey…a man would have to be blind not to see that she was a stunner.

But if he went home with Dan, Molly would ply him with soup while she talked up her latest "find," a single woman who was, she'd assure him, everything he wanted in a woman.

And if he went home with Lacey, he'd just complicate his life. She'd ply him with the lush pleasures of her body, and afterward, she'd expect…what? Maybe just a smile. Then again, based on the looks she'd been tossing at him lately, maybe more than that.

More was the last thing Luke wanted. As the saying went, he'd been there, done that—done it legally, moreover, marriage license, chapel and all—and it hadn't worked.

So he was, as Dan had pointed out, thirty-five and single. He liked it that way. Besides, he wasn't the kind of guy who could do a one-night stand with a woman who wanted more, and then keep seeing her day after day, which was how it would go with Lacey. Nine-Thirty-One was a hangout for the precinct detectives, so he'd had to pass—if reluctantly—on Lacey's generous offer.

Luke flushed the toilet, went to the bathroom cabinet and caught a glimpse of himself in the mirror. Hell, what a mess.

His green eyes were red-rimmed, his nose was pink, and the light stubble on his jaw made his high cheekbones stand out in stark relief.

Forget a pair of aspirin. Four was more like it. He dumped the tablets into his mouth, turned on the faucet, cupped his hand under the water and gulped some down. Then he shucked off his white boxers, stepped into the shower and turned the water as hot as he could stand it.

Hands flat against the tile, head bowed so the water could beat down on the nape of his neck, Luke gave himself up to the heat and the steam. Steam wasn't chicken soup. Nor was it an old-fashioned sweat lodge, the kind he'd tried years ago while visiting an Oglala Sioux cousin in North Dakota. But after a few minutes, between the aspirin and the warmth, he began to feel better.

Naked, just a towel wrapped around his hips, he walked into the kitchen of his condo, took a container of orange juice from the refrigerator and lifted it to his lips.

One thing about living alone, you could do stuff like that.

Back in his bedroom, he pulled on a pair of running shorts, ancient Nikes and a faded T-shirt emblazoned with a Thunderbird clasping a whale in its talons. Then he pulled his long black hair back from his face and caught it at the base of his neck with a narrow length of rawhide.

The rain had slowed to a drizzle. Not that it mattered. Luke ran in all kinds of weather. Besides, he thought wryly, a run in the rain would either cure his cold or give him pneumonia…and at least there was a cure for that.

An hour later, he came puffing back into his apartment, soaked to the skin but feeling closer to human. The light on his answering machine was blinking. Luke hit the play button. The message was probably from Molly, calling to scold him for not coming home with Dan for a cup of her homemade penicillin last night.

But it wasn't Molly, it was the captain's clerk, calling to tell him that Lieutenant McDowell wanted to see him at 8:00 a.m. and would that be convenient?

Convenient?

Luke shot the answering machine a look that some of the suspects he'd questioned during the past four years, ever since he'd made detective, would have recognized. The lieutenant or the clerk must be having a good laugh—except that nobody had ever seen either of them smile, much less laugh.

Maybe he'd heard the message wrong.

He toed off his Nikes, tugged his soaked T-shirt over his head and stripped off his shorts. The phone rang just as he reached toward the play button.

"Sloan."

"Molly wants to know how you're feeling."

Luke smiled, tucked the phone between his ear and his shoulder and headed for the bathroom.

"Better than yesterday, and curious about today."

"Why? What's up?"

"I just got a message from the captain's clerk. The lieutenant wants to see me when I get in."

"And?"

"And…I don't know anything more than that." Luke hesitated. "Dan? You think maybe the lieutenant developed a sense of humor?"

"See, I knew you should have come home with me last night. You need Molly's soup, Luke. You must be running a fever."

"You could be right. Either I'm hallucinating, or the message on my machine says I should see him at eight…if it's convenient."

"If it's…?" Dan gave a gusty sigh. "Man, you're in deeper do-do than usual. What'd you do to piss him off this time?"

Luke grinned. "Nothing more than usual. Why?"

"Well, last time I know of he used the word *convenient* was maybe three, four years ago. Right before you got made. He asked Rutledge if it was convenient for him to stop by his office at six one evening. You ever know Rutledge? Tall, mustache— looked like John Q. Public's idea of a detective."

"Yeah, I heard about him. The guy who couldn't have found an elephant in a phone booth with a sack of peanuts in his pocket."

"That's the one."

"So? What happened?"

"McDowell told Rutledge he was putting him on a special detail."

Luke opened the shower stall door, turned on the water, then closed the door again.

"Which was?"

"Which was, handing him over to that TV anchor with the hairpiece for a PR stint. Well, he wasn't an anchor then, but you know who I mean—the guy who can't walk by a mirror without kissing his reflection. After a week, even Rutledge was going nuts."

Luke sat down on the closed commode. "In other words," he said slowly, "'convenient' is a polite way of saying 'smile and grab your ankles, pal. You're about to get screwed.'"

"Yeah," Dan said mournfully, "and not by a babe like that lady last night. What? No, Molly. Honey, I was just—of course not. Would I even notice another woman when I can come home to you? Molly. Baby…"

Luke chuckled. "See you in an hour."

He put down the phone, stepped into the shower and turned the water on full force.

Dan tended to look at the down side of things. Rutledge had always been an ass; he'd deserved an assignment that paired him with another ass. But Luke knew he was—well, without being too immodest, he was good. He cleared most of his cases and he had an impressive arrest record.

During his five years in uniform, he'd taken down more than his fair share of the lowlifes he encountered. Once he'd been made a detective, he'd busted burglars, pornographers, a child kidnapper and a killer.

Turning his face up to the spray, he let the warm water do its job.

No way would the lieutenant waste him on some idiotic PR thing.

No way whatsoever.

BY EIGHT-FIFTEEN, LUKE KNEW he was right.

The lieutenant didn't want to waste him in an idiotic PR

thing. He wanted to use him in something worse. He hadn't said so. Not yet, but Luke could feel it coming.

First there'd been a handshake and congratulations about yesterday's collar. He and Dan had put in two months working on a dozen cases of home-invasion robberies and finally caught the vicious SOB who'd been busting into the homes of the elderly, stealing whatever he could, and beating up the frail victims just for kicks.

"Good job, Sloan," McDowell said, to start their meeting.

Then he motioned Luke to a chair and made what was supposed to be some meaningful small talk along with lots of serious eye contact.

The lieutenant, like most of the bosses, had taken a management seminar on how to encourage subordinates to feel like part of the team. The looking-deep-into-the-eyes thing was one of the techniques.

Luke knew that because he'd leafed through a syllabus he'd found lying around.

Lieutenant McDowell wasn't particularly good at the deep eye contact. He'd come to the department from the mayor's office, and if he had something to tell you, he had a tendency to yell and get red in the face.

That he wasn't even raising his voice, but was doing this by the syllabus, made Luke nervous.

Then he offered Luke a cup of coffee. Starbucks, by the taste of it, and one thousand percent better than the sludge they brewed in the squad room.

"Cream?" the lieutenant asked, and that was when Luke knew that whatever came next would not be pleasant.

"No," Luke said politely, "I'm fine."

"Sound a little husky, Sloan. Got a cold?"

"I do, yeah."

"My wife swears by horehound drops. Might want to try some."

A polite invitation, coffee, an offer to add cream to that coffee, and now some fatherly advice. No, this was not good.

"I'll do that," Luke said, and waited.

McDowell sat back in his chair and tented his fingers under his chin. ''Well,'' he said, ''you must be wondering why I called you in today.''

Luke said nothing. Back when he was a marine, he'd learned the drill. Keep your mouth shut and wait. You'd find out what was going on sooner or later. That worked in a cop's world, too.

McDowell cleared his throat, rose from his desk and walked to a wall map of Seattle. He stabbed a finger at the northwestern section of the city and raised an eyebrow at Luke.

''Some very expensive real estate up here,'' he said.

Luke muffled a sneeze. ''Uh-huh.''

''I guess you've heard about the robberies in the area the last few months.''

Now they were getting down to it. Luke began to relax. Maybe he'd misjudged things. Maybe McDowell was the victim of another management seminar, this one on issuing summonses to his office that didn't sound like summonses.

''I heard something about a cat burglar doing his thing.''

''At first. But our perp's gone from playing it cool and careful to strong-arm tactics. Comes in when he knows somebody's home, frightens them half to death, roughs them up if they don't move fast enough.''

''Sounds like a real nice guy.''

''Uh-huh. His taste is good, too. He takes only what they call estate jewelry, meaning it's old and expensive.''

''What more do we know?''

''Well, we had a report of one of the missing pieces possibly turning up on the market.''

''Possibly?''

''Yeah. And not in your usual kind of market, Sloan. This wasn't a pawnshop.''

''What was it, then?''

The lieutenant sat down behind his desk. ''Ever hear of the Emerald City Jewelry Exchange?''

''Sure. Big place, expensive by the looks of it. On a street over in Belltown.'' Luke cocked his head. ''Wait a minute. Are you saying somebody at Emerald City is fencing stolen jewelry?''

The lieutenant allowed himself a quick smile. ''I'm not saying a thing. Not yet.''

''But?''

''But a lady called last week, all upset. Said she'd just come from there and swore she spotted a necklace that was the duplicate of one stolen from her. It was lying in a corner of a display case.''

''And?''

''Let's put it this way. The lady in question is ninety-three, wears a hearing aid in each ear and glasses thick as Coke bottles. During the original interview, she told the detective who took the squeal that she's being pestered by aliens from outer space who talk to her through her Persian cat.''

Luke grinned. ''Uh-huh.''

''The detective paid her another visit, chatted with a maid who said the old girl's okay most of the time but, well, every now and then she has a little trouble with reality.''

''Not the world's most reliable complainant,'' Luke said with a nod.

''On the other hand, the maid was with her that day. She says when the old woman gasped and pointed at the corner of the case, she looked, too, and she thinks maybe it really was the necklace.''

''Maybe?''

McDowell shrugged. '''Maybe's' about it.''

''Did they say anything to anybody in the store?''

''No, not a word. They went straight outside and phoned us.''

''So, what we've got is an old lady with a screw loose, and a maid who thinks maybe she saw something...and maybe she didn't.''

''Exactly. That's why we have to move carefully on this.''

''I assume somebody checked the display case in the store.''

''Sure. The detective went in, she took a look, didn't see a thing.''

"And she interviewed the people who work at the exchange?"

McDowell shifted uncomfortably in his swivel chair. "The place is owned by Julian Black. Name ring any bells? No? Well, Black's at the top of the food chain. Good-looking guy, rich, supposed to be as honest as George Washington...and he's active in civic affairs."

Luke folded his arms. "You mean, he knows all the right people."

"You say that like it's an obscenity, Sloan, but that's how things work. Black's on a first-name basis with the governor, he served on the mayor's recent ad hoc arts commission, and I'd be a fool to drag this department into a swamp until I know how deep the mud's going to get."

"Simply interviewing his clerks wouldn't be..."

"It would," McDowell said firmly. "Seattle's best families buy their toys at Emerald City. The last thing people like that want is cops swarming over the place, giving it a bad name."

"Yeah. Okay. I can see that."

"I thought you would. That's why you're going to set up a surveillance."

Luke nodded. He hated doing surveillance. It was almost as dull as watching grass grow, but that was where he'd figured this was going.

"Okay."

"You'll have a camcorder so you can get tape of anything that looks interesting."

"Where am I doing this? In a van on the street or is there a parking lot?"

For the first time since their meeting had started, McDowell looked uncomfortable.

"We've arranged for you to set up the camera and equipment across the street, at a place where you can have an unimpeded view of the exchange, where you can hang around for hours and nobody will figure you for a cop."

Luke frowned, thought about the street the exchange was on, and came up with what he assumed was the place he'd be setting up shop.

"I've got it. That café—what's it called? Caffeine some-thing." He snapped his fingers. "Caffeine Hy's. Yeah, I guess that'll work." He grinned as he began to rise from his chair. "Although I'll probably swear off coffee by the time I—"

"Not the coffee shop."

"No?" Luke sank into the seat again. "Maybe I'm thinking of the wrong street."

"You've got the right street, Sloan, just the wrong spot for the stakeout." McDowell picked up a pencil and tapped it on the edge of his desk. "You're going into the Forrester Square Day Care Center."

Luke blinked. "What?"

"I said, we're setting you up in—"

"A day care center?"

"Right."

"Day care for what?" Luke said slowly. "Dogs? Cats? Ca-naries?"

"Very funny." McDowell's voice was flat. "Kids. Babies through kindergarten. You're going to be a teacher's aide."

Luke stared at the lieutenant. He thought about what he knew about kids, which was exactly zero. He thought about what he *wanted* to know about kids, which was even less than that.

"Is this a joke?"

"The center is directly across from the exchange. It has a window in a fairly quiet location that looks out on the street." McDowell tugged a file toward him, opened it and quickly scanned the top page. "There are three owners—Hannah Rich-ards, Alexandra Webber and Katherine Kinard. Our people have spoken with them—well, more specifically, with the Kin-ard woman and her attorney. She's agreed to cooperate."

"Lieutenant, whoever came up with this plan is crazy. Ex-cuse me, sir, for being blunt, but setting up a surveillance in a day care center, asking me to deal with babies is—"

"I came up with it," McDowell said, his eyes riveted to Luke's. "And I'm not asking you, Sloan. I'm telling you."

"I don't know the first thing about kids."

"You'll learn."

"I don't *like* kids."

"Ever spent any time around them?"

"No!"

"Well, that's why you think you don't like them. You're a quick study, Sloan. Just pay attention to what Ms. Kinard tells you, you'll be fine."

"Lieutenant," Luke said desperately, "a female detective would—"

"The place is open Mondays through Fridays, so you won't be able to use it for surveillance of the jewelry exchange on Saturdays. Dan Shayne will take Saturdays. He'll set up in a van on the street. Other times, he'll do whatever legwork, paper stuff you might need."

"Lieutenant. Really, a woman would—"

"Here's what little we have on the Emerald City Jewelry Exchange, its employees and Julian Black."

McDowell got to his feet and held out the folder, indicating the meeting was over. Luke stared at him for two or three seconds. Then he stood up, too.

"Susan. Susan Wu," he said desperately. "She's one hell of a good detective, she has grandchildren, she *likes* kids."

"An excellent choice."

Luke let out his breath. "Well, then, sir…"

"Unfortunately, Wu is in the hospital with appendicitis." McDowell shoved the folder at Luke and fixed him with the sort of look he remembered from his days in the corps. "Anything else, Detective Sloan?"

Luke had taken on men twice his size, fought battles he'd never expected to win, but he wasn't a fool. There was no way to win a war with McDowell unless he wanted to find himself in uniform again.

"No, sir," he said, took the folder and went to meet his fate.

AN HOUR LATER, LUKE SAT in a chair, staring at a woman seated behind the business side of a desk so neat and uncluttered it made him nervous.

Katherine Kinard wasn't making him nervous, however. What she was doing was pissing him off. From the look on her face when he'd walked into her office and introduced him-

self as the detective who'd be working undercover at her day
care center, he might as well have been Ivan the Terrible.

"You?" she'd said, her eyes round with shock. "*You're* the
undercover police officer? But my attorney—Daniel Adler—
said you'd be... He spoke with someone in your department,
and they promised him you'd be a woman."

Luke lifted one dark eyebrow. "Trust me, Ms. Kinard. I'm
not."

"He said you'd be middle-aged and motherly, someone the
children would love."

"Believe me, I'm no happier about this than you are."

"What do you know about children, Officer—Officer...?"

"Detective. Detective Luke Sloan. I don't know a damned
thing about them."

"We don't curse at Forrester Square Day Care, Detective."

"I'll bet you don't." Luke glared at his supposed new employer. She glared back. "Look, I told you, I'm no happier
than you are, but—"

Katherine held up her hand, reached for the phone and
punched a speed-dial button. "One moment, please, Detective.
No, don't bother getting up. I'm going to call Mr. Adler and
see what he...Daniel? Yes, it's Katherine. I'm fine, thank you.
Look, Daniel..." She rolled her eyes. "That's great. Yes, it is
difficult to get tickets for... Alexandra is fine, too, thank you.
Yes. Much better. She's even starting to talk about moving out
of my place and getting an apartment of her own. Right. I do
see that as a good sign."

Luke tried not to listen, but it was impossible. Besides, he
wasn't hearing anything he didn't already know. The "Alexandra" Katherine Kinard was talking about was undoubtedly
Alexandra Webber. McDowell had told him Forrester Square
Day Care was run by three women: Alexandra Webber, Hannah
Richards and the woman sitting at her desk, who was doing
her best to get rid of him.

He could only hope she managed to pull it off.

Luke rose to his feet. The Kinard woman looked up inquir-
ingly.

"Take your time," Luke said politely. "I'll just stroll around your office and try to get a feel for what the place is like."

It took less than ten seconds to decide that what the place was like was the inside of a loony bin after the art therapist finished a session with the inmates.

Luke stood, transfixed, before a sheet of paper tacked to a beaverboard wall. The paper was covered with swirls and stripes of red, yellow and blue and was only one of what looked like a hundred similar sheets of paper.

Slowly, he walked the length of the wall. What were all these brushstrokes supposed to represent? That thing had to be a tree. And a dog...well, no. He'd never seen a blue dog with six legs. That had to be a house. A man, a woman, a child. And a bird in the sky...or was it an airplane?

Hell, he thought, and walked toward the window that looked out onto the Emerald City Jewelry Exchange, directly across the street. The floor space all around him was crowded with stacks of books and boxes.

The lady needed a good carpenter. Some shelves, some cabinets and cupboards—

"Detective?"

Luke swung around. Katherine Kinard was staring at him and trying to smile. She was a nice-looking woman, not his type at all, but he'd kiss her smack on the lips if it turned out she and her lawyer had enough clout to get him taken the hell out of here.

"Well, Detective, it looks as if you're going to be working here for a while."

Luke groaned. Kinard looked startled, and then she laughed.

"My feelings, exactly. Understand, it's nothing personal."

"The same here, Ms. Kinard."

"Please, call me Katherine. If you're going to be an aide here—"

"I have to admit, I was pulling for you and your attorney."

Katherine sighed. "Seems they really did have a female detective lined up, but she came down with—"

"Appendicitis. I know."

"Mr. Adler called your lieutenant while I was on the

phone.'' She pushed back her chair. ''I guess we'll just have to make the best of it. I've already had my partners, Hannah and Alexandra, relocate upstairs for as long as you're here.'' She waved a hand at the two vacated desks in the room. ''They share this office with me, but we decided you'd be able to work better with fewer people around. They'll be in and out from time to time, of course. Now, we thought that you could work with one of our teachers and a group of about ten children, and— What's the matter?''

''I have a job to do, Katherine. I don't know how much they told you....''

''They told me nothing whatsoever. Police business, they said. That was it.'' She cocked her head. ''I don't suppose you'd like to tell me more?''

''Sorry. All I can say is that my work here involves steady surveillance. I can't possibly do what I'm here to do and work with ten kids at the same time.''

''Well, then, Detective, I don't know—''

''Call me Luke. Nobody here must know I'm a cop.''

''Yes, but you just said—''

''I have an idea,'' Luke said slowly. He jerked his head toward the window. ''Were you planning on turning that area into something particular?''

''You mean, something instead of a disaster zone?'' Katherine sighed. ''Someday, when I have the time and the money, we'll put in shelves and—''

''And cabinets and cupboards.'' Luke nodded. An idea was slowly coming together in his mind. If he brought in some tools, some wood... ''How'd you like that stuff built right now?''

''I'm afraid I don't understand.''

''I wasn't always a cop. There was a time I was pretty handy with a hammer and saw. Suppose I come in as a handyman instead of a teacher's aide? That way, I can keep my attention where it's supposed to be—and you won't have to worry about me scaring the kiddies out of their skin.''

''Oh, I wasn't...'' Katherine smiled. ''Okay. Maybe I was a little concerned. And I have to admit, your idea makes sense, but how long will your assignment here last? Will it be long enough to complete shelves and cabinets?''

Luke grinned. ''Sounds like a plan, huh?''

''It does—but what if you can't finish the job?''

''If I can't, you'll have to hire a real carpenter to do the rest of the work. Look, Katherine, I know this is an imposition, but we're both stuck with it.''

Katherine nodded. ''You're right, Detective—Luke, I mean. Just remember, please, that children are in and out of my office all the time. Parents, too, so if you'd try to, um, to, uh—'' She licked her lips. ''You're so big. The kids might find that overwhelming. And if you'd, uh, if you'd smile more often, and watch your language…''

''I'll be charming, I'll clean up my language, and if I can find a way to shrink from six foot two to two foot six, I'll do it,'' Luke said without a smile. ''All right?''

''I'm not trying to be inhospitable, Detective—''

''Luke,'' Luke said again. ''And I'm not trying to be unpleasant. I just think we're both going to have to make accommodations for a situation neither of us likes very much.''

Katherine Kinard nodded glumly. ''I guess you're right.'' She forced a smile; he could almost see the wheels grinding as she searched for a couple of friendly words. ''That cold of yours,'' she finally said, ''you might want to try vitamin C.''

Advice from Dan. From a barmaid. From the lieutenant, and now from Katherine Kinard. What he really needed was somebody to jump out and say, *Surprise! This is all just a bad dream.*

But it wasn't, and he let his polite smile fade a couple of minutes later as he headed for the main door and tried not to sneeze, not to acknowledge the headache that had returned, big time, not to step on any of the munchkins zipping around.

He'd head home, change his clothes and pick up his old carpentry tools. Then he'd stop by the squad room and sign out a camcorder plus some other stuff he'd need, and hope to hell he caught somebody fencing jewels at Emerald City in record—

The door swung open just as he reached for it. Next thing

he knew, he was doing the two-step, trying to avoid walking through a woman and a little kid, but he ended up bumping into the woman, anyway.

"Isn't he s'posed to say he's sorry?" the kid said, looking up at her mother.

Luke gritted his teeth. Great. Now he was getting lessons in etiquette from a preschooler.

"Sorry," he growled, but the kid was no fool.

"He doesn't sound very sorry, Mommy."

The kid's mother hauled her back against her legs. "Emily," she said quickly, "hush!"

Luke looked at the woman. She was a hazel-eyed brunette, maybe five six, five seven. No more his type than Katherine Kinard was, but he had to admit she was pretty.

In fact, maybe she *was* his type. Maybe under normal circumstances he'd have given the woman a slow, appraising look and an even slower smile. He wasn't interested in playing around close to the job, but he wasn't dead, either. When he saw a good-looking woman, he was interested.

But his mood was foul and both the kid and her mother were looking at him as if he might morph into a monster who ate children for breakfast. Why disappoint them?

"Emily didn't mean—"

"Save it," he growled. "And maybe you ought to teach the kid not to talk to strangers."

The brunette gasped, the little girl's mouth began to tremble, and Luke headed for his car feeling pretty much as if he'd just kicked a puppy.

It was a bad feeling for a man who'd never kicked anything except a bad guy who'd been trying to kick him. Still, he'd given the woman good advice....

Who was he kidding?

Luke got into his car, pulled away from the curb and told himself he was going to have to improve his attitude, or both he and Forrester Square Day Care were in for a really miserable time.

CHAPTER TWO

Abby Douglas stared after the man.

Even from the back, he looked as rough as he'd sounded. Tall. Big shoulders. Long black hair caught at the nape of his neck. And a way of walking that said he owned the world and everything in it.

Maybe you should teach your kid not to talk to strangers.

She *had* taught that to Emily, drummed it into her head over and over. Her little girl knew that litany better than most four-year-olds.

She had to, because there was always the chance that Frank, or someone hired by Frank, might be out there trying to find her.

Trying to find the both of them.

If a stranger comes up to you, she'd told Emily, walk away. Don't answer any questions. Don't listen to stories about daddies wanting to find their little girls, or strangers wanting help finding lost puppies. And if somebody tries to touch you, run, run, run.

But that wasn't what had happened. The man hadn't sought Emily out. He hadn't even spoken to her, not until he overheard her childish comment.

Still, the incident had shaken Abby.

She'd thought she was long past that rush of terror, the thump in her chest, the suffocating panic that came of suddenly being confronted by a glowering man who was physically intimidating....

Who really hadn't done anything but react to a child's innocently made comment.

"Mommy?"

The man hadn't showed interest in her or in Emily. He was just an unpleasant stranger and he didn't have a damned thing to do with her ex-husband. All true, but logic didn't matter. One snarl, one growl, and all the old fears came right to the surface.

Damn it, Abby thought angrily, could she still fall apart that easily?

"Mom?"

A little hand tugged on her skirt. Abby blinked, looked down into her daughter's upturned face and saw the telltale glimmer of tears on her lashes.

"Oh, honey!" She bent down, clasped her child's shoulders and dropped a gentle kiss on her forehead. "Don't be upset, Em. That man was just—"

"He yelled at you."

"No. He wasn't exactly yelling, baby. He was just…"

"Daddy used to yell." Emily's voice quavered. "I 'member."

Abby's heart turned over. How could her little girl remember that? She'd left Frank when her baby was two…but children sometimes stored up things subconsciously.

A social worker had mentioned that at the shelter back in Eugene. Katherine Kinard had said something similar during a parents' coffee klatch. A worried-looking father had mentioned that his son had had a bad experience in day care when he was only a couple of years old, and that he still remembered it.

That happened, Katherine had said calmly. Children's memories went back further than many people thought. What mattered was letting a child admit bad things had happened, and then helping the child leave those things behind.

Abby nodded. "Yes," she admitted gently, "he did. Sometimes people yell when they're angry at each other."

Emily's face scrunched up in serious thought.

"Sam says his daddy never yells."

Abby smiled. Sam was in Emily's play group. "That's good. People shouldn't yell."

"Was that man angry at me?"

"Well, he didn't like what you said, Em."

"But I was right. He should have said he was sorry."

"Yes, but… Maybe he got up on the wrong side of the bed this morning."

"Or maybe it was 'cause he has a cold."

Smiling, Abby smoothed the frown line from between her daughter's eyes.

"You think so?"

"Yup. His nose was all red, like Lily's when she got sick. She had to drink lots an' lots of orange juice an' she didn't come to day care for a whole week. Remember?"

"I remember." Abby hesitated. "Em. Do *you* remember what I said about talking to strangers?"

"Uh-huh. And not helping anybody look for their little girl or their puppy."

Emily's expression was solemn. As she had so many times during the last two years, Abby wondered where to draw the line between keeping her baby safe from the man who'd fathered her, and letting her enjoy the innocence of childhood.

"Yes. That's right."

Emily tucked a finger into her mouth. "I didn't talk to that man, Mommy."

"You did, baby."

Her daughter shook her head so emphatically that her braids flew around her face.

"I talked to you."

One point to the four-year-old, Abby thought. She sighed and rose to her feet.

"Right. Technically, anyway."

"What's technically mean?"

Abby smiled. "It means you're right and I'm wrong."

Emily's light brown eyebrows rose in confusion and Abby gave another deep sigh. "Okay, how about this? You shouldn't say things about other people so they can hear them."

"Yesterday, you said Lily's new dress was pretty. You said it to me, but Lily was right there. She could hear you."

Two points for the four year old, Abby thought, and grinned.

"Right again. How's this? You shouldn't say things that aren't nice. Got that?"

"Yes." Emily wrinkled her freckled nose. "You should whisper them."

Abby began to laugh. One thing she'd learned since fleeing Oregon and her ex was that no matter how rough things seemed, her baby could always brighten her day.

"I give up." Abby retied the blue bow around one of Emily's braids. "Go on. Have fun, drink all your milk at lunchtime, and I'll be back for you after work."

"Okay, Mommy."

Mother and daughter exchanged hugs just as the door swung open again. A blond woman and a little girl who looked enough like Emily to be her sister stepped inside.

"Lily!"

"Emily!"

The children fell on each other as if they'd been parted for years instead of overnight, exclaiming happily at braids identically tied with blue ribbons, at blue jeans, blue sneakers and blue T-shirts.

"See, Mommy?" Emily said happily. "Lily wore blue everything, same as me."

"Was there ever a doubt?" Faith Marshall, Lily's mother, smiled at Abby. "'Today we're wearing blue,' my daughter announced this morning." Faith shook her head. "You think maybe we've got twins who were mysteriously separated at birth?"

Abby chuckled. "Sometimes it seems like we do." She bent down, gave Emily another quick hug. "Now, scoot. Otherwise, you'll miss morning storytime!"

The little girls kissed their mothers and skipped off, hand in hand. Abby turned to Faith and smiled.

"They're quite a pair."

Faith grinned. "Two peas in a pod."

"I was going to call you and see if Lily can come over tomorrow and spend the night. I promised Emily we'd bake chocolate chip cookies."

"You're off tomorrow?"

"That's the other thing I was going to tell you. I'm off Saturdays from now on."

Faith grinned. "Will miracles never cease?"

"My manager called me in and gave me the news just yesterday. I'd asked for that when I first began working at Emerald City, but Mr. Black—my boss—said it was impossible."

"What changed?"

Abby shrugged. "Who knows? My manager simply said she's decided to work Saturdays." She grinned. "Mine not to reason why—"

"Yours just to reap the trickle-down benefits. The guys on top always get what they want."

"In this case, that's fine with me. I'd much rather have a normal weekend—and you won't have to watch Em for me Saturdays anymore."

"Lily and I will miss her."

"Just remember, you can still leave Lily with me anytime you have a freelance job nights or weekends."

Faith smiled. "Trust me, Abby. I won't forget."

"So, how about it? Want to bring Lily by tomorrow?"

"Sure. What time's good?"

"One, two, whatever works for you."

"Fine." Faith pushed open the front door and she and Abby trotted down the steps to the gate in the wrought-iron fence that surrounded the day care center. "You have time for coffee?"

Abby shook her head. "Sorry. I'm almost late as it is." She looked across Sandringham Drive at the big windows of the Emerald City Jewelry Exchange. "My boss is probably already wondering where in heck I am."

Faith nodded. "Another time, then."

"Absolutely," Abby said, and wondered if the word sounded as false as it felt. "See you tomorrow."

"Sure. See you then."

The women exchanged smiles. Then Abby checked for traffic and ran across the street.

Their daughters had grown close, and she and Faith Marshall had quickly discovered that exchanging occasional baby-sitting duties was a lot less expensive—and a lot more reassuring—than paying strangers to watch their children for them.

Still, the women hadn't moved beyond a superficial friendship. It wasn't Faith's doing, it was Abby's. Of necessity, she'd settled for something less.

There was too much risk in getting involved with people. When you'd run away from a man who'd sworn never to let you go, you never really knew who you could trust.

Abby stopped before the Emerald City door and tapped lightly on the glass. Bill, the security guard, smiled, opened the lock and let her in.

"'Morning, Abby. Lovely day."

"'Morning, Bill. Yes, it is," she agreed as she hurried up the main aisle of the exchange.

It was a couple of minutes before ten and all the counters—fine watches, gold and platinum jewelry, gemstones, sterling and china—were staffed and ready for customers. Well, all except hers. She sold estate jewelry at a counter right up front in one of the big windows that looked out on the street.

She wasn't late. Not really, she thought, and glanced up at the loft. Yes, her boss was there, tall and distinguished-looking, his hands clasped behind his back.

He smiled pleasantly.

Abby jerked her gaze down.

Mr. Black had never given her a hard time about being a few minutes late. She'd explained she was a single mother, that she had to drop her daughter off at the day care center every day, and he'd been wonderfully understanding. But sometimes he looked at her in a way that made her feel…uncomfortable.

Silly, she knew.

It was just that *any* man looking at her made her feel uncomfortable, whether they were polite like Mr. Black or surly like the stranger at the day care center. Frank had taught her enough about men to make her more than cautious.

As far as she was concerned, she didn't want a man anywhere near her, ever again.

To that end, Abby had made certain rules for herself and Emily when she left Eugene, though "left" wasn't exactly the right way to put it. What she'd done was just grab Emily and run as if the devil was on her heels, with only one suitcase crammed with clothes and baby things, and the last of the money she'd inherited from her parents in her purse—money Frank hadn't been able to get his hands on.

At two, Emily had thought their flight was a great adventure.

"We goin', Mommy?" she'd kept asking.

"Yes," Abby had answered, "we're going somewhere special."

That was better than the truth, which was that she'd had no idea where they were going until they got there. At first, she'd fled to a shelter, then to Portland, because it was familiar. But Frank found her there, and when she ran next, it was to San Francisco, where she'd figured on the security quotient of being swallowed up by a big city.

Wrong. San Francisco was *too* big. Too expensive. Within a week, she'd abandoned it for Seattle. The city was large enough to get lost in, small enough to make her feel comfortable. She'd loved the waterfront on sight, and when the clouds parted and she saw Mount Rainier shouldering up against the sky, she felt as if she'd come home.

Abby opened the door to the back room and went to her locker.

She'd been in the city a year now and she still loved it. She'd found an apartment in a converted Victorian house in a nice neighborhood. The apartment was tiny, but how much space did she and Em need? Plus, it included a small porch and use of a handkerchief-size yard. The rent deposit had taken a big bite out of her remaining funds and she'd gone searching for a job right away.

Who'd have imagined she'd luck out and find one like this so quickly?

Abby put her purse on the bench that ran the length of the lockers. The door swung open and Bettina Carlton strolled in. Bettina had handled the estate jewelry counter before Abby. Now she was Emerald City's manager.

As always, she looked elegant. Cool and ladylike.

"Good morning, Abby."

"Hi, Bettina. I know I'm late, but— "

"Not yet," Bettina said pleasantly. "The front door's still

locked.'' She opened her locker, took out a nail file and worked carefully at one perfectly manicured nail. ''We'll be short one clerk today, Abby. Phil's out with a cold, so I'll have to relieve you a bit later than usual for lunch.''

Abby closed her locker. Looking at Bettina always made her want to check her hair for flyaway strands, her panty hose for runs.

''No problem.''

Bettina gave the nail one last brush with the file. ''Is one-thirty okay?''

''Fine.''

''Great. I have a private client coming in at noon.'' Bettina put the file away and looked at Abby. ''I noticed you're doing well.''

''Sales have been good,'' Abby said.

''Better than good.'' Bettina paused. ''That's one of the primary reasons for the scheduling change we implemented.'' She smiled. ''Sort of a bonus for you. I know you have a little girl. Emily, isn't it?''

''Yes, that's right.''

''I recalled that you'd originally asked for Saturdays off, so when I had the chance to juggle things a little…''

''It was very kind of you, Bettina.''

''Oh, I'm not any kind of saint, I assure you. I like working Saturdays. You know, lots of customers in and out. Gives me the chance to keep up my sales skills.''

Abby nodded. In truth, Bettina's sales skills were incredible. She still handled private customers, the rich and the eccentric. They would occasionally come in and demand to deal with Bettina and nobody else.

Someday, Abby hoped to be just as invaluable to the store. Her job, this job, was important to her.

She'd been lucky to find it, especially since she didn't have any real work skills. But she was good with people and she knew a little bit about fine jewelry, thanks to the few pieces her mother had owned—pieces she still cherished and knew she'd never sell, no matter what. Estate jewelry, it was called now.

Maybe that was why the ad for a clerk at the Emerald City Jewelry Exchange had leaped at her from the classifieds.

The bell announcing the start of the day pealed politely. Abby smiled at Bettina, who was smoothing back her hair. Then she took a breath, as she always did before manning her counter, stepped out of the back room and made her way up the aisle to the front of the store.

Look busy, Mr. Black always reminded his clerks, *even if you're not.*

Taking a cloth and a bottle of Windex from behind the counter, Abby sprayed the glass tops of the cabinets and wiped them clean. Mr. Black walked by, nodded at her and smiled pleasantly.

Frank had never smiled pleasantly. Only in the beginning, when she was naive, when she was just weeks past her eighteenth birthday and her parents' death had turned her world upside down. Back then, Frank had seemed wonderful.

Not that her ignorance had lasted long. A year into the marriage, he'd begun losing his temper with her, demanding to know how she spent every minute of her day. Two years into it, he'd hit her for the first time. Afterward, he'd begged her forgiveness, sworn he'd never hurt her again....

But he had.

She'd called the police, they'd taken him away, and when they let him out of jail the next day, Frank had wrapped her in his arms and wept. He adored her, he'd said, and she'd wanted to believe him, so she'd taken him back.

By the time he hit her again, she was twenty-two. His rage terrified her, and she waited until he left for work, then began to pack her things. She was going to leave him...but she was overtaken by a wave of nausea, and she began to bleed. Somehow, she'd managed to call 911. An ambulance took her to the hospital; a doctor who kept asking her questions about her blackened eye told her she was pregnant. When she told Frank, he fell on his knees, kissed her still-flat belly, and swore the news had changed him forever.

How could she leave him then?

For a while, it seemed as if he'd spoken the truth, though

sometimes she could tell he was bottling his anger inside him. It finally exploded on Emily's second birthday when Em spilled her milk. Frank spoke sharply to the baby and slapped her hand. Em began to cry and Abby rushed to comfort her.

"Let her be," Frank yelled, and when she didn't obey, he went for her.

"No," she remembered screaming, "not in front of the baby."

Frank dragged her out of the room and beat her, and that was when Abby knew she had to leave—before he turned his attention to their daughter.

It took months to squirrel away enough money to make her escape, and she'd tried not to think about how she'd support Emily and herself after that. She had no skills—she'd been in her first semester of college when her parents died, and her grades slumped to Ds and Fs. With Frank's encouragement, she'd dropped out.

"You don't need a degree, Abigail," he'd said. "I'll take care of you. You'll always belong to me."

He'd reminded her of those words the night their divorce became final.

You'll always belong to me, he'd said, and turned the statement into a promise with his fists.

That was when she'd known he was right, and she'd packed up, dressed Em, hustled her into the car and fled Oregon for good.

And all the time, all of it, she'd been sure if she'd turned around, she would see Frank coming after her.

Abby put the cloth and window cleaner away. As she bent down, she caught a glimpse of herself in one of the oval mirrors that were arranged along the countertops throughout the store.

What she saw was a woman who'd come a long way since she'd been foolish enough to fall for Frank Caldwell's promises.

She stood up straight.

Her ex would hardly recognize her. Oh, he'd probably be able to look past the shorter hair, artfully applied makeup and sophisticated clothes—clothes she bought in a consignment shop in the city's upscale Queen Anne Hill area—and find the girl he'd once known, but he'd never recognize her independence, her determination to make something of her life.

He'd surely not recognize her conviction that she'd never go back to him or the kind of life she'd been forced to lead as his wife.

And if she sometimes awoke in a sweaty panic in the middle of the night, or felt her heart climb into her throat because a man looked at her the way the man at the day care center had, if she overreacted just because an oversize jerk with cold eyes, a turned-down mouth and a surly disposition snarled…well, time was on her side.

Someday, she'd get beyond all of that. She'd learn not to let silly things spook her so she wouldn't feel she was jumping at shadows, the way she did now.

The door to the street opened and the soft scent of rain drifted to Abby's nostrils as a white-haired matron stepped inside the shop. Abby smiled pleasantly as the woman approached her counter.

"Good morning, Mrs. Halpern. How nice to see you again."

The older woman's face relaxed in a smile.

"Ms. Douglas. How have you been?"

"Very well, thank you. Is there something I can help you with this morning?"

Mrs. Halpern sank her teeth gently into her bottom lip. "Well," she said, with the sort of coy smile that still looked good on her despite her years, "there might just be, yes. Our anniversary's coming up and my husband wants to buy me a little gift."

"That's lovely," Abby said. "Did you have something special in mind?"

"As a matter of fact, I do. I was in last month, remember? And you showed me a charming little diamond and ruby pin…."

"Of course."

Abby unlocked a case, drew out the correct tray and reached for the pin.

A movement, a flash of color caught her eye. She straightened, turned her face to the window and saw the front door to the day care open. One of the teachers came down the steps, followed by six children, all holding hands so that they made a twelve-legged caterpillar.

Abby smiled.

Emily was one of the children in that chain. They appeared to be headed for the front yard. The rain had stopped, and the sun had peeped out. The kids were probably going to play outside for a little while.

Another movement. Another flash of color.

Abby caught her breath.

A man, his back to her, was trotting across the street toward the children.

He was big. Six one, six two. His long black hair was tied at the nape of his neck, and he was wearing jeans and a leather jacket this time, not a suit, but she recognized him in an instant.

The ruby and diamond pin fell from her hand and landed on top of the display case. Abby scooted around the edge of the counter and flung open the door.

"Ms. Douglas?" she heard her customer say, and the guard called her name, but Abby didn't stop.

She was already flying toward Emily, her heart solidly lodged in her throat.

CHAPTER THREE

ABBY DARTED THROUGH A HOLE in the traffic, ignoring the blare of a horn.

Still, she wasn't moving quickly enough to catch the man. He had a head start, and his longer stride ate up the distance at a startling rate.

The teacher paused at the foot of the steps and said something to the children. Abby could see them moving into a neat little two-abreast line; Emily and Lily clasped hands and grinned at each other.

"Emily," Abby shouted, just as the man reached the gate and opened the latch. "Emily," Abby yelled again, and all the children looked toward her. Emily's face split in a joyful grin and Abby knew her daughter had spotted her.

"Mommy?" she said happily, and in that instant Abby realized she'd made an awful mistake. Emily suddenly let go of Lily's hand and started running toward the gate, moving away from the relative safety of the teacher and the group of children.

"No! Em, stay where you are—"

Too late. The man swung the gate aside and stepped into the yard. Emily ran straight into him. She staggered and he caught hold of her, lifted her off the ground....

Abby shouted, ran the last few feet and deliberately barreled into him as hard as she could.

It was like hitting a stone wall and bouncing off.

"Put her down!"

The man swung around, still holding Emily, and looked at Abby as if she were crazy.

"What's the matter?" he said.

She stepped in close, her breath ratcheting in her lungs, the adrenaline pumping through her blood so hard that she could feel the surge of it in her muscles. The man towered over her, just as he had this morning.

This morning, she thought bitterly. What had he been doing then? Sizing up the situation?

She had to tilt her head back to make eye contact.

"Damn you, put her down!"

"Mommy?" Emily said, and began to cry.

"Put…my…daughter…down!" Abby demanded, punctuating each word with a fist to his shoulder.

Baffled, Luke lowered the little girl to her feet, then watched as she flung herself at her mother and clasped her skirt.

It was the same pair, the kid and the brunette from this morning. The woman had looked cool then, almost icy. Now her face was flushed. Strands of hair had escaped from the combs that held it back from her temples and curled against her cheeks. She was glaring at him; the kid was sobbing….

What in hell had he done to deserve this?

"Take it easy, lady," he said.

"Take it easy? *Take it easy?* You try to—to steal my little girl—"

"Whoa! What are you talking about?"

"I saw you try to take her."

Luke took a step back. "Listen, lady, I don't know what your problem is, but I didn't—"

"I saw the whole thing. You—you—" She caught her breath and shoved the child behind her. "But you won't get away with it."

Luke blinked. Backpacking through the Wonder Mountain Wilderness one time, he'd come face-to-face with a black bear and her cubs. The look in the bear's eyes had been the same as the look in the brunette's. *Hurt my baby,* the look said, *and I'll rip you apart.*

A four-hundred-pound bear was a tough adversary, but even though the woman facing him probably didn't weigh much more than a quarter of that, he knew he'd rather face the bear. The bear had seen him as a threat to her cubs. The woman saw him the same way, though he'd be damned if he knew why. Still, he tried to see the situation from her viewpoint.

Luke held up his hands, palms out, and tried for the tone he'd learned on the streets his first months on the job, the one meant to convince a nut coming at you with murder in his eye that you weren't the enemy.

"Easy," he said quietly. "I don't know what you think is happening here, but just calm down, okay?"

Calming down didn't seem to be on the agenda, not for the fire-breathing brunette or the kid, who began to wail. Luke heard another couple of little sobs from behind him, which caught the interest of some of the passersby, enough so they stopped to join the growing cluster of gawkers.

Just what he needed, Luke thought in disgust, and shot a glance over his shoulder. The teacher had gathered the children in front of her. The sobs were coming from a little boy whose face had gone so pale his freckles stood out, and a little girl whose braids were tied up with blue ribbon, same as the kid hanging on to the brunette.

All of them, teacher, kids, the boy with the freckles and the girl with the braids, were staring at him as if he'd just dropped in from the one hundred and fiftieth remake of *Friday the 13th.*

Great. Just great. No doubt about it, this was definitely the textbook approach to blending quietly and unobtrusively into the background.

Who'd have believed it? He was here to find out who was fencing jewels in the Emerald City Jewelry Exchange. Instead, he was being accused of child molestation or kidnapping or who knew what by a woman who was clearly a certifiable psycho. Cops had to deal with crazies as part of their job, but until now, the crazies he'd dealt with all had that otherworldly shine in their eyes.

The only thing shining in this woman's eyes was fury.

Nine years of on-the-job experience dealing with people who were in direct contact with talking dogs and creatures from the planet Mongo kicked in fast.

"Listen," he said, as calmly as he could manage, "I can understand your concern."

The woman snorted in disbelief.

"Honest, I can. But I think you're making a mistake here."

"You saw Emily this morning."

"Emily," he said, trying for a smile. "Is that her—"

"Don't give me that innocent routine! You saw Emily this morning!"

"Well, yes," he said, working at keeping it together, "I guess I did, but—"

"And then you watched the center, saw my baby come out the door, ran over and—and grabbed her!"

"That's not what happened. Your little girl ran into me. I didn't want her to fall down, so—"

"Marilyn," the woman said, her eyes never leaving his, "take the children inside and dial 911."

Luke almost groaned. That was all he needed to make things perfect. A patrol car showing up. Odds were that whoever caught the call would recognize him.

And even if he got lucky and they didn't blow his cover, he'd never live it down. Detective Luke Sloan couldn't handle a good-looking brunette who stood no higher than his chest without making a bunch of kids cry their hearts out...

Jesus.

He knew how stuff like that went. Cops would be talking about it every time somebody mentioned his name, just the way he and Dan had talked about Rutledge this morning.

"No," he said quickly, "don't do that, Marilyn." He took a breath, forced a smile. "Look, I can understand your concern, Mrs...."

"Don't you try and placate me!"

"I'm simply saying I understand why you might be upset. In today's world..." He shot a look at the kid. She was peeking out from behind her mother, hanging on to her skirt and looking as if she expected him to bare a set of fangs any second. "What I'm telling you," he said carefully, wanting to avoid specifics because he still didn't really know what was going on, "is that whatever you think I was doing, I wasn't."

The brunette's mouth thinned. And why wouldn't it? If a

suspect made that kind of statement to him, he'd guarantee the guy was guilty.

"I mean, I don't know what you think was going on here, but—" He paused. "Actually, now that I think about it, I *do* know what you think was going on, but I assure you—"

"You were taking my little girl," the woman said. Her voice quavered. "That's what was going on here."

"No," Luke said again, even more adamantly. "Try listening, okay? I just told you, I was coming through the gate, your kid ran into me, and—"

"I was running toward my mommy," the kid said defiantly. "Not you."

"Okay. Fine. She was heading for you and I was in the way, and instead of letting her run into me, I picked her up and—"

"That isn't what happened."

"Yes, it is," Luke replied, his tone no longer quite so conciliatory. "It's exactly what happened. And if you don't stop making wild accusations, I'll—"

What? Blow his cover all by himself?

"Is there a problem here?"

Luke looked around. Thank God. Katherine Kinard was coming down the steps.

"Yes," the brunette said. "This man—"

"—is a bad man," the little girl said, her mouth trembling.

Puppy-kicking time again, Luke thought in disgust, except this time, he wasn't to blame.

"Okay," he said through his teeth, "that's it." He took a step toward Katherine. As if on signal, the teacher and the kids with her stepped back. "Ms. Kinard, something happened here. This little girl ran into me, and…" He shook his head. The Kinard woman looked as puzzled as he felt. "The kid's mother saw me pick up her daughter instead of letting her fall down, and now she has me pegged as everything but a serial killer."

"For all I know, you're that, too."

"Ms. Kinard," Luke said, ignoring the brunette, "will you please tell her who I am?" He saw the quick puzzlement in Katherine Kinard's eyes and silently cursed himself for being a fool. "That I'm the carpenter you hired yesterday," he added quickly, "and I'm going to be working here for a while."

"He's the what?" the woman said, her voice racing up the scale in disbelief. "Katherine? Does this man work here?"

"He does, yes." The day care director smiled at Luke's accuser but still managed to pin him with a glare that said he was an idiot to have gotten himself into this situation. Hell, he already knew that. "This is Luke Sloan," Katherine continued dutifully. "He's a carpenter, putting in some shelves and cabinets in my office."

"No!"

"Yes," Luke said coldly. "Disappointed?"

"Then, why did he try to grab my daughter?"

"What's wrong with you, lady? Haven't you been listening to a thing I said? I was coming to work, your kid slammed into me, and…damn it, I don't believe this!"

"Ooh," a small voice behind him whispered, "the bad man said a bad word!"

There was a heartbeat of silence. Then Katherine turned a beaming smile on the teacher.

"Marilyn," she said briskly, "isn't it time for juice break?"

"Is it?" Marilyn stared blankly, and then she shook herself. "Oh. Oh, yes, of course, Katherine. It's time for juice break! Kids," she said, smiling brightly, "let's go in and have our juice."

The kids didn't move. Why would they? Luke thought glumly. They were as transfixed by the scene as the still-gawking crowd beyond the gate.

"Tell you what. How about cookies with your juice, as a special treat?"

The little boy who'd been whimpering leaned toward the girl with braids and whispered in her ear. The girl nodded.

"No juice," she said firmly. "We want ice cream."

Luke laughed. He couldn't help it, though all it won him was a withering look from the brunette.

"Ice cream," Katherine repeated happily, as if the child had just spoken words that held the wisdom of the ages. "That's a wonderful idea, Lily. Marilyn? Ice cream for everybody."

That did it. The teacher went up the steps and opened the door, and the children trooped obediently inside. Then Katherine slid her arm gently around Abby's shoulders.

"Abby," she said softly, "I can understand your fear."

"You can?" Abby's pulse rate went into high gear.

"Certainly." Katherine gave her a quick squeeze. "All these awful kidnapping cases in the papers lately... Nobody could blame you for worrying about Emily, but I promise you, she's safe here."

Abby looked from Katherine to the stranger. He was a carpenter. That's all he was, just a man headed for work. He'd turned up twice in one day, and she'd written a story that had nothing to do with reality.

Letting that happen was like letting Frank still control her.

She bent down, cupped Emily's face and smiled.

"Go on inside, baby. You don't want to miss that ice cream."

Katherine held out her hand. "Emily?"

Emily shook her head. "I want to stay with my mommy."

Abby's throat tightened. She'd frightened her little girl. That was the last thing she wanted to do, ever.

"Em honey, everything's fine now. You go with Katherine."

"But the bad man..."

"Listen, kid."

Luke squatted down until he and the girl were nose to nose. Out of the corner of his eye, he saw the brunette jerk forward, but Katherine Kinard caught her by the arm and stopped her. The only one who didn't move was the kid. He had to give her credit. She figured him for some kind of scum, but she wasn't going to budge an inch.

"Don't call me 'kid,'" she told him. "My name is Emily."

"Emily. That's a really pretty name."

She gave him a look that said flattery, if she'd known what it meant, wasn't going to work.

Luke couldn't blame her. This was hardly a good scene for a child to endure.

"Emily," he said in the same tone he'd have used with an adult, "I'm not a bad man."

"My mommy said you were."

"Your mommy made a mistake. Think about what happened from start to finish. You and the others came out of the day care center. You went down the steps and—"

"And," Emily said, her face puckered in thought, "I heard my mommy call me. An' I looked up and saw her. An' I ran to the gate, but you was there first an' I ran into you, an' you said 'Whoa, kid,' like I was a horse instead of a girl, an' I bounced off your legs an' I kinda started to fall, an' you grabbed me to keep me from falling, an' then my mommy started yelling."

As the kid paused for breath, Luke rose to his feet. "I rest my case," he said smugly, and folded his arms across his chest.

"But you didn't say sorry to us this morning," Emily added.

"This morning?" Katherine echoed, frowning.

"Yes," said Abby. "We met this—this gentleman as we were coming into the center."

Luke heard the twist Emily's mother put on the word "gentleman," but decided to let it pass and respond only to the child.

"You're right," he told her. "I guess I wasn't very nice. I was in a bad mood and I took it out on you. I apologize."

"Mommy said you got up on the wrong side of the bed, but I said it was 'cause you got a bad cold."

"You noticed that, huh?" Luke asked with a grin.

The child nodded. "You were sneezing. And your nose was all red, like it is now."

"Well, that's all true, Em. I have a cold and I was grumpy this morning." He bent toward her and tapped his finger lightly against her nose. "And I said a bad word a couple of minutes ago, but that's it. None of that makes me a bad guy."

Emily rubbed the tip of one sneakered foot against the other and regarded him with sober interest.

"What's a carpenter?"

The non sequitur almost threw him. Then he remembered that Katherine Kinard had just explained what he was. What he was pretending to be.

"A carpenter's a person who makes things out of wood."

"Like boats? I saw a man make a boat on TV. The Discovery channel."

Luke smiled. "That must have been cool. Nope, I don't make boats. I build houses." It wasn't a complete lie; he had done just that a long time ago, on the reservation. "And I build things that go inside houses, like shelves and cabinets."

"Can you make toy chests?"

"Emily!"

The little girl looked at her mother. "I need a toy chest, Mommy. You said so. And you said you couldn't find one to buy that didn't look like it was made out of garbage."

"Emily," the brunette said again, and blushed.

She'd blushed this morning, too, Luke recalled. It was a nice thing to see in a woman. As far as he knew, women didn't blush much anymore.

"I'd be happy to make you a toy chest someday, Emily." Luke shot a quick look at the brunette. "Your mom and I can discuss it."

"We cannot," Abby said quickly. "I mean, thank you for the offer, Mr.—"

"Sloan. Luke Sloan."

He held out his hand. She looked at it. For a couple of seconds, he thought she was just going to let it go at that, but then she held out her hand, too. His fingers closed around hers, swallowing them up.

"Abigail," she said, with what he knew was reluctance. "Abigail Douglas."

"Abigail. Nice to meet you."

He smiled. She hesitated, then offered a smile in return. It wasn't a real smile, but it pleased him. Not because she was a good-looking woman, but because he didn't need the mother of one of the kids at Forrester Square watching his every move just to make sure he wasn't some kind of pervert up to no good.... Although he supposed some might say the "no good" part could be construed as accurate, considering he was lying about who he was and why he was here.

"My mommy's name is Abby," the little girl said helpfully. "Nobody calls her Abigail."

"Well," Katherine said, clearing her throat, "why don't we all go inside?"

Suddenly Abby thought of how she'd run out of the jewelry shop, dropping the pin on the counter, leaving the case unlocked, leaving Mrs. Halpern standing there in confusion....

"I really can't," she said. "I mean, I don't..."

"Please, Mommy?"

She looked down at Emily. The child's cheeks were flushed. Her daughter had spent a bad few minutes, and it was her fault. For the past two years, she'd lived in fear of Frank coming after them or sending someone else to do the job. Despite that, despite her lectures to Em about not talking to strangers, she'd never frightened the girl. Now she had, and for no reason. Luke Sloan was just a carpenter. He was harmless.

She looked around. Luke was making eye contact with the couple of people still standing outside the wrought iron fence, watching the scene and waiting for the action to start again.

"It's all over, folks. Move it."

He spoke softly, but it was enough. He was big. Leanly muscled. Powerful-looking.

People scurried away.

Harmless, Abby thought again. She'd thought Frank was harmless, too.

"Mommy?"

She looked down into Emily's pleading face.

"Come inside, Mom, just for a minute."

Abby nodded. "Just for a minute," she said, taking her daughter's hand.

They all went into the center and made small talk about nothing in particular for a few minutes. Then one of the teachers called out to Katherine, who made her apologies and went to talk with the woman. Emily gave Abby a big hug and a smacking kiss, and ran off to join her play group.

Abby watched her go.

Her little girl was going to eat ice cream.

She was going to eat crow.

She'd had one faint hope—that Luke Sloan would wander off once they were alone. He had work to do, after all. But he didn't move. He stood there, motionless, his hands tucked into the pockets of his jeans, his eyes fixed on her.

"So," he said, "we all squared away?"

Abby nodded. "Yes."

He took his hands out of his pockets and folded his arms over his chest.

"You're sure?"

Abby nodded again. "Yes."

He was waiting. She knew the reason, knew she had to get it over with.

"I guess—I guess I owe you an apology. I'm sorry."

"Excuse me?"

"I said…" Abby lifted her chin. "You heard me, Mr. Sloan."

He had. He'd also heard the way she'd delivered that apology. What was it with this woman? Better still, what was it with him? Last night, a babe with twice her looks had practically thrown herself into his lap. This one had taken a tenth of a second to decide he was little better than something she might see floating belly-up in the bay.

So what? Why should it bother him? As long as she wasn't going to point her finger at him and scream loud enough to call attention to him whenever their paths crossed, what did it matter?

Luke gave a sigh, relaxed a little and tucked his hands back into his pockets.

"You're right, Mrs. Douglas. You apologized already. I should have accepted it the first time. It's just… Here's the thing, Mrs. Douglas—"

"Ms."

"Sorry?"

"I said, it's Ms., not Mrs."

"Ah." He nodded, wondering what that meant, whether she was divorced, widowed, had never been married…. He wondered, too, why it should matter to him. "About what happened here…"

"I already said—"

"I know. I just want you to understand why I reacted so

strongly. I'd never hurt a kid. Never. If you only understood how—'' *How cops feel about the kind of man you thought I was,* he wanted to say. *How we wish we could take the law into our own hands when we arrest the bastards who get their kicks out of hurting women and children...* ''I come from a big family,'' he said, knowing that would have to suffice. ''I have lots of cousins, a couple of them probably just about Emily's age. So when you thought...''

''I'm sorry,'' Abby said, and he could tell that she really meant it this time. ''It's just that it's such a crazy world....''

''Sure. I understand.'' Luke smiled. ''Okay, then. Now we really are squared away.''

Abby smiled, too. ''Yes. We are.'' She was the one who held out her hand this time. ''Goodbye, Mr. Sloan.''

Once again, Luke's fingers closed around hers. ''Luke.''

''Luke.''

''Goodbye, Abby.''

She tugged lightly on her hand. He let go of it and she turned quickly, went through the door and was gone.

Luke stared after her. Then he smiled, pursed his lips and whistled softly as he made his way to Katherine's office, where his good mood vanished in an instant.

''Mr. Sloan,'' Katherine said in a voice that was enough to freeze him in his tracks.

''Luke,'' he offered as she stepped past him and slammed the door shut.

''*Detective* Sloan,'' she said with deliberate emphasis, ''if you think you can come to Forrester Square and disrupt everything—''

''Hold on.'' Luke held up his hands. ''I didn't disrupt anything. That woman—Abby Douglas...''

''Yes?''

He'd been going to say Abby had overreacted, but how could he know how a mother would feel if she thought her child was in danger? He'd been on the police end of a couple of child-missing cases, and as hard as such things were on cops, they had to be twice as tough on parents.

''It was a screwup,'' he said. ''Nobody's fault, just one of those things that happen. Trust me, Katherine. You don't want the kids upset, and I don't want to call attention to myself. Okay?''

"This is exactly why I said I'd only cooperate if they sent me a female officer.''

"Yeah,'' Luke said, straight-faced, "but could she build you shelves that will make you drool?''

Katherine stared at him. Then her lips twitched. "They'd better.''

"They will, I promise.'' He took the leather bag he carried from his shoulder and walked to the back of the office. "As a point of information, is the Douglas woman widowed, divorced, what?''

"I don't see what that has to do with anything.''

"It's a cop thing,'' Luke said casually. "Filling in all the blanks, you know? Okay.'' His tone turned brisk. "I understand there's a vacant apartment on the third floor.''

"Yes. My brother lived up there, but now that he's married, he moved to a house. Eventually the day care will be taking over the space.''

"Good.'' Luke zipped open the bag and took out a small black object. "I left my carpentry tools in my SUV. I'll go get them in a little while. Meanwhile, I'm going to set this up.''

"What is it?''

"A camcorder. I'll put it in one of the third-floor windows.''

"A camcorder? I thought you were here to do surveillance.''

"I am, but the camera can do it nonstop, and if something—somebody—interesting goes into the jewelry exchange, we'll have a record we can view.''

"And you'll still be here, in my office?''

Luke glanced up and smiled. "Yeah. Sorry about that.''

"No, that's okay.'' Katherine sighed. "Although, to be honest—''

"To be honest, the sooner I'm gone, the better. I agree. We're just lucky that this window, this building, gives me such a perfect—''

"A perfect what?''

"Huh?" Luke turned toward Katherine. "A perfect view of the jewelry exchange," he said, but what he'd just had a perfect view of was Abby Douglas, standing inside the exchange, behind the counter nearest the window.

CHAPTER FOUR

BY THE END OF THE DAY, Luke was starting to wonder how he was going to survive this assignment.

Between the day care director's active disapproval of him setting up his equipment in her office, the kids trooping in and out of the room, and a noise level that approached that of a hen-house under attack by a weasel, he felt the kind of headache coming on that would rival any he'd ever experienced after some of the bachelor parties he'd attended.

"Don't you ever close your door?" he'd said to Katherine Kinard.

"No," she'd replied.

End of discussion.

He'd looked up a dozen times and found munchkins wandering through, though now that Kinard had hurried off to a meeting, the kids didn't come all the way into the office. They crowded into the doorway instead, staring at him as if he was some exotic species of animal.

He knew it was because he was a male in female territory. The teachers, the aides, everybody who worked here was a woman. Still, he had to fight back the god-awful desire to look at the kids and yell "Boo."

He didn't do it. He'd learned his lesson about frightening small children this morning.

Instead, he endured.

It was like being in the Gulf with the corps and finding yourself in enemy territory

Usually, police surveillances were the dullest things on earth. Just you, a camera, maybe a tape recorder, if you'd planted a bug, and whatever it was you were watching. A cop's life consisted of ninety-nine percent boredom and one percent mind-numbing terror, where you hoped your training and instincts would be enough for you to survive. It was never the bang-bang, shoot-'em-up existence like you saw on TV, the one where the good guys solve the crime and save the heroine in the last three minutes, but at least it had some variety—except when you were doing surveillance.

On the other hand, working undercover was a high. You put on clothes to suit the character you were playing, got caught up in another kind of life, dealt with people who thought you were one of them when you weren't. Luke had always liked that part of his job, and he was good at it. Pretending to be a druggie, to be a dealer, even to be a gun for hire—he'd played that role, too—could be dangerous as hell.

That was probably why it was so much fun.

But this? Sitting around, pretending to be a carpenter... This was Dullsville. What could possibly come of it? That was what he'd thought, anyway.

Except it turned out there might be another way to get information about the jewelry exchange, and that other way's name was Abby Douglas.

Maybe she knew something. Maybe she knew more than Luke wanted to think about, which was crazy, because what was Abby Douglas to him? Nothing. Well, okay, a good-looking woman, but the world was full of good-looking women.

It was just that this one had a little girl who adored her, and a look in her eyes that said something, or somebody, had once given her a bad time.

Luke sighed, took the container of coffee he'd bought next door at Caffeine Hy's, sat down in a chair beside the window that looked out at the exchange, and stretched out his long legs. The coffee had cooled down some, but it was still hot, strong and good.

He smiled, remembering the look on the face of the kid behind the counter when he'd stepped up to place his order.

"One coffee to go," he'd said, "extra large, black."

The kid had shifted a wad of gum from one side of her

mouth to the other as she stood behind the cash register, fingers
poised over the keys.

"And?"

"And...that's it."

"You don't want a latte?"

"No."

"Whipped cream?"

"No."

"Shaved chocolate?"

"No," he'd said again, politely. "Just the coffee, black, extra large."

"How about today's special? Café Kava Java Lava Mo-
cha?"

"No," he'd repeated, and he'd damn near felt every eye in
the place settle on him.

Dan often teased him about his preference in coffee. He said
Luke could wind up being banished from the city if he kept
ignoring all the exotic brews served up in Seattle's coffee bars
and insisted on sticking to plain old high-test.

His ex had laughed about it, too. "You're so predictable,
Luke," Janine had said, and he'd smiled and replied, well, so
was she, because she always ordered Café Killa Vanilla Something-or-Other...

Luke's jaw tightened.

That predictability had marked the end of his marriage. Stop-
ping at home one night to pick up some notes on a case, he'd
found two take-out coffees on the kitchen table, one sending
up the scent of vanilla, the other with a milky froth floating on
top.

He'd known right then what he'd only suspected for weeks.
He'd headed straight for the bedroom, heard the sounds before
he pushed the door all the way open....

And what in hell was he doing, sitting here and thinking
back to something that had been dead and gone for three years?

Luke drank some of his coffee.

He had too much time on his hands, that was the problem.
He'd go nuts if this detail lasted more than a few days.

Okay. He'd think about something else. Something pleasant,

like what would he do once this surveillance ended? He had time coming to him. Lots of it. Maybe he'd go somewhere. Drive to Oregon, go up the coast. Or take a couple of weeks, head for his cabin at Neah Bay, do some of the fix-up work he'd started last year about this time.

Neah Bay. He'd run from the place as soon as he was old enough, first into the marines, then into working construction here in the city while he took the test for the Seattle PD.

Now he wasn't quite sure why he'd run so far or so fast.

He'd gone back to the rez only a few times during those first years, but he returned to it more and more often lately, even though there was nobody to draw him there anymore. His aunts, his uncles, the extended family that had raised him were all gone. Even his cousins had moved away.

Still, he went back.

There was something about the beauty of the place, the cool green of the forest, the thunder of the ocean on the rocks, the piercing blue of the sky, that drew him. A tribal elder had once told him that no matter how you tried to deny it, ancestral memories beat forever in your blood…even if that blood was half white.

Or maybe it was because, sometimes, just being where he'd grown up could evoke memories of his mother, how it had been when he was a little kid and she was alive.

She'd been a good mother. Warm. Loving. Devoted. He was sure she'd have defended him from harm, real or imagined, every bit as fiercely as the Douglas woman had defended her kid this morning.

Abby Douglas was some piece of work. No question about it, she'd have taken him apart if she'd had to. Well, not really, but she'd have tried.

Luke drank down the last of his coffee.

Was it fear of the predators who seemed to roam the streets of towns and cities, preying on the innocent, that had made Abby come at him as she had?

That kind of fear was valid. It was a new, terrible reality in American life, but somehow he had the feeling there'd been more behind Abby's reaction than a concern that he was a child molester. He thought again about that look he'd seen in her eyes, the set to her mouth that suggested she'd been expecting trouble to come looking for her and the kid, and that she'd been expecting it for quite a while.

Sure, he had nothing to base that observation on, but he'd been a cop for too long to discount intuition, a sort of sixth sense you developed after a few years on the job.

His told him there was more to the Douglas woman's response than met the eye.

He'd have to check it out. He'd have to check out Abby Douglas, anyway, now that he knew she worked in the Emerald City Jewelry Exchange.

Damn.

Luke sat up straight, aimed the empty cup at the trash can near Katherine Kinard's desk, then smiled when he sank the basket, stopped smiling when he remembered the director's words as she'd watched him setting up his stuff.

"I can't believe I'm letting you spy on people," she'd said with all the righteous indignation of a civilian who wanted safe streets but didn't want to know how cops kept them that way.

What would Abby Douglas think if she knew he was a cop? Would she look on him as a necessary evil, the way Kinard had? Or would she see him as a sexy knight standing between her and all that was bad in the world.

Lots of women did.

He shut his eyes and thought about their first meeting.

This morning, he'd imagined she wasn't his type. How could he have thought that? She was definitely his type. Curvy. Fiery. She smelled good, too. He'd noticed when she'd come at him like a tiger. She smelled of sunshine. In a city like Seattle, that was one very appealing scent.

If things were different, if he wasn't here to do a job, if she was just a woman he'd met somewhere…

Except, she wasn't.

Luke sat up straight, opened his eyes and put them to better use by leaning forward and peering through the lens of the miniature camera, a tiny marvel of silicone chips hidden inside what looked like a perfectly normal box of nails he'd stood in just the right place on the windowsill...

"Whatcha doin'?"

Luke jerked his head back so fast he slammed it on the window frame. A little boy stood in the doorway, one finger jammed up his nose.

How many kids were in this building? Fifty? A hundred? A million, easy, and every last one of them seemed determined to find his or her way in here.

"I'm working," Luke said shortly, and reached for a tape measure.

"Are you Katherine's husband?"

Luke shot the kid a look. "No."

"Are you her boyfriend?"

"No."

"Are you Emily's daddy?"

"Am I... No, I'm not. Why would you think I was?"

"'Cause she's tellin' everybody you're big and brave and smart."

Luke gave a weary sigh. "Don't you have a place you're supposed to be, kid? Isn't it juice time, or milk time, or bathroom time?"

At first, he'd been more polite to the wanderers who drifted in to see him. They asked questions like, where were the apples? The chalk? The Scaredy Cat Scooby-Doo doll—whatever in God's name that was. His answers had ranged from "What?" to "I don't know," and back again.

After a while, he'd stopped answering at all. Maybe if he pretended the munchkins weren't there, they wouldn't be.

It was a clever idea, but it hadn't worked. This kid was living proof of that.

Luke flashed him another look. "Did you ever hear of a handkerchief?"

The kid yanked his finger from his nose, checked it for signs of life, then hid his hand behind his back.

"Emily thinks you're nice, but I don't."

Well, at least he'd made a good impression on somebody.

"I'd be nicer if you took a tissue from that box on Ms. Kinard's desk and used it."

The boy shuffled his feet. Then, to Luke's surprise, he edged over to the desk and plucked what looked like most of the tissues from the box.

"Her name's Katherine."

The kid wiped his finger on the tissues, dug around in his nose a little, then dropped the mass of paper in the trash.

"Emily says you're a carpenter."

"She's right." Luke measured the wall, marked off a couple of spots. "That's what I am."

"Whatcha doin'?"

"Working," Luke said irritably. "I just told you…"

He paused. Was that a different munchkin voice? He looked around and saw that it was. The first kid had been joined by another. This one had a smear of jelly on his chin and wore pants that sagged in the seat.

"Yuck," the nose-picker said, and took off.

Yuck? Luke frowned. Surely a case of the pot calling the kettle black…except the new kid shuffled forward, and Luke's nostrils crinkled as he caught a whiff of something.

He had the sudden unhappy feeling he knew the reason those pants were so saggy.

"I gotta go potty."

"Right." Luke stood up. "Well, that's not my problem. Where's your teacher?"

"I gotta go now," the boy said, and jiggled from one foot to the other.

Luke muttered something. He put down his tape measure, grabbed the kid's hand and marched him out of the office.

"Hello," he called to the world in general.

"Luke?" Katherine Kinard came quickly toward him. "What are you doing?"

"Looking for help. This kid—"

"The children are not your responsibility."

"Damned right, they aren't."

"Your language…"

"Maybe you want to discuss my language later. Or would you rather do it now, while this kid poops all over your floor?"

Katherine's eyes widened. "Joshua," she said, "do you have to go to the bathroom?"

"Uh-uh. Not anymore."

Luke laughed. He couldn't help it. Katherine gave him a baleful look and held out her hand.

"Come with me, Joshua. I'll take you to the toilet and then we'll find your play group."

"'Kay."

"Mr. Sloan, wait in my office for me, please."

The "please" changed nothing. The words were an order. Luke thought of telling the director what she could do with her orders, but he knew that would be a mistake. He needed her cooperation for however long he was going to be here. So he kept his mouth shut, strolled back to the office and settled a hip against the desk.

The lady wanted to talk? Fine. So did he. By the time she returned minutes later, he was more than ready.

"Ms. Kinard."

"Mr. Sloan."

Katherine closed the door, clearly a sign she meant business.

"Mr. Sloan, this isn't going to work."

Luke nodded. "Agreed."

"I cannot have children streaming in here all day."

"And I," Luke said, folding his arms over his chest, "am not here to play nursemaid to a bunch of toddlers."

"They're not all toddlers, Mr. Sloan, and the very last thing I wish you to do is play nursemaid."

"Amen to that."

"Good." Katherine let out a breath and gave him a polite smile. "We agree, then."

"We do."

"I'm sorry this didn't work out, Mr. Sloan...Luke. Shall I inform your lieutenant, or will you?"

"Inform him of what?"

"Why, that you won't be doing your surveillance from our center anymore."

Luke's smile was tight. "I'm not leaving."

"But you just said—"

"I said that I couldn't do my job and play nursemaid."

"Yes, but in that case—"

"Make up some rules. Tell the kids your office is off-limits until I finish here."

"I'm afraid that's impossible. As you said, this is *my* office."

"And this is a police matter," Luke said coolly. "I can't get anything done with kids hanging on my neck." He paused. "And when I get around to using tools—"

"Tools?"

"Tools, Katherine. Saws. Hammers. The things I'll need to do the job right. As far as everyone else knows, I'm a carpenter, remember? I'm going to be building those shelves, and I don't think you'll want rug rats underfoot when I do."

Katherine stared at Luke. Then she sighed and sank into her chair.

"I'm not going to get rid of you that easily, am I?"

"You're not going to get rid of me at all. Go on. Call your attorney. He'll tell you I'm here to stay."

Katherine nodded. The truth was, she'd already spoken with Daniel again and he'd told her the same thing. Nobody would give her much information on what was happening across the street, but it seemed to be important.

The detective was right. They'd need some rules.

Katherine picked up a pencil, tapped it against her lower lip. "Rule number one. Kids can come in during breaks."

"Meaning?"

"Meaning, morning juice, lunch, afternoon snack, late-day snack…"

Luke ran a hand along the back of his neck.

"Goddamn it, Katherine…"

"No bad language."

"Sorry. Look, with all those scheduled breaks, kids will be in and out all the time."

"I'm not going to change the way we run this place, Luke. Besides, I thought it was important to keep things looking as normal as possible. Isn't that why you're representing yourself as something you're not?''

He scowled. That was an accurate description of undercover work, but Luke didn't much like hearing it defined that way. There was something, well, unpleasant in knowing you were deliberately misleading people. People like Abby Douglas—unless she was somehow involved in the fencing operation.

His scowl deepened. Katherine mistook it as an indication he was going to argue and forged ahead.

''And when those break times occur, you will, of course, not use any dangerous tools.''

''Fine.''

''I think it might be a good idea, too, if you spoke to the children in the events room. Explained what a carpenter is, what a carpenter does…show them some of your tools, that sort of thing.''

''Talk to them? But I don't know the first thing about kids.''

''They don't know the first thing about carpenters, either. Or what it's like to have a man in the center all day. We're an all-female staff, in case you hadn't noticed.''

''I noticed,'' Luke said dryly.

''I'll be honest. Nothing personal, but the sooner you're done here—''

''I agree.'' Luke cleared his throat. ''And you can help speed me on my way.''

Katherine leaned back in her chair and tossed her pencil on the desk. ''Just tell me how.''

''Doing surveillance is kind of like doing a giant jigsaw puzzle. At first, all you see are the pieces. Then, gradually—with luck and time and a little bit of skill—the pieces begin to come together.''

It sounded fascinating, but Katherine wasn't foolish enough to let him know that.

''And?''

''Well, you know that I'm watching the jewelry exchange across the street.''

''Yes,'' she said politely. ''But I don't know why. And that's another thing. Being asked for cooperation without being told why is irritating.''

''I'm sure it is,'' Luke said, just as politely, ''but that's standard procedure. What I'd like to do is get as much help as I can in finishing this case so that I can make both of us happy and disappear.''

Katherine winced. Good. Luke would have laid odds that she was a polite woman by nature. She was willing to stand up to him, but letting him see her as inhospitable took some doing. He'd counted on that.

''Detective Sloan…Luke. Honestly, I'm not trying to be difficult.''

''I appreciate that, Katherine.''

''It's just that, well, the parents, my staff—these people all trust me. I hate dragging them into a police operation without them knowing I'm doing it.''

''You aren't dragging them into anything.'' Luke waited a beat. ''I'm sure that virtually all the people you deal with will never need to know what I'm doing.''

''Well, that's good, because… *Virtually* all?'' Katherine narrowed her eyes. ''Why the qualifier, Detective?''

''I can't guarantee anything, that's why. Anything is possible.''

''I really don't follow this. My understanding was that this surveillance had nothing to do with us, that your department only wanted my cooperation because of the location of Forrester Square Day Care to the Emerald City Jewelry Exchange.''

''That's basically correct.''

Katherine threw up her hands. ''Another qualifier! Surely you don't suspect someone here of being connected to whatever is going on across the street?'' She paused and gave an uncomfortable laugh. ''Just listen to me! I'm talking in riddles like you.''

''Here's the point, Katherine. You can help me make this entire procedure move more quickly.''

''How?''

''Well, if I knew something about the people who work

here…'' He paused. ''Or about the people who send their kids here, it would be a big help.''

Katherine looked puzzled, but only for a couple of seconds. Luke could tell the minute she figured out what he meant.

''No.''

''Katherine…''

''You think one of our parents or teachers is involved in something criminal.''

''I didn't say that.''

''You didn't have to. The answer is still the same. No.''

With a sigh, Luke eased away from the desk and tucked his hands into the pockets of his jeans.

''All I want is a quick look through your files.'' Untrue. He'd need more than a quick look, considering that he didn't know what he was looking for, exactly, but then, he hadn't expected to glimpse a parent from Forrester Square working inside the Emerald City Jewelry Exchange, either.

''Absolutely not.''

''Katherine,'' Luke said pleasantly, ''I can subpoena those records if I have to.''

''I don't think so,'' she said, just as pleasantly. ''But if you think you can do it, by all means, Detective, go for it.''

Luke wasn't really disappointed. He'd figured she'd turn him down…and she was right. He didn't have any legal grounds for gaining access to her records. Not yet, anyway.

Well, you couldn't blame a man for trying…and he was going to try one last time.

''That's that, then.'' He started to turn away, then swung toward Katherine. ''One last thing,'' he said casually. ''Is Abby Douglas the only parent here who works at Emerald City?''

Katherine smiled blandly. ''Does Abby work there? I had no idea.''

''You didn't, huh?''

''Is that all, Luke? If it is, I have some calls to make.''

''How long has she had her child enrolled here?''

''Ask Ms. Douglas, why don't you?''

''Is she married?''

The words were out before he could call them back. Katherine looked surprised, but she couldn't be any more surprised than he was. He hadn't intended to ask that question. Abby Douglas's marital status had nothing to do with his investigation.

Still, he'd asked. Now he wanted an answer.

"Is she?"

Katherine puffed her cheeks with air, then blew it out.

"As far as I know, she's not."

"Never? Or is there a man—"

"Uh, uh, uh." Katherine wagged her finger at him. "The interview's over, Detective. And if I were you, I'd get as much work done as I could in the next few minutes because—" she looked at her watch, then flashed him a grin "—the next break is only twenty minutes away."

Luke groaned. "What did I do to deserve this?" he said, raising his eyes to the ceiling.

Katherine laughed as the undercover cop headed back to the corner he'd filled with tools, sawhorses and lumber. She didn't want him here, but she was a pretty good judge of character.

Try as he might to appear tough-skinned and hard-hearted, Luke Sloan seemed like a nice guy.

He had a job to do, though, and she hoped that job didn't include anything about Abby Douglas.

From the little she knew about Abby, Katherine had already concluded that Emily's mom had trouble buried somewhere in her past.

The last thing she needed was more.

CHAPTER FIVE

ABBY COULD HARDLY WAIT for the day to end.

It was better to have the ax fall quickly than to wait for the kiss of the blade.

At a few minutes to six, she'd surely be called to Julian Black's office so he could tell her she was fired.

Abby hoped he'd leave the deed to Bettina. Bettina was single; she didn't have children, but she was a woman and there was always the chance she'd understand how desperately Abby needed this job.

Julian Black would keep that cool, polite smile on his face, but even if she pleaded for another chance, he wouldn't give her one. He made it clear that he expected his clerks to be dependable and to put their job responsibilities ahead of everything else.

Tossing aside a pin worth ten thousand dollars wasn't exactly a sign of dependability. Neither was walking out on a valued customer. But she'd do it all over again if she thought her daughter needed her.

She'd known that even as she'd rushed back to the store, felt the eyes of all the clerks on her as she went inside and saw Bettina standing behind her counter.

Abby had felt her heart sink to her toes. Somehow, against all logic, she'd hoped no one had noticed the way she'd raced from the store.

Impossible, of course. She knew that, just as she knew that soon she'd pay the price.

"Everything all right?" the security guard had asked her.

Bettina was fussing with a tray of rings, arranging them to best advantage.

"Yes. Yes, everything's fine," Abby had said with a nod.

The guard's voice had fallen to a murmur. "Don't you worry about that pin, Abby. I got it back into the case where it—"

Bettina had looked up. "Abby! There you are."

"Bettina." Abby licked her lips and tried to find a way to phrase an explanation that might save her job without giving away too much. "I'm terribly sorry about—"

"Is everything okay? Bill said you thought something might have happened to your daughter."

"No. I mean, she's fine. It was all a misunderstanding."

"Ah. I'm glad to hear it."

"Bettina, I know I left my customer…"

"Mrs. Halpern. Yes. She's quite loyal to you, Abby. I offered to help her, but she said she'd be back later in the day so you could wait on her."

"Oh. That was—that was kind of her. Bettina, look, about what happened…"

"We'll discuss it later." Bettina had glanced at the diamond watch on her wrist, then stepped out from behind the counter. "I have a call to make."

"Of course," Abby had replied, and ever since, she'd waited for Bettina or Mr. Black to come by and say they wanted to see her.

So far, neither of them had appeared.

She'd waited on several customers, sold a gold locket inscribed with a date from the 1950s, sold the ruby and diamond pin to Mrs. Halpern, who seemed to think it was perfectly normal for a clerk to race away in the middle of a sale, and now it was five minutes to six.

The day was over.

The customers were all gone, warned by the discreet tone of a chime ten minutes ago that Emerald City would be closing soon.

Abby checked to make sure her cases were locked, whisked a spot of lint from one of the black velvet display trays as she put it away for the night…and looked up to see Bettina coming toward her.

The moment of truth had arrived.

She felt her belly knot.

"Abby? If you're finished straightening up, I'd like to see you for a minute."

Abby nodded. The other clerks were heading for the back room to collect their coats and bags. She'd be doing the same thing soon, but for the very last time.

She started to come around the counter, but Bettina motioned her to stay where she was.

"We can talk right here," she said.

Yes. They could. After all, how much privacy did someone need to say, You're fired.

Bettina came around to Abby's side of the counter, took Abby's elbow and walked her to where the counter made a ninety-degree turn. There was a little more privacy at that end.

"Now that we have some privacy... What happened this morning? All I know is that one second you were here, and the next you were gone."

At least she'd had time to refine the story, Abby thought, clearing her throat. She'd tell the truth, but not the details. Nobody knew she'd run away from Oregon, that she was hiding from a violent ex-husband. Nobody would ever know. She'd learned that in the shelter. The less people knew about your circumstances, the better your chances of not being found by the man who wanted to hurt you.

"I, uh, I thought my daughter was in danger."

"What? Emily in danger? Doesn't she go to the day care right across the street?"

"Yes"

"My God, Abby! Is she okay?"

"She's fine. It was all a terrible misunderstanding."

The other people who worked in the store began filing by, bundled in raincoats and jackets. Abby could see them just beyond Bettina's shoulder. One gave her a thumbs-up; another offered a sympathetic smile.

"What sort of misunderstanding?"

Abby looked at Bettina. "Well, it began this morning, when I dropped Emily off. She almost collided with a man, someone I'd never seen at Forrester Square before."

"And?"

"He was—curt, I guess you'd call it. I didn't think much of the incident at the time, but later, when I was waiting on Mrs. Halpern, I happened to look out the window. Emily's play group was coming out of the front door…and I saw the same man heading straight for her."

Bettina's delicately arched eyebrows lifted. Abby felt her cheeks redden. As she recounted the story, even though she knew the darker details behind it, she realized just how badly she'd overreacted.

"I know. It sounds ridiculous. But—"

"No. I mean, I don't have kids, but I can put myself in your place. You read so many terrible things in the papers lately about children being abducted…."

"Exactly," Abby said gratefully. "That's why I didn't think. I just reacted."

"Still, you have to view this from our perspective."

Time for the ax to swing, Abby realized.

"You left your counter," Bettina said with a little wag of her finger. "Unlocked, Abby. Unlocked and unstaffed."

"I realize that, and I'm terribly—"

"I'm sure you are, but that doesn't change the facts. Mrs. Halpern said you were showing her a pin. At least you had the presence of mind to put it back in the case."

Abby flushed. *Bless you, Bill.* "Bettina, I know I behaved badly."

"Irresponsibly."

"Yes, but under the circumstances—"

"Under the circumstances…" Bettina sighed. "Under the circumstances, I'm going to overlook this incident."

Abby could almost feel the brush of her guardian angel's wings against her face.

"Thank you," she said quietly.

"But if something like it happens again…"

"It won't."

"You have an enormous responsibility here, Abby. We pride ourselves on the quality and variety of our estate jewelry."

What Bettina meant was that their estate collection made lots of money, but nobody at Emerald City was crass enough to use words like *money*.

"Mr. Black wanted me to let you go." Bettina looked around and leaned in closer. "But when I explained how valuable you were to us, I was able to change his mind."

"That's—that's very kind, Bettina."

The store manager stood back. "Just think about what happened with Mrs. Halpern. She's a valued customer. She's been coming to us for years, and now she's come to rely on your judgment."

"That's nice of you to say, but—"

"Nice? It's the truth." Bettina smiled. "She preferred to come back later when you were here rather than let me wait on her or go to one of our competitors."

Uh-oh. That smile didn't hide the sudden glitter in Bettina's eye. Maybe it wasn't such a good thing to have a customer make a point of saying she preferred you to the manager.

"I'm sure she was only being kind," Abby said carefully, and Bettina laughed.

"*We* are obligated to be kind to our customers. *They* are not obligated to be kind to us. Sometimes, however, if you're lucky, you can establish rapport with a customer. When that happens, he or she will want to deal with you and nobody else." Bettina smiled. "Your Mrs. Halpern, for example. Of course, the longer you're in the business, the better your chance of developing a loyal customer base."

Unsure where this was going, Abby was growing concerned about the time. Emily would be waiting for her inside the day care. Abby tried to pick her up by six-fifteen, though sometimes she was delayed by a private customer, but after this morning's upsetting scene, she didn't want to alter Em's routine.

"I'm working toward that," she said, "and I'm very glad Mrs. Halpern feels that way, but my little girl…"

"Is waiting for you. I should have realized." Bettina slid her arm around Abby's waist and the women moved from behind the counter and started toward the back of the store. "I didn't mean to keep you. I just want to be sure you know that

Mr. Black and I appreciate how well you're doing. Building a loyal customer base is a sign of success, Abby.''

"Thank you.''

"I'm fortunate enough to have several customers who feel that way about me.''

They'd reached the end of the aisle and came to a stop under the loft where Julian Black's office was located. Abby knew it had to be her imagination, but she could almost feel his eyes on her.

"I'm sure you do,'' she said politely.

Bettina gave a tinkling laugh. "I'm not fishing for compliments, I'm simply telling you that if I should be away from the estate jewelry counter... You do recall that I'm going to work it with you Fridays from now on?''

"Oh.'' Actually, Abby had forgotten all about it. "Of course, Bettina. And I understand.''

"Do you?''

"Well, I assume if anyone asks for you and you're not here, you want me to tell them when you'll be back.''

"Right. And I'll put a little stack of note cards and envelopes in the drawer under the register, so they can leave a message for me.'' Bettina made a face. "You know how eccentric some of our customers can be.''

Abby nodded. She didn't, not really, but why argue?

"Good. That's taken care of.'' Bettina smiled and reached into her pocket. "I almost forgot. Here's your paycheck.''

"Thank you.''

"Go on. Pick up your little girl. And have a great weekend.''

Bettina headed for the stairs that led to Julian Black's office. Hurrying into the back room, Abby put on her coat, grabbed her purse, then rushed to the front of the store.

Bill opened the door and winked. "I take it you've still got a job.''

Abby grinned. "Yes. Bill, thanks again for—''

"Go on, Abby. No need to thank me. I have a daughter just about your age, working hard to support herself and her kids. I just hope someone would do the same for her.''

Impulsively, Abby reached up and kissed the guard's grizzled cheek before dashing out the door.

The intermittent rain had finally stopped, leaving the sidewalk wet and glittering. Abby gave a quick check for traffic and ran across the street to the wrought-iron fence that marked the entrance to the day care center.

Children and parents were coming down the steps, the kids babbling happily about their day, the parents doing their best to look as if they were devoting all their attention to the chatter instead of listening with half an ear and thinking about what they could fix for dinner after a hard day at work.

Abby thought about the leftover chicken from last night as she stepped inside the building. No, that wouldn't do. Emily didn't like cold chicken and she didn't have the things she'd need to put together a chicken casserole. If she made a stop at the market now, she could get the cream of mushroom soup and frozen peas for that, plus she could pick up everything for the chocolate chip cookie sleep-over party tomorrow and save herself an early morning supermarket foray—

"Oof!"

Even before she looked up, Abby knew that the stone wall she'd walked into was really Luke Sloan. Nobody else could be as big, as solid....

Nobody else would have Emily clinging to his hand.

She reprimanded herself for the quick bite of panic she felt, and did her best to smile politely when Luke clasped her shoulder to steady her.

"Hey," he said with a little smile. "Looks like we're starting to make a habit of this."

"Sorry. I was late, and...Em? What are you doing, honey? You're supposed to wait with Marilyn until I come for you."

She'd tried to keep her tone light, hoping she didn't sound half as crazed as she had this morning, but the look her daughter gave her said she wasn't fooling her one bit.

"I *am* waiting with Marilyn, Mommy. See? We're all together."

Oh, Lord. Abby felt heat climb her cheeks. Emily was right.

She and Luke were part of a group that included Marilyn and a couple of the other kids whose parents had yet to show.

"Oh. I didn't— Sorry, sweetheart. I didn't—"

"The children had some more questions about power tools for Mr. Sloan," Marilyn said, coming to her rescue.

"Power tools?"

"Yeah." Luke cleared his throat. "We had a little assembly this afternoon. It was Katherine's idea. She thought it would be a good idea if I explained the work I'll be doing here for the next few weeks."

"Oh. Well. Well, that sounds…interesting. Um, well, thank you for keeping Emily busy."

"Mom?"

"Yes, honey?"

"Can Mr. Sloan come home to have dinner with us?"

Abby's head shot up. She stared at Luke and was relieved to see that he looked as stunned as she felt.

"No," he said quickly. "I mean, thank you, Emily. That's a very nice suggestion, but I have, uh, I have —"

"We weren't very nice to Mr. Sloan today, Mommy."

"Emily." Abby bit her lip and tried not to notice the fascinated expressions on the faces of the children—and the teacher, for that matter. She squatted in front of Emily, who let go of Luke's hand. Abby clasped the edges of her daughter's bright yellow raincoat and tugged her closer.

"Honey," she said softly, "Mr. Sloan probably has other plans."

"He doesn't," Emily informed her.

Abby flashed a look at the man towering over her. His high cheekbones were turning a dark, embarrassed red.

"The kids were talking before," he said, his words a desperate rush, "about the weekend. You know, their plans, what they'd be doing. And they got to discussing tonight, and one little guy said he was going out to dinner with his parents, and one of the girls said she was going to her grandmother's, and they asked what I was doing tonight, and I said I wasn't…" His voice faltered. "I said I wasn't doing anything, but I didn't mean…"

"See?" Emily stepped back and reached for Luke's hand. "He's not doing anything tonight, Mommy. And we were mean to him today, and that time I was mean to Lily, remember, before we were good friends? You said I had to let her know I was sorry by doing something really nice."

"Yes, but that's…"

Different, Abby was going to say, but how was it different, exactly? And how was she ever going to dig her way out of this hole with such a fascinated audience, she thought, biting back a groan.

"Em." It was Luke who squatted down in front of Emily this time, an earnest look on his face. "Look, your invitation was very generous. But—"

"Don't you want to have supper with Mommy and me?"

Oh, crap, Luke thought. Whatever answer he gave was going to be a mistake. The kid's lip was starting to quiver, her mother looked as if she wanted to find the nearest mouse hole to hide in, the teacher and kids were paying such rapt attention that he could almost hear this miserable little story being told over the entire city. What was he supposed to do, damn it? He was a cop on a case, and the first rule—okay, maybe not the first, but an important rule was Don't Get Personally Involved.

"Tell you what," he said quietly. "What if I take a rain check?"

"What's a rain check?" Emily asked in a wobbly voice.

"It means that Mr. Sloan—"

"Luke."

Abby nodded as Luke rose to his feet. "It means Luke can have supper with us some other time."

"I bet he won't," one of the children said.

The kids giggled, Marilyn snickered, and Luke decided that enough was enough.

"Okay," he said cheerfully. "Em? Ms. Douglas? Why don't we discuss this outside? I'll, uh, I'll walk you to your car. How's that sound?"

"It sounds like a fine idea." Abby snatched at the lifeline and rewarded Luke with a quick smile. "Em? Honey, say good-night to everybody and let's get going, shall we?"

"G'night," Emily murmured.

Her mouth was turned down in a perfect half moon, but Abby acted as if she hadn't noticed. She took one of her daughter's hands, Luke took the other, and they went out the door and down the steps.

Luke glanced at Emily, then at Abby. "Does she know her face might freeze like that if she keeps that expression long enough?" he asked conversationally.

Abby looked at him. "What?"

"The kid," he said, and winked. "I was wondering if you ever told her that you have to be careful making a face, because you might end up with it for the rest of your life."

He saw the glint of humor in Abby's eyes. "No," she said in a matter-of-fact tone, "I don't believe I ever got around to telling Em that."

"Ah," Luke said as he opened the gate. "Well, never mind. Maybe she's just one of those people who likes to look as if she just bit into a lemon."

"What people?" Emily asked, still glowering.

"Oh, you know. The ones who don't mind going around with their eyes all scrunched up and their mouths skinny as slits."

"I don't look like that."

"Lemme see." Luke jogged ahead a couple of paces, bent down and peered into her face. "Yeah, you do."

"Do not!"

"You do, Em. But if you don't mind having your face freeze that way, hey, it's your business."

"Faces don't freeze," Emily said with confidence, then reconsidered and looked up at her mother. "Do they, Mommy?"

"Well, I'm not sure, Em. My mom used to tell me that they did, but I have to admit, I never saw anyone whose face had frozen."

"Then you never met my aunt Mary."

Emily and Abby both looked at Luke. He nodded wisely.

"Aunt Mary got mad at Uncle Jim one day, made a really ugly face behind his back, and that was it." Luke gave a deep sigh. "Never could take her out in public again."

Emily stared at him. "You made that up."

"Guy in our village carved my aunt's likeness into a totem pole."

The child's eyes widened. "Are you an Indian?"

"Emily," Abby said quickly, but Luke just nodded.

"Yup. Half of me, anyway." He looked at Emily. "You know what they did with that totem pole?"

"What?" Emily said, enraptured.

"They set it just outside the village to scare away the bears."

"No they didn't." Luke's expression remained bland, and Emily began to giggle. "You *did* make that up!"

A smile curved Luke's mouth. "Well, maybe I exaggerated a little, but it did the trick and made you laugh. You look a lot prettier now than you did a minute ago. I bet your mom thinks so, too."

He looked over Emily's head at Abby. She was smiling, and for some crazy reason, he felt pretty good about being the one who'd put that smile on her face.

"Thank you," Abby said.

"No problem." He held his smile, and her eyes, until he saw her cheeks start to pinken. When she looked away, so did he, and wondered what in hell he was doing, flirting with a woman who could very well turn out to be instrumental in his investigation.

The rain, ever-dependable, chose that moment to pick up in intensity.

"Where's your car?" Luke said.

Abby jerked her head toward Emerald City. "Behind the jewelry store."

They clasped Emily's hands tightly and ran across the street, moving so quickly they all but lifted her off her feet.

"Whee," Emily said happily.

Abby laughed as they dashed into the lot. Here she was, getting wet and laughing about it. Amazing, considering how her day had begun.

"That's it. The black Focus right over there."

She stuck her key in the door, hustled Emily into the back

seat and tucked herself behind the wheel. Luke slammed both doors shut and she put down her window.

The rain was falling steadily now, glinting against his black hair and his black leather jacket. Luke Sloan, Abby thought suddenly, was an incredibly good-looking man.

Her heart gave an unsteady lurch. She couldn't recall the last time she'd looked at a man and thought anything remotely like that.

"Well," she said, "well…can I give you a lift?"

"No, that's okay. I'm parked right over in the day care lot."

"In that case…"

"Mommy," a small voice piped up from the car seat behind Abby, "you an' Luke didn't talk about when he's gonna come over for dinner."

Abby bit her lip. Now what? Actually, the "now what" was simple. She could arrange for Luke to come to dinner some evening right now…,

Or she could just give in for Em's sake, say, *Okay, let's have your Mr. Sloan come home with us, Emily.* She'd stop at the market, as she'd intended, blow the life out of her budget by buying three steaks. Well, just two. She and Em could share one. Steaks, and salad, and potatoes for baking. That was a man's meal, and surely Luke Sloan would enjoy…

"We'll discuss it another time," she said briskly. "Em, say good-night to Mr. Sloan."

"But, Mommy…"

"Say good-night, Emily."

"But you said…"

"Emily," Luke said gently, "don't argue with your mom."

"But—"

"Hey, you want me to drown out here?" Luke smiled, reached in and ruffled Emily's bangs. "See you tomorrow, okay?"

"Monday," Emily said. "I won't see you for the whole weekend."

Emily's voice was small, but she made the word "whole" sound like forever. Abby glanced in the mirror and sighed. If there was one thing she always tried to do with her little girl, it was keep her promises.

"How's this for a plan?" she said.

Em's expression brightened. "What?"

"Well, next Parent Day, if Mr. Sloan is still here, we'll all have lunch together."

Emily hung her head. "That's not the same thing."

No, Abby thought, it wasn't, and what kind of mess was this turning into? If Luke Sloan were short, fat and bald, would she be making such a fuss over Em's misguided invitation, or would she simply go with it?

She didn't want to think about the answer. Instead, she stuck her key in the ignition.

"We have to go, Em. And Mr. Sloan—"

"Luke."

"And Luke really is getting drenched, so, Emily, say goodnight."

The child snuffled. "G'night."

Luke nodded. "Good night, kid." He leaned down, folded his arms on the open window and smiled at Abby. She got a whiff of an indefinable woodsy scent as well as a deeper glimpse into those fantastic green eyes. "Sorry about this," he said softly.

"Me, too. It's not that I don't want to... I mean, it isn't because..."

"I understand." He straightened up and tapped the roof of the car lightly with his hand. "Well, goodbye."

"Goodbye," Abby said, and turned the key. And turned it again.

Luke had started to walk away, but he looked back at the sound of the engine whining.

"Problem?"

"Yes. No. I don't..." Abby slapped the wheel with the heels of her hands. "I just had it serviced a couple of weeks ago. Some sort of problem with the timing, the mechanic said."

"Pop the hood," Luke said, walking to the front of the car.

Abby did as he asked. Luke raised the hood, then peered into the car's innards, poking at this and that while she tried to remember exactly what the mechanic had said about the timing. The truth was, talk about anything mechanical flew right over her head.

Her parents had kept her sheltered. Frank had, too. At least, that was how he'd made it seem, except what he'd really done was control her every breath.

She'd taken charge of her own life since leaving him. She could balance a checkbook without blinking, make a budget and keep to it, take a handful of chicken and some rice and turn it into a meal, but she was lost when it came to anything mechanical.

Luke slammed the hood and brushed off his hands. "I can't tell much," he said, "not without some tools."

With a groan, Abby leaned her forehead against the steering wheel. She'd been too quick to think this day would end well, after all. A hundred bucks to the mechanic last week. Another hundred this week, probably even more.

At least she didn't need the car for work tomorrow, but meanwhile, how was she supposed to get home?

"Mr. Sloan could drive us," a little voice from the back seat said, as if Emily had read her mother's mind.

Luke nodded. "That's just what I was going to suggest."

Abby lifted her head. "I couldn't impose like that."

"Where do you live, Abby?"

"Over in Magnolia."

"Well, that's no problem, then. You guys can just walk home. Take you, what, an hour?"

He said it so seriously that she had to laugh. "All right. Thank you. We'll accept your offer, Mr...,"

"Luke," he said as he opened her door and then Emily's. "Considering the fact that I'm going to give you a lift home, come back tomorrow and see what I can do to fix your car, I think we really ought to stay on a first-name basis, don't you?"

"I'll pay you, of course."

"I don't take money from friends."

"But—"

"But," Luke said, looking at Abby's flushed face, "I'm willing to make an exception."

"Just tell me what it costs—"

"Dinner," he said softly. "Whatever night you like. How's that sound?"

Abby sighed. "It sounds like I'm going to get the better end of the deal."

"Hey, for a guy who lives on frozen dinners, getting a home-made meal is like winning the lottery."

She laughed, just as he'd hoped she would. The last thing he wanted was for Abby to think he was taking advantage of the situation…even if he was.

"In that case," she said, "it's a deal."

"Good." Luke straightened up. "I'll get my car, drive back here and collect you and Em."

"We could go with you."

"Yeah, you could, but there's no reason for all of us to get soaked. You stay put. I'll be right back."

It sounded like an order and Abby almost bristled. But Luke was smiling, and before she knew it, she smiled back.

He turned away, put up his collar and trotted from the lot.

She watched until he disappeared around the side of the building.

Then she sat back and wondered what, exactly, she was getting herself into.

CHAPTER SIX

SATURDAY MORNING, LUKE opened one eye, saw the gray light seeping through the vertical window blinds, punched his pillow into shape and turned on his side.

It was the weekend and the sun was playing hard to get. Both were fine reasons for sleeping in.

A couple of minutes later, his eyes shot open.

Abby's car. He'd promised her he'd check it out, see about getting it started, and deliver it to her, one way or the other.

Luke stretched, yawned, rolled onto his back, folded his hands under his head and stared up at the ceiling.

"I don't want you to spoil your Saturday plans," she'd told him as he drove her home last night.

He'd assured her he had no plans.

It was true.

When he and Dan weren't working a case that kept them going Saturdays, he usually kicked around the condo, taking care of whatever needed to be done. Laundry. Bills. Shopping—although it didn't take very long to hit the supermarket's frozen food aisle and flip a week's worth of dinners into the cart. Then he'd head over to Dan's late for a little one-on-one, maybe get together in the evening for poker with some of the guys from work.

Once in a while, he'd even get himself together enough to take a woman to dinner and a movie.

But that part happened only once in a while. If a woman was interesting enough for more than a couple of dates, you were heading into deep water. Commitment, for lack of a better word. And commitment hadn't been on his agenda since his divorce.

You found your wife in bed with another man, it sort of made you wary of getting involved again.

Molly was great at scolding him about that.

"You can't stay single forever," she'd say. "You'll end up a lonely old man."

And he'd say with a smile that she might have something there, but the only woman in the world he'd even consider was already taken, and she would laugh, tuck a graying strand of hair behind her ear and tell him he had more blarney in him than either she or Dan.

What he didn't tell her was that even though he was a long way from being old, there were times he was lonely already. He and Janine had lived separate lives in a lot of ways, but it had been nice, seeing her across the table at breakfast, knowing she was waiting for him when he came home at night.

And, separate lives or not, they'd always been faithful to each other.

Luke scowled at the ceiling.

Correction. *He'd* been faithful, and until the night he'd stopped at home unexpectedly and found her in bed—*their* bed—with another man, he'd believed Janine was faithful, too.

"You didn't know her," Molly had told him once. Dan had tried to shush her, but Molly had forged ahead. "Sharing a bed isn't enough," she'd said bluntly. "Marriage is about sharing your hearts."

Was she right? Had he and Janine kept a wall between them? Had they subconsciously been unwilling to share themselves with each other?

They hadn't shared many interests, that was for sure.

Janine didn't like sitting around on a cool winter evening, watching old movies. She wanted to be up and out all the time, seeing people and things, dancing in the newest clubs. He liked that, too, sometimes, but the truth was, he preferred quieter moments, quieter places.

Janine said he was antisocial. It was, she figured, because he was a cop.

Maybe she had something there. And maybe that was why he liked the cabin up on the peninsula, near Neah Bay.

It was little more than a fishing shack, really. It had belonged to his grandfather, and he'd gone there with the old man several times after his mom died, when he was a little kid. The fishing was fun, but the best part was just sitting on the sagging porch at night, looking at the stars and listening as his grandfather told him stories about the old days and the old ways.

His ancestors had been a proud, brave, warlike people, his grandfather said, and he told Luke about the whale hunts they'd asked to begin again, and how important it was to understand that the whales gave themselves up to the Makah because the Makah had respect for the whales' souls.

Luke sighed.

He wasn't so sure about the hunts and the whales giving themselves up, but he was positive that those times at the cabin had been special.

He'd gone back to the place for the first time in years after he and Janine had been married a few months. No special reason, really, just that he'd thought about the cabin and the forest and the ocean, and then he'd thought, well, why not take a look, see if he could fix the place up a little?

Even then he'd been thinking that maybe he and his wife needed a getaway spot, someplace where they could leave the world behind and just be together.

Janine had gone with him twice, the first time out of curiosity, the second time under protest.

What was there to do all the way up on the Olympic Peninsula? she'd said petulantly. She liked shops, and bright lights, and the buzz of people. And since when did they have to do everything in lockstep? Luke liked it up there in the middle of nowhere? Fine. He could head for Neah Bay whenever he wanted.

She had her life. He had his. It was one of the things they'd both liked in their marriage, wasn't it? Independence?

Yes, Luke thought, answering the question for himself just as he had when Janine posed it. He'd wanted a woman who could deal with a cop's life. The irregular hours. The ever-present danger.

There was nothing wrong with a little emotional self-sufficiency.

If his mother had possessed some, maybe she wouldn't have fallen apart after his father left for parts unknown. Maybe she could have stood up to life a little better. Maybe...

Maybe it was time to get moving.

Luke sat up and ran his hands over his face.

Why waste time rehashing the past? He had better things to do, like dealing with Abby's car.

And if that meant spending some time with her today, well, that was good. He'd have the chance to get a feel for who she was, what she was like, maybe find out a little bit about Emerald City and what might be going on there. At the same time he'd be helping her out.

It wasn't every day a man could play Good Samaritan and cop at the same time.

That was definitely the only reason he was feeling good about today.

It had nothing to do with Abby as a woman.

Nothing at all.

Luke reached for the phone and hit a speed-dial button. It was still early enough to catch Dan before his partner left to do surveillance on the exchange for the day.

Dan answered on the first ring.

"I already heard," he said.

Luke raised his eyebrows. "Good morning to you, too."

"Yeah, yeah. Good morning, all that stuff. Now that that's over with, I already know."

"You know that I need you to give me a lift this morning? What are you, psychic?"

"A lift? What're you talking about?"

Luke sighed and swung his legs to the floor. "Okay. Let's start again. What is it you already heard?"

"That the Emerald City Jewelry Exchange is closed today for inventory. The owner and manager are going in at noon, but they won't be opening the doors to the public, meaning I don't get the exciting experience of sitting in the spy-mobile, trying to stay awake while I watch the place."

"That's not why I called."

"Yeah, so you just told me. You need a lift. Don't tell me that brand new SUV of yours broke down."

"You're just jealous that I'm driving a big, bad gasaholic truck while you're still driving a station wagon," Luke said, smiling.

"Wait until you have two kids away in college, pal. You'll be looking for ways to cut corners, too."

It was a takeoff on an old routine, Dan kidding Luke about being a bachelor, Luke kidding Dan about being an old married man, but underneath it all, Luke could hear the pride his partner had in his sons.

It must be nice to feel that way, Luke thought, and then he scowled and explained why he needed Dan's help.

AN HOUR LATER, the two men sat opposite each other in a booth at a diner near Luke's condo.

"Molly's waffles are better," Dan said, dragging a forkful of waffle through the pool of maple syrup on his plate.

Luke, finished with a toasted bagel, bacon and two eggs over easy, sat back with his hands wrapped around a mug of coffee.

"Is that why you ate every bite of what was on your plate?"

Dan grinned as he laid his knife and fork across his plate.

"Wouldn't want to insult the cook," he said, dabbing at his mouth with his napkin. "Besides, a man needs to start the day with a breakfast that'll stick to his ribs."

"Uh-huh. And two breakfasts are even better," Luke raised an eyebrow at Dan's wide-eyed look. "You don't really expect me to believe Molly let you out the door without feeding you first."

"Yeah, but I had to be sociable here, right? Keep you company while you ate? I mean, otherwise, what are friends for?" Dan smothered a burp, spooned sugar into his coffee and stirred it. "So, tell me again why I'm driving you to Belltown at eight in the morning on a Saturday neither one of us is supposed to be working."

"I told you. One of the women who works at the jewelry store—"

"—has a kid at the day care center, and her car broke down last night when she was about to head home."

"That's right."

"And you're involved in this because…?"

"I told you that, too. I was walking the lady and her kid to her car."

"Uh-huh. So you walked this babe to her car, drove her home, and now you're going to see if you can get her car started, after which you're going to drive it to her house."

"And you're coming along for the ride so I don't end up having to ask her to drive me back to the lot so I can pick up my car, which I'd have to leave there."

"I figured that part by myself."

"Yeah. Anybody can tell by the way you gather facts that you're a trained investigator," Luke said dryly.

"Well, here's a fact for *you,* my man. Playing Sir Galahad is not part of a surveillance."

"Abby works at the jewelry store."

"Abby?"

Luke could feel his face heat. "Just seems senseless to keep referring to the lady without using her name."

"Gotcha. You're expanding the surveillance? You're investigating this babe?"

"She's not a babe."

"Sorry. Figure of speech, that's all."

"Look, I told you, she works there. So if she mentions something useful about Emerald City, that's cool. Basically, though, her car wouldn't start, it was pouring cats and dogs, it would have cost her big bucks for a tow and a taxi, and I was standing right there with my truck parked across the street. You'd have offered a woman and a little kid a lift, too."

"You're probably right."

"I'm definitely right."

"But I wouldn't have offered to go back and see to her dead car the next morning."

"No," Luke said, "you certainly wouldn't, because you're a married man."

"A married man can't do a good deed?"

"Not for a woman who's a babe."

"I thought you just said…" Dan saw the smile his friend was trying to conceal and grinned. "She is, huh?"

"Yeah, she is, but I'd have made the same offer if she wasn't."

"Like I said—Sir Galahad." Dan dug some bills from his wallet and put them on the table. "Breakfast's on me."

"Fine. The check's mine next time."

"Darned right, it is." Dan opened the diner door and the men walked toward his car. "The lieutenant told me all that stuff about the old broad thinking she saw her stolen necklace in that display case."

"Uh-huh."

"You think she really did? I had an aunt and uncle lived in L.A. We used to go visit once a year or so. Went down to celebrate my aunt's ninetieth birthday. She wanted us all to give my uncle a hug."

"So?"

"So, he'd been dead twenty years."

Luke chuckled as they got into Dan's car. "Yeah, I agree. The old lady's not the most reliable witness, but it's too soon to know much of anything. I set up a couple of cameras, the usual stuff. We'll give it a little time and see what happens."

"Maybe you'll luck out and this…Abby, was it? She might give you a lead."

"Anything's possible."

"You might *really* get lucky, and it'll turn out you've already fingered the fence, and we can get the names of her customers from her."

"Like I said, anything is possible."

Dan flashed him a look of curiosity.

"You're not, you know, getting into something here?"

"Getting into what?"

"Some personal involvement?"

Luke rolled his eyes. "I told you, I'm helping Abby with her car."

"Yeah, but you sound as if you'd rather not imagine her helping the scum that steals the stuff."

"She's a single mother, Dan. And she seems like a nice woman. Yeah, I guess I do hope she's not involved."

"We've both been cops long enough to know that you can't judge a book by its cover."

"That works both ways. Maybe we forget that sometimes."

Dan nodded. "Sure." He looked at his partner, searching for a way to lighten what threatened to become a sticky moment. "I was just afraid all that management-seminar touchy-feely stuff might be catching."

Luke grinned. "No way, man. And if you ask me to share my feelings, I'm liable to punch you out."

"That's a relief," Dan said, laughing.

"Okay. Take a left at the next corner, go straight for two lights, then hang a right."

"I could hardly believe it when McDowell said you were set up inside a day care center."

"Tell me about it," Luke said dryly.

"On the other hand, Molly thought it was a fine idea."

"Your wife thinks being around a bunch of rug rats will make me feel domestic."

"She said you were terrific with our boys when they were home."

Luke smiled. "How're they doing?"

"Fine. And as long as I can manage to come up with the tuition payments every year, it looks like we're gonna turn out an accountant and an engineer. Who'd have thunk it?"

"Your kids were, what, ten and eleven when you and I met?"

"Yeah, just about."

"Well, that's why I did okay with them. I mean, kids are human by that age," Luke said.

Dan laughed.

"You know what I mean," Luke protested. "Old enough to talk with, joke with, stuff like that. But some of the kids at Forrester Square Day Care are still in diapers. There's the second light, up ahead."

"The babe... The woman's kid—Abby's kid—is that young?"

"Emily is four." Luke shrugged his shoulders. "Nice little girl. Sweet. Smart, too."

"Almost human, huh?" Dan said sardonically.

"Okay, so maybe I was wrong when I said that. It's just that I've never spent much time with little kids, except for a passel of cousins, and I haven't seen them in years. Anyway, Emily's a charmer. Tough on the outside, too, except there's something under the toughness, same as with her mother."

"Such as?"

"I don't know." Luke folded his arms. "It's like Abby's guarding a secret, and the stress of carrying it is somehow weighing on the kid."

"Something to do with jewelry, maybe? I'm not saying the lady's a suspect," Dan added quickly. "Just thinking out loud, is all."

Luke let a long minute go by. "I'm keeping my mind open, Dan. You know me well enough for that. It's just... I have this gut feeling Abby's clean. Plus, back to square one. We don't know for sure that somebody really is fencing stuff through Emerald City."

"True." Dan looked at Luke and assumed a solemn expression. "Your mission, Detective Sloan," he said, his voice deep and dramatic, "should you choose to accept it...."

Luke grinned. "Take the next right," he said, and Dan pulled into the parking lot where Abby had left her car the night before. "Over there. That Ford..."

He fell silent. There was another car in the lot, a Mercedes Roadster, parked parallel to the curb near the store's rear door. Its trunk lid was up.

Luke glanced at his watch. It was twenty after eight. Based on what Dan had told him, nobody was supposed to be here for another four hours.

"Dan," Luke said softly.

"Yeah. I see it."

Sudden awareness stretched between the men like a high-voltage line. They'd worked together long enough that neither had to explain what he was thinking.

This was a store filled with a fortune in jewels, a store that was supposed to be closed right now. Nothing else was stirring all along this piece of Sandringham Drive, and here was a car, snugged up to the back door, its trunk open.

"Probably nothing," Dan said, pulling up alongside the Ford but never taking his eyes from the Mercedes.

"You're right." Luke eased open his door. "Could be the owner decided to come in early."

"Bound to be that," Dan said, opening his door, too.

Luke nodded. He reached under his jacket, routinely felt for the comfort of his automatic, and muttered a short, sharp word when he found nothing. He was working undercover; a man didn't carry a weapon when he was masquerading as a carpenter.

Dan unzipped his Mariners jacket, touched the small of his back and nodded.

"Nothing to worry about," he said in a low voice. "We both know this is—"

"Probably nothing."

They walked slowly toward the Mercedes, spreading apart as they reached it. The door to the jewelry store was closed. Luke signaled to Dan; he'd knock on the door, Dan would back him.

Without warning, the door swung open. A man and woman stepped into the gray light, the man holding an attaché case. Luke saw the color drain from his face when he saw them. The woman gave a shrill little cry and grabbed the man's arm.

"Everybody just take it easy," Dan said.

"Julian," the woman whispered. "Julian, who are these men?"

"An excellent question, Bettina." The man glared at Luke and Dan. "Who are you, and what's your business here?" His voice carried the authority of someone accustomed to being obeyed.

"You first, pal," Dan said. "Who are *you,* and what are you doing here?"

Luke said nothing. The guy wasn't showing a weapon. Neither was the woman. If they had a legitimate reason for being inside the store, then he couldn't afford to blow his cover.

"If this is a robbery…"

"This is the police," Dan said sharply, and hauled out his shield. He looked from the man to the woman. "Who are you?"

"Julian Black." The man seemed to stand taller. "I own this store."

Dan shot Luke a look. Luke gave an imperceptible shrug. Same as Dan, he knew the name but he had no idea if this was Black or not.

"I'm Bettina Carlton," the woman said in a quavering voice. "The manager."

"You got ID?" Dan asked.

"Yes," Bettina said quickly. "My driver's license, credit cards…"

Luke looked at the man who'd identified himself as Julian Black. He wanted to ask him the same question, but maybe it was best to keep quiet and let Dan deal with this. He had a gut feeling that he was better off not letting these people know he was a cop.

Dan checked Bettina's ID. "Okay. Now, how about you, mister?"

Black fixed him with a piercing stare. "In my pocket."

"Which pocket?"

"Are you aware that the mayor is a personal friend of mine?"

"The ID, please."

"This is ridiculous. I've a mind to— " Black huffed out a breath. "Left rear trouser pocket."

"Take it out."

The man yanked out his wallet, flipped it open and held it toward Dan, but his eyes kept darting to Luke. Dan peered at the driver's license inside, then nodded.

"Okay. You're Julian Black."

Dan let out a breath. So did Luke. Bettina gave an audible moan of relief. Only Black went on scowling.

"Explain yourselves," Black demanded. "What is going on here?"

"We, uh, we…"

Dan fell silent. Luke knew he'd realized that whatever they might say could give the game away. The odds were he'd never see Black or Bettina again, but all cops knew how easily the odds could change, especially since he'd be right across the street for the next few weeks.

"We saw your car," Luke said quickly, "and I mentioned that the exchange was supposed to be closed today."

"And just how did you know that?"

"I work across the street."

"At the day care center?"

"That's right."

"So, you decided to investigate?"

Black's voice was oily with sarcasm. Luke could hardly blame him. It was a thin story, at best.

"It's my job," Dan said coldly. "Or would you prefer cops look the other way when they see something out of order?"

Black hesitated. Slowly, his expression softened.

"Perhaps I overreacted, Officer…?"

"Detective. Detective Daniel Shayne."

"And you are…?"

"Luke Sloan."

Luke smiled politely. He could see the color returning to Black's face. For a couple of minutes there, the man looked as if he were going to pass out. Well, why wouldn't he? He'd been working inside his own store and walked out of it to find company waiting. For all he knew, that company could have been a pair of thieves.

"You're right. It's good to know our city's finest—" Black smiled "—and even friends of our finest keep their eyes open all the time." He tossed the attaché case in the trunk and closed the lid. "But I think I should warn you to be careful about springing surprises outside jewelry stores in the future."

"We're always careful, sir," Dan said politely.

"Yes, but if I really were a thief, I could have pulled a gun on you."

"You carrying one?"

"I'm not, but many owners of stores like Emerald City go armed for self-protection. In fact, you're lucky I'm driving my-

self today. My chauffeur *is* armed. And licensed,'' he added.
''And he's very quick.''

''We'll keep that in mind.''

Black nodded. ''Please do.'' He turned his attention to the
woman, smiled and closed his hand around her elbow. ''Bettina?''

''Yes, Mr. Black.''

''It's time we got moving.'' Black opened the door on the
passenger side, then went around to the driver's side and slid
behind the wheel. ''Thank you again for your well-intentioned
interference, gentlemen.''

Smiling, he held out his hand. Dan shook it, then Luke.

''Sorry about this,'' Luke said. ''I guess we just never figured anybody would work on his day off.''

Black chuckled. ''Ah. Well, that's what happens when
you're your own boss,'' he said pleasantly. ''You never actually have a day off.''

''Must be a problem,'' Dan said.

''Oh, it can be. There's always the tendency to overdo.'' He
put the car in gear. ''That's why my manager and I had to
come in today.''

''Doing inventory?'' Luke said, just to make conversation.
''That's what I heard, anyway.''

''Yes. I hate the job, but it has to be done, and you really
need extremely responsible people to do it. That's why Bettina
and I get stuck with it.''

''Makes sense.''

''We decided to get an early start, take a long break for
breakfast, then pick up where we left off.'' He paused. ''You
know, you gentlemen never did explain what *you're* doing
here.''

''One of your employees couldn't get her car started last
night.'' Luke jerked his head toward Abby's Ford. ''We came
to pick it up.''

''Ah. I noticed that car last evening and again this morning,
but I didn't think much of it. This lot's private property, but
it's a busy neighborhood. Parking's tight. People leave their

vehicles here all the time.'' He paused. ''Whose car is it, anyway?''

''Abby Douglas's.''

''Abby Douglas. She's one of our best salesclerks, isn't that right, Bettina?''

''One of our best,'' Bettina said pleasantly.

''Well. Is there anything I can help you with? Shall I stop at a garage and send back a tow truck for Ms. Douglas's vehicle?''

''No, we're fine,'' Luke said. ''But thanks for the offer.''

''In that case… Again, my thanks to you, Detective, for being so conscientious.''

Dan nodded. Black put a finger to his forehead in a salute and then goosed the Mercedes, which gave a deep-throated purr as it roared away.

Luke and Dan watched it go. They exchanged glances, then, without a word, started back toward the Ford.

''You got the keys for this thing?''

Luke shot a look at the exit from the parking lot. The Mercedes had already disappeared into traffic.

''Yeah.'' He tossed Abby's keys to Dan, who got behind the wheel and turned the key in the ignition.

Nothing happened.

''Okay,'' Luke said, ''pop the hood.''

He peered inside the engine compartment. There'd been an advantage to the old monsters he'd driven on the rez when he was a kid. You could make sense of what you saw. Not anymore. Everything was computers and chips.

Sighing, he straightened up. Sometimes the simplest things worked.

''Let's try jumping it.''

Dan got the cables from his trunk and attached them. He signaled Luke, who turned the key.

The jump worked like a charm. The Ford sputtered and came to life.

''Problem solved,'' Luke said.

Dan nodded. ''Great. I'll follow you to—what's her name again?''

"Abby. Abby Douglas."

"I'll follow you to her house, you drop off the car and I'll take you home."

"No," Luke said after a second or two, "don't bother. I need to take a better look, make sure this was all the car needed."

"Well, then, give me a call when you're finished and I'll pick you up. Molly says to tell you she's making corned beef and cabbage for dinner."

"Tell her she's the love of my life."

"If I do, she'll just get a swelled head." Dan grinned and dumped the jumper cables in the back of his station wagon. "So, I'll see you later."

"Yeah, I'll call you."

Dan started the car, then leaned out the window.

"Luke?"

"Yeah?"

"Was he serious? Julian Black? Is he pals with the mayor?"

"That's what the lieutenant said."

"Crap. I just hope he meant it, all that stuff about deciding we were really the good guys, just doing our job."

Luke grinned. "What's this 'we' stuff, *kemosabe?* You were doing your job. Me? I'm just a carpenter, tagging along with my buddy."

"Thanks for the vote of support."

"Hey, man, you know you can always count on me."

The men smiled at each other. Luke tapped the roof of Dan's car with his hand, then stepped back.

"See you later."

"Later," Dan echoed, and drove off.

Luke stood watching as the car merged into the slow early-morning traffic. After a minute, he got into the Ford and wrapped his hands around the steering wheel.

He'd met Emerald City's owner and manager. Now he was busy trying to decide what he thought of them after a five-minute conversation.

Crazy? Maybe, but he was a cop. He'd spent years sizing up people, making what anybody else would call snap judgments. Besides, assuming there really was a fencing operation going on at Emerald City, everybody in the place was a suspect, even the owner and manager.

But he wasn't supposed to be a cop now, not for the rest of the day. He'd drive to Abby's, just a guy who'd offered to help a woman with a problem.

Whistling softly through his teeth, Luke headed the car out of the parking lot.

CHAPTER SEVEN

ABBY SMILED AS SHE CLEANED up after breakfast.

Emily was singing a song about flowers and showers and bowers as she straightened up her bedroom in anticipation of Lily's visit later in the day, and her warbling soprano drifted down the hall.

After she'd put the orange juice in the fridge and wiped up the crumbs around the toaster, Abby suddenly heard the familiar sound of her car's engine coming up the driveway, a rumbling counterpoint to Em's voice.

Surprised, she looked up at the clock. It was just past eight-thirty. Luke hadn't said when he'd be coming by, but somehow she hadn't expected him this early.

She wiped her hands on a dish towel, untied her apron, dropped it on a chair and flung open the door to the broom closet. She'd nailed a mirror to the inside, just at Emily's height, so her little girl could check herself before they went out the door each morning.

Face clean. Hair combed. Smile bright. That was their daily litany.

Now Abby scrunched down and stared at herself in that same mirror. Her hair was loose, damp and drying in unmanageable waves from her shower. Her face was scrubbed shiny. She had yet to put on mascara or even a dab of lipstick. And maybe she should have worn something other than jeans and a Save the Rain Forest T-shirt....

Abby stood up straight.

What on earth was she thinking?

She didn't need to dry her hair or put on lipstick to go outside and say thank-you to Luke for bringing her car here. This wasn't a social call.

Still, she paused when she got to the door and found that she needed to take a deep breath before she could open it.

Such foolishness, she thought, and stepped out onto the tiny porch that went with her ground-floor apartment in a rambling old Victorian just as Luke climbed out of the car.

He was wearing his leather jacket and faded jeans, and he must have heard the door shut because he turned around and looked at her, so early-morning handsome that it caught her by surprise. Abby felt as if a quick hot wind had come out of nowhere to scoop her off her feet.

Luke's mouth curved into a smile. "Good morning."

"Yes, isn't it? I mean, it's definitely a good…" She laughed and shook her head. "Sorry. Good morning. I guess I'm still not wide awake. I didn't expect you so early."

"My fault. I never thought… Look, if my timing's bad—"

"No. It's fine. I didn't mean…" She swallowed and came down the steps. "I just meant that it's bad enough I'm taking a piece of your Saturday morning without making you get up early, too."

"Hey, I've been falling out of bed at six for so long that it's habit by now. Don't worry about it."

His eyes made a fast sweep from her mop of unruly hair down to her sneakers, then back to her face. He smiled in a way that was purely male, and she felt that long-forgotten frisson of male-female awareness again.

Flustered, she put her hands to her hair and smoothed it back behind her ears.

"Well…" she said.

"Which rain forest?"

Abby blinked. "Excuse me?"

"Your T-shirt."

She looked down and saw the words Save the Rain Forest marching across her chest.

"Oh. Oh, you mean…"

"Uh-huh." Luke tucked his hands into the back pockets of

his jeans. "I just wondered if you had any special rain forest in mind."

She looked down at her shirt again, as if the answer might be printed there, and told herself to say something before he decided she was an idiot.

"Not really. I, uh, I bought this at a street fair. There was an environmental booth, and…"

She stopped in midsentence. Luke didn't actually care why she was wearing the shirt. It was just man-woman banter, and she certainly didn't want to encourage him to think that was why she'd agreed to let him give her a hand last night.

The sooner he got that message, the better for them both.

"Rain forests in general," she said briskly.

"Ah. Well, at the risk of being branded a tree hugger, I have to admit I'm all in favor of saving them, too."

"That's nice."

That's nice? Was that the best she could do? Abby moistened her dry lips with the tip of her tongue and went for a polite smile.

"I can't tell you how much I appreciate this," she said. He arched a dark eyebrow and she waved a hand at the Ford. "For getting my car going. And driving it here."

"You're welcome."

"Did it start right up, or what? It occurred to me later last night that maybe the rain…" *Why did he keep looking at her like that?* It was disconcerting. "I knew someone years ago, back in high school—one of the boys in my home ec class had this ancient car…" She was babbling. Abby took a deep breath. "Anyway, thanks."

"You had guys in your home ec class, huh?"

"Don't tell me you went to a place where they got away with the boys taking shop and the girls home ec."

"They called it Woodcraft and Skills for Living, but I lucked out. I got to miss them both. I played football and had to have time to practice." He folded his arms across his chest, crossed one sneakered foot over the other. "So, where'd you go to school?"

"I went to school in…" Abby froze. Two years of being

careful, two *days* of knowing this man, and look how close she'd come to making a dangerous admission. "San Francisco," she said, sticking with the details she'd invented after moving to Seattle.

"Great town."

Great town, big mistake. What if he knew San Francisco well? What if he began asking questions? What if, what if, what if?

"Well," she said in breezy dismissal, "thank you again, but I don't want to keep you."

"You're not. I told you last night, I don't have anything on for today." He paused, as if he were waiting for her to say something. When she didn't, he arched that one eyebrow again. "Don't you want to know what was wrong with the car?"

God, Abby, you are making a mess out of this.

"Oh. Yes, of course. I just didn't…" She gave a little laugh. "What was it?"

"Well, it's more like what *is* it than what was it." Luke leaned inside the open window, popped the hood release, then walked to the front of the car. "Your battery was dead. I gave it a jump and it started right up."

A new battery. How much would that cost? Maybe she asked the question out loud, or maybe her face was easy to read, because Luke answered it.

"You can get a new one for anywhere from, say, fifty bucks to a hundred."

She nodded. A cool breeze had picked up and she felt goose bumps rising on her arms, or maybe it was the thought of having to spend more money that did it.

"The thing is, though, I suspect there's more to it than a dead battery."

Worse and worse. Abby wrapped her arms around herself and walked toward Luke and the car.

"Like what?"

"Like maybe it's your alternator."

She looked at him blankly.

"The alternator," he repeated. "It's kind of the link between the engine and the battery. I guess you could think of it as a different kind of generator."

Still she just stared at him.

"The alternator charges the battery."

Abby nodded. "Okay."

"Have you noticed any problems starting up lately?"

"No," she said slowly, "not that I can—"

"Last week, Mommy," Emily said as she came skipping down the steps. "'Member?" She paused and shot Luke a beaming smile. "Hi, Luke."

"Hi yourself, princess. How are you this morning?"

"I'm fine. Thank you for bringing us our car."

Luke smiled. The kid was something special, not just little-girl cute, and she often showed a maturity beyond her years. She was happy to see him, which was nice. Happier than her mother, who'd been doing her polite best to get rid of him. Although for a couple of minutes there, when she'd first come outside, he'd had the feeling she was as pleased to start the day with him as he was to start it with her.

"You're very welcome," he said.

"Mommy, we did have trouble with our car." Emily looked up at Abby. "Remember? That day we were going to the lib-erry."

"Library," Abby said automatically, and frowned. "Yes, I remember now. Em's right. It took me a couple of minutes to get the engine to turn over."

"Any problem with lights flickering? Or lights not coming on? The horn not working, stuff like that?"

"Well, now that I think about it, the dashboard lights seem a little dim lately." Abby put her hands on Emily's shoulders. "Does all that add up to an alternator problem?"

"The definitive answer is 'maybe.'"

"Wonderful." Abby gave a weak laugh. "I just love diagnoses like that. What you really mean is expensive."

"No, not necessarily. If it is the alternator, I can get a rebuilt one fairly cheap."

"Trust me. The guy at the service station doesn't have that word in his vocabulary."

"You won't need him." Luke cleared his throat. "I'll install it for you."

"Oh." *Damn it, Abby, how many times are you going to use that word this morning?* "I couldn't let you do that."

"Why not?"

"Well, it would be an imposition."

Luke grinned at Emily and bent down, and she went straight into his arms so he could scoop her up.

"Your mom seems to think I have this packed social calendar, princess."

"What's a social calendar?"

"It's when you need a private secretary to remind you that the queen of England is coming to call."

"The real queen?"

Emily's question made Luke laugh. He hoisted the little girl over his head and she squealed with delight.

"The only queen in my life is the Dairy Queen," he told her. "Do you like hot fudge sundaes?"

"With whipped cream an' a cherry?"

"Of course, with whipped cream and a cherry. Is there any other way to have a sundae?"

"Sometimes they put nuts on them." Emily crinkled her nose. "I don't like nuts."

"Well, then, we won't have any." Luke put the child down and looked at Abby. "What do you say, Ms. Douglas? Shall I see what's doing with your alternator, or would you rather worry about imposing on a guy who's missing out on the important things in life, like doing his laundry?"

Abby hesitated. She looked at her daughter's flushed, happy face, at the car that seemed to eat money, and at the man smiling at her as he waited for an answer.

"Have you had breakfast yet?"

Luke felt a little kick of delight. He was tempted to say he hadn't, if it meant spending half an hour sitting at a table in this woman's kitchen, just watching her and wondering why she was trying so hard to keep from looking at him the way he was looking at her.

"Yeah. Don't worry about me. I'm good to go. I'll just poke

around in the engine for a while, then head for a place I know to get things tested out, see what we need... If that's okay with you.''

"Of course. Then...thank you, Luke. This is—it's very kind of you.''

"Hey,'' he said lightly, "it's a guy thing. You know. Cars, engines, dirt and grease. What man could walk away from a challenge like that? I should be thanking you.''

Abby laughed, really laughed, the skin around her eyes crinkling, her mouth curving up, and Luke wondered if maybe Dan was right and he was getting into something he hadn't planned on.

A OUPLE OF HOURS LATER, Abby was still telling herself there was nothing unusual about seeing a man in a driveway, working on a car.

Not in this neighborhood.

This was the kind of family street where you could almost always see men puttering with automobiles on weekends. They washed them, waxed them, did whatever it was men did to cars that made them look happy while they did it.

Nothing unusual there.

What *was* unusual was seeing a man working on a car in the driveway outside her place. The driveway was a perk that came with the first-floor apartment. That made it *her* driveway, *her* car, and a man she'd only met yesterday morning.

A man so good-looking that the woman next door had come out to walk her dog three times since Luke's arrival.

Abby smiled. The last time, her neighbor had all but dragged the dog out of the house. By then, probably the last thing the poor animal wanted was another trip to the fire hydrant.

Luke was the big draw. Even the gray-haired widow across the street kept pulling back the curtains for a peek.

Who could blame them?

Luke Sloan was a handsome man. Oh, hell. He was gorgeous. Big. Macho. All rippling muscles and tanned skin.

Lots of muscles, lots of skin, now that he'd peeled off his jacket.

Not long after he'd begun poking at the engine, he'd straightened up, slammed the hood shut and driven off. An hour had gone by, maybe more, and then he'd pulled into the driveway again, opened the hood and gone back to whatever it was he was doing.

By then, the sun had pierced the clouds and the day was warm for November. Luke had taken off his leather jacket, which meant he was working in his jeans and a faded blue T-shirt.

His biceps flexed under the shirt's short sleeves; the body of the shirt clung to his torso like a second skin. Each time he bent over, the shirt rode up in the back, exposing a tantalizing inch of taut, golden flesh....

"Mom?"

A small hand patted Abby's leg. She swallowed hard and looked down at her daughter.

"Yes, baby. What is it?"

"What's Luke doing now?"

"The same thing he's been doing all morning, Em. Trying to fix our car."

"I know that. I mean, what's he *doing?*"

Abby smiled and ruffled Emily's hair. "I don't know, sweetie. Something with the alternator, I guess."

"Is this the new one? Is that what he got when he drove away?"

"I don't know."

"Well, can I ask him? Can I watch?"

Abby sighed. It was almost eleven o'clock. Emily had asked the same question just about every five minutes. A fine pair they were, she thought wryly, the two of them so amazed at the sight of a man right under their noses that they could hardly concentrate on anything else.

"Mom? Can I go outside and watch Luke?"

"*May* you go outside, Em."

"May I?"

"No, you may not."

"Why? Luke said—"

"It doesn't matter what Luke said. *I* said no."

Emily's bottom lip pushed forward. "That's not fair."

"Emily, you have thousands of toys in your room."

"I don't have thousands of toys," Emily said sulkily.

"It's just a figure of speech, Em. My point is—"

"What's a figure of speech?"

Oh, Lord. "It's a way of saying something, but you shouldn't take it seriously."

"Like when Luke said he'd have our car fixed in no time, you mean?"

Abby bit back a laugh. "Yes. Like that." She turned away from the window and smiled at her daughter. "Lily will be here pretty soon."

"Uh-huh."

"Is your room all straightened up?"

"Yup."

"Toys all put away?"

"Uh-huh. But Lily and me are just gonna take 'em all out again."

"Lily and I."

Emily wrinkled her nose. "You aren't gonna play with Lily, Mommy. You're gonna sit in here and have coffee with Lily's mom."

Abby burst out laughing, squatted down and opened her arms.

"C'mere."

Emily went into her mother's embrace and the two of them hugged.

"What would I do without you, Emily Douglas?"

"You'd be lonely," Emily said solemnly, "same as I'd be without you."

A sudden dampness formed on Abby's lashes. She shut her eyes, hugged the child again, then turned her loose.

"Tell you what," she said brightly. "Why don't you go outside and bring Mr. Sloan—"

"Luke."

"Right. Bring Luke a glass of water. He must be thirsty by now."

"Can't he come in for some water?"

Abby opened her mouth, then shut it again. What was wrong with her today? Her daughter kept exhibiting grown-up manners, while she seemed to have forgotten them.

"Yes, of course. Why don't you go ask him if he'd like to come in and have something cold to drink?"

Emily was through the door in a flash. Abby stood by the window, watching as the child ran to Luke and shouted his name. He stood up too fast and Abby winced in sympathy as he banged his head on the open hood. Still, he managed a smile for Em, who skidded to a stop beside him.

The child gestured to the house and said something. Luke glanced up toward the window. There was a look on his face, a tension, a hint of longing....

Abby felt her face heat and took a quick step back, then reminded herself that he couldn't possibly see her from this angle, with the sun in his eyes. She moved toward the window again, just in time to see Em hold out her hand.

Luke made a face and held out both his hands, palms up. Abby could almost hear him telling her daughter that he was grubby, but Emily was persistent. She chattered away, her hand still outstretched, and finally Luke shrugged his shoulders, carefully wiped his hands on the seat of his jeans, and took Em's hand in his.

Together, they started toward the house.

Quickly Abby ran a hand over her hair, held back neatly now with a pale yellow ribbon, then tucked her shirt into the waistband of her jeans, even though it was already tucked in.

She'd lived in this apartment for almost two years, and in all that time, the only man who'd ever set foot inside was a middle-aged plumber with a beer belly and droopy jeans.

Taking a calming breath, she turned the doorknob and smiled as Luke and her daughter crossed the threshold.

"Hi," Luke said.

His forehead was beaded with sweat. He smelled of it, too, but not unpleasantly, sort of a basic male scent that reminded her of hot afternoons and tall grasses.

"Hi," Abby replied. "Em thought you might be thirsty."

"Yeah, I guess I am. I didn't realize it until she asked if I'd like something to drink."

"Oh," Abby said. *Oh* seemed to be her word of the day. "Well, please, sit down. I'll get you some iced tea. Or water. Or orange juice. I don't have anything else, I'm afraid. I mean, I don't have any beer or soda. Soda's bad for Em, and I don't drink…" She blushed, hating herself for the runaway flow of words. "What would you like?"

"Iced tea would be fine, but I don't think you want me sitting at your table. I'm kind of messy."

"Don't be silly. Sit down, by all means." Abby took a glass from the cupboard, filled it with ice and poured the tea over it. She held out the glass. He took it, and when his fingers brushed hers, she pulled her hand back as if his touch had scalded her. "Sugar? Lemon?" Rushing over to the refrigerator, she peered inside. "I think I have some lemon in here somewhere."

"Sugar is all."

"Well, that's good. I can't seem to find…" She turned as the refrigerator door swung shut. Luke was staring at her. "What?" she said, laughing a little, touching a hand to her face.

"Nothing. Just—you pulled your hair back."

Do not say "oh" again, Abigail! "Right. It gets in my eyes if I leave it loose."

"Yeah." Luke cleared his throat. "It looks great either way. Loose or tied back."

"Luke thinks you're pretty, Mommy," Emily said. "Isn't that right, Luke?"

"Em, why don't you go get ready for Lily's visit? Make sure that pillowcase with the butterflies is on the pillow on the top bunk bed. You know, the one she likes so much?" Abby waited until her daughter had skipped from the room. Then she leaned back against the counter and looked at Luke. "Emily's at that age—the one where she says whatever she's thinking."

"Well, she was right. I do think you're pretty." Luke grinned. "Now I've made you blush."

"I'm not used to—I mean, it's a long time since—" She

took a deep breath. "I'm divorced," she said, as if that explained everything.

"Ah. Well, there's lots of that going around, I guess." He studied her blank expression. "I'm divorced, too," he explained.

"Kids?"

"No. I suppose that's a good thing. I mean, it's not good for a kid to grow up without two... Damn. Sorry. I wasn't trying to suggest—"

"That's okay. I agree with you. Kids should have two parents, whenever possible, but sometimes—sometimes things just don't work out." Abby waved a hand at the table and chairs. "Please, sit down. I feel guilty for not having realized how warm you must have gotten, working out there on my car."

"No reason to feel guilty. And if you don't mind me needing a shower, I'll be happy to sit down if you'll join me."

She hesitated, almost as if he'd invited her out on a date instead of simply asking her to sit at her own kitchen table. Then she smiled, poured herself a glass of tea, and sank into a chair.

Luke sat across from her.

"To that most amazing of occurrences," he said, holding out his glass. "A sunny November day in Seattle."

With a soft laugh, Abby touched her glass to his and took a sip. Luke tilted his head back and took several long swallows of the cold tea. She watched the muscles in his throat contract and felt a sudden dryness in her mouth, dryness another gulp of tea did nothing to ease.

"Well," she said briskly, "what's the verdict?"

"That you make great iced tea."

His reply made Abby laugh again. Luke thought she had a nice, easy laugh, but it had an unused quality to it. He had the feeling she didn't do much laughing, except with Emily.

"Thanks, but I'm talking about my car. Was it the alternator?"

"Yup, it was. I took it over to a shop I know, had it tested. The thing was on its last legs."

Her face fell.

"But it's all fixed," he said quickly. "I took out the old one, put in a new one. A rebuilt one, to be accurate. It'll give you almost as much wear as a new one for much less money."

"I hope much less money isn't still a king's ransom."

Luke thought about what he'd paid for the alternator, recalled how his mother had had to watch every dollar, then halved the true cost and named that price to Abby.

Her face lit with relief.

"That's wonderful! But what about your time? Surely that's worth something."

"I like to think so," he said, smiling.

"Well, you tell me what I owe you, and—"

"Dinner."

"No, that was for driving me home last night."

"Right. You and Emily are going to have me here, to dinner, to pay for that. Now it's my turn. You want to pay me for today, you'll let me take you and Em to dinner another night."

Abby stared at him as if he'd suggested flying them to Borneo.

"We couldn't possibly let you do that."

"Because?"

"Well, because— because I owe you, not the other way around."

"You don't understand." Luke finished the tea in one long gulp, pushed back his chair and stood up. "I wasn't joking before. About guys and cars, you know? I haven't had the chance to get my hands dirty in too long a time."

"That's a very polite lie, Luke Sloan." Abby smiled and rose to her feet. "But we both know you work with your hands every day."

Hell. She thought he was a carpenter. How could he have come so close to forgetting that little detail? And why should he feel so lousy about letting her believe the lie?

"Sure," he said, sliding over it, "but it's not the same as tinkering with engines. Seriously, this was fun. So, what do you say, Abby? Can I take you two out to dinner one night next week?"

"I don't—I don't—"

"Hi."

Abby swung around. Faith Marshall stood in the doorway, holding her little girl by the hand. She looked from Abby to Luke, then to Abby again.

"Sorry. I knocked, but nobody…"

"Faith." Abby took a deep breath. "Faith, this is Luke Sloan. Luke, this is my friend, Faith Marshall."

Faith smiled. "The famous Luke Sloan," she said, extending her hand. "Lily's told me all about you."

"I'm grimy," Luke warned, looking at Faith's hand.

"And I just came from an hour in the darkroom, so we're a good pair. You're grimy, and I smell like a tray of developer."

Luke chuckled, shook Faith's hand and smiled at her daughter.

"Hey, I know you. You're the moppet who wanted to know all about how to use a saw."

Lily blushed, nodded, and ducked her head. Luke grinned at Faith.

"We had an assembly, I guess you'd call it, so I could explain things to the kids. Lily here wanted to know if she could use my tools."

"That figures," Faith said. "Lily, honey, why don't you go find Emily? Abby, I have to get going, but I'll be back tomorrow at—"

"No," Abby said quickly. "I mean, stay for a little while. Have some iced tea, why don't you, while the girls get settled in?"

"Well…"

"I'm the one who has to get going," Luke said.

"Oh, I didn't mean to intrude. Really, I can just—"

"Luke was kind enough to fix my car," Abby said, even more quickly.

"Yeah. And I have a couple of things to do to the beast before I go. Abby? Will it be okay to leave your keys in the car?"

"Fine…but how will you get home?"

He patted his back pocket. "I have a cell phone. I'll call the same guy who gave me a lift to the jewelry store this morning.''

Abby nodded. ''Thanks again.''

''No problem. Ms. Marshall...''

''Faith.''

''Faith. Abby. Give the princess a hug for me and tell her I'll see her Monday, okay?''

''Okay.''

Luke went out the door and Abby watched him head for her car, then bend under the hood again. Slowly, she turned back to Faith, who gave her a smug grin.

''Nice,'' Faith said.

''Very,'' Abby agreed, deliberately misunderstanding the comment. ''He gave Em and me a lift home last night, then went back this morning to give my car a jump to get it started today. He worked on it all morning to find out what was the matter with it and—''

''I meant the man, not the good deeds. Mr. Sloan is mucho macho.''

Abby blushed. ''He's just a man who was nice to us.''

''Uh-huh.''

''That's all there was to it.'' Abby bustled around the kitchen, emptying the ice from Luke's glass into the sink. Taking down a fresh glass, she filled it for Faith, then topped off her own glass of iced tea. ''He's just a really pleasant guy who believes in old-fashioned courtesy.''

''That, too.'' Faith smiled over the rim of her glass. ''But it doesn't negate the fact that he's also one gorgeous hunk of masculinity.''

Abby stared at Faith. The corners of her mouth began to twitch. ''He is, isn't he?''

''He most certainly is. The last time somebody fixed *my* car, he had a cigar stuck in his face, a belly hanging over his jeans that made him look like he was eighteen months pregnant with triplets, and each time he leaned forward—''

''—you got a view of fat, hairy cleavage.''

The women looked at each other. Abby snorted; Faith made a choking sound. They both began to laugh.

''What's so funny?'' Emily demanded as she and Lily came into the kitchen.

''Life,'' Abby said, though there really wasn't anything funny about life, not when it dropped a man in your path and you knew, absolutely knew, you'd better avert your eyes and quicken your steps when you turned your back on him. There was no room in her life for a man. Not now, maybe not ever.

The years she'd lived with her ex had convinced her of that.

CHAPTER EIGHT

EMILY LOOKED CONFUSED at seeing her mother go from laughing to looking sad so quickly.

Maybe getting started on the baking would distract her, Abby thought.

"How about we start the cookies now?" she suggested, bending down and giving Emily a hug. Emily's eyes shone in anticipation. "Hooray!"

Lily looked up at Faith and tugged at her skirt.

"Will you help us, Mom?"

"Well," Faith said carefully, "I didn't really intend—"

"Please stay," Abby said softly. "I'd like it if you would."

"In that case—sure. I was going to do some shopping, but I can get that done later."

"Great." Abby smiled. "There's one stipulation. You have to promise to take some of the cookies home."

Faith laughed. "You drive a hard bargain," she said, snatching up her daughter and kissing her. "Okay, toots. Let's bake."

"Em, you get out the butter. I'll get down the sugar."

"And the chocolate chips!"

"Oh-oh, we can't make chocolate chip cookies today. How do sugar cookies sound?"

Emily's face fell. "You said—"

"I know I did, honey, but Luke drove us home last night, remember? We didn't get to stop at the supermarket to buy chocolate chips."

"No chocolate?" Lily said, crestfallen.

"Lily." Faith put her daughter on her feet. "Hush."

"But chocolate chip cookies are the best, Mom. Everybody knows that!"

"Lily, did you hear what I just said?"

"It's okay." Abby sighed and blew a strand of hair back from her forehead. "They're right. I promised they could bake chocolate chip cookies, and a promise is a promise. Okay. Here's what we'll do. We'll all pile into my car and take it for a test spin."

"What's a tesspin?" Emily asked.

"It's a short drive to see if everything's working right."

"It has to be if Luke fixed it," Emily said. "Luke can do *anything!*"

"And do it extremely well, I'd bet," Faith said.

Abby looked at Faith. Her expression was one of total innocence, but laughter glinted in her eyes, and Abby felt her lips twitch in response.

"Not even Luke Sloan can be perfect, Faith."

"Maybe not, but I'll bet he'd come close."

"He would, Mommy." Emily looked up from under her lashes. "I like him. He's very nice."

"Yes. Yes, he is." Abby cleared her throat. "All right, here's the plan. We'll go buy a bag of chocolate chips. Then—"

"Then we can go to that pizza place," Emily said happily, "an' we can bring a pizza home for lunch."

"Oh, no," Faith said quickly. "I only stopped by to drop Lily off."

"Let's do it," Abby said.

"You sure?"

Abby nodded. She knew what Faith was really saying, that she had rejected all such suggestions in the past. But today was different. First she'd had a man in her kitchen, and now she was reaching out to a friend—someone who wanted to be her friend, anyway.

"Yes. I'm positive."

"Well, in that case…" Faith grinned. "Who's up for anchovies on their pizza?"

"Yuck," everyone answered, and they were all laughing as they went out the door.

THE "TESSPIN" WAS A huge success.

Five minutes into it, Abby knew that Luke must have done

more than replace the faulty alternator. She'd bought the car used, with considerable mileage on it, and it had always run a little rough.

"Nothing I can do about that," the guy at the garage had told her.

Luke had done something about it, though. The engine was quieter, and it didn't labor as she went up the hill that led to the market.

Good grief, she hadn't paid him for the alternator.

The man had done so much for her and she'd said thank-you by offering him a glass of iced tea and inviting him to supper, but only after her four-year-old had pushed her into doing both. And when Luke had invited *her* to dinner, she'd accepted so grudgingly that she was embarrassed thinking about it.

Had Emily done any of those things, she'd have given her a stiff lecture.

It was a relief to reach the supermarket and fill her muddled brain with decisions about whether to buy dark or milk chocolate chips.

"Both," Lily stated with the conviction of a connoisseur.

Then they stopped next door to pick up the pizza they'd ordered when they'd first reached the mall.

Faith insisted on paying for it, and adding a big bottle of Coke and a family size, take-out garden salad.

"The major food groups," she said by way of explanation. "Fat, sugar, carbs and veggies."

As they all got back into her car, Abby realized she'd laughed more today than in what seemed like forever, and it was a wonderful feeling.

At home, the girls set the table, while Faith poured the Coke and Abby dished out the salad. They all sat down, dug into the pizza, pronounced it delicious and proved it by scarfing down every crumb.

Faith sat back. "I don't know about you guys, but I'm stuffed!"

"Same here." Abby put a hand over her belly. "I couldn't eat another thing."

"I could," Em said. "I could eat cookies!"

"Me, too," Lily said eagerly.

Abby and Faith both groaned.

The kids cleared the table, and Abby and Faith washed the dishes. Then they set up the bowls and wooden spoons their daughters would need to make the cookies. The girls measured and mixed while the mothers supervised, and in less than an hour the cookies were baked, cooled and heaped high on the biggest platter Abby owned. Emily and Lily selected a few for the plastic bowl they were taking into Emily's room.

"See?" Emily said, shoving the bowl toward Abby. "We're gonna eat the sad ones first, so they won't feel bad."

Abby peered into the bowl and saw an assortment of rejects, misshapen cookies that were too small or too big, or were burned around the edges. She looked at her little girl and felt a tug at her heart.

"That's good, baby. That's a nice thing to do."

Emily nodded. "Lily and me don't think anybody should be sad."

Lily and I, Abby thought, but right then, grammar didn't seem very important.

"You're right," she said softly, "nobody should."

The kids took the cookies down the hall to Emily's bedroom, came back for glasses of milk and announced that they'd be busy for a while, having their tea party.

Abby gave a dramatic sigh as the children's footsteps faded.

"Let's be busy, too—busy doing nothing. How about some coffee?"

"I'd love some, but…" Faith hesitated. "Look, I know you didn't expect me to hang around."

"No, I didn't." Abby smiled over her shoulder as she filled the pot with water. "But I'm glad you did. Let me start the coffee and then we'll see if we were telling the truth about being too full to eat any of those cookies."

Faith laughed. "It's a deal."

By the time the coffee was ready, Faith had loaded the bowls and cookie sheets in the sink, but Abby wouldn't let her wash them.

"I can do all that later," she said firmly. "Besides, the coffee's ready and I'm dying for a cup."

"Me, too."

Abby filled two mugs and put them on the table. "Milk?"

"Black is fine."

"Sugar? Or the blue stuff?"

"The blue stuff, definitely. Every calorie counts, especially now that I've blown a week's worth on that pizza."

"And on these gourmet cookies," Abby said, sitting down and reaching for one at the same time as Faith.

"Yeah," Faith said, "but how can we resist? These are great."

"Well, they should be." Abby dropped her voice. "I used an old family recipe."

"Care to pass it along?"

"I'd have to kill you if I did." Abby grinned. "Let's just say the magic is in the words *Toll House*."

Laughing, Faith reached for another cookie.

The women sipped and munched and chatted companionably about inconsequential things. Abby topped up their mugs with hot coffee, then sat down again and plucked another cookie from the platter.

"I'm really glad we did this."

Faith nodded. "So am I."

"I guess—I know I must sometimes seem kind of unsociable. I mean, our kids became such close friends so quickly..."

"No need to explain. I know how it goes. It's the same for me. Between having a child to raise on your own, a home to keep, a job to go to, time just gets away from you."

"Yes." Abby traced the rim of her mug with her finger. That wasn't the reason, but it was simpler to let it go at that. "It must be interesting, what you do. Photojournalism, right?"

"Uh-huh."

"Sounds exciting."

"Well, it can be." Faith smiled. "On the other hand, I spent the morning photographing people bringing recyclables to the dump for an article in *Parade*.''

"Okay, so maybe *exciting*'s not the word," Abby said. "Still, working for yourself must be great. No set hours, nobody to answer to…"

"No steady paycheck, no employee benefits, no way to know what you'll be doing from one day to the next."

"I guess the grass is always greener," Abby admitted.

"You're right. I think about you working in that jewelry store, handling all those beautiful things…"

"Not forever. I've been thinking about going back to school, taking some night classes at the university."

"In what?"

"Art history. Well, jewelry history, or whatever it is you'd call a specialty like that. See, one thing I've discovered, working at Emerald City, is that while I don't much like jewelry—"

"What!" Faith said, laughing.

Abby grinned. "Don't tell a soul," she said dramatically, "but it's the truth."

"Are you serious?"

"Absolutely. I only like the old stuff, pieces that have been through lots of hands."

"You're a romantic at heart, huh?"

"Not me. Romantics see life through rose-colored glasses. Sunglasses are the only tinted lenses I wear, and how often do I need them in Seattle? What about you? Are you a romantic or a realist?"

Faith looked down into the black depths of the coffee in her cup as if she might find the answer to the question.

"I don't know. What would you call a woman who fell in love with the wrong man?"

Abby sighed. "I'd call her Abigail, except I'm not so foolish as to think I'd be alone. Besides, to be honest, I'm not sure what I really felt was love. 'Comfort' might be closer to the truth."

"Well, I tumbled head over heels for this guy. He was like nobody I'd ever met in my entire life."

"And that was good?"

"Well, here I am," Faith said, "and he's gone, so, no, I guess it wasn't good. On the other hand, he gave me Lily, and that part's wonderful."

"It's the same for me," Abby said in a low voice. "My husband gave me Emily. She's the joy of my life. How could I ever regret my marriage?"

"Actually, I don't have a marriage to regret. Ethan—that was his name—Ethan and I were lovers, but—"

"Faith." Abby placed her hand over the other woman's. "I'm sorry. I didn't mean to get personal. I never talk about Frank or my marriage, or anything like that. I just...I don't know. I guess it just feels good to share a little of all this for the very first time."

"You're right, it does. And I'm the one who started the conversation." Faith sat back and sighed. "Anyway, it's not as if I keep it a secret. Lily knows that I loved her father, and that he loved me, but that he could no more change the person he was than I could change the face of the moon."

"It's wonderful that Lily knows you loved each other." Abby caught her lip between her teeth. "I wish I could tell Em that, but it wouldn't be true. I thought I loved my husband and that he loved me, but it didn't take long for me to realize that we had very different ideas about the meaning of love."

She was saying far too much, Abby realized. This was exactly why she'd avoided making friends with anyone. It was dangerous to tell people things like this. Frank was clever and determined. The less people knew about him, about her marriage and divorce, the safer she'd be.

"Let's just say ours wasn't a storybook romance," she said with a quick smile.

"Well, how many romances really are? I'd bet happy endings in real life are as scarce as hen's teeth."

Silence fell over the kitchen. Faith was the first to break it.

"On the other hand," she said, with a smile that made it clear she was trying hard to lighten the mood, "there are storybook heroes out there."

"Name one."

"Well, your guy."

"*My* guy?"

"Uh-huh. Mr. Wind in his Hair. You know, that character in *Dances with Wolves*." She laughed at the look that spread over Abby's face. "The guy with the long black hair in that movie? That's who your knight in shining armor reminds me of."

Abby blushed. "We've gone over that already."

"Oh, right. What did you tell me? He drove you home, went back today, got your car, brought it here, took out the old battery—"

"Alternator."

"Whatever," Faith said with cheerful indifference. She put her elbows on the table and propped her chin in her hands. "And the way he looks at you…" She sighed and rolled her eyes. "It's enough to make the temperature rise."

Abby stared at Faith. "That's not so."

"It is."

"But—but I don't want—"

"You do. Deep down inside, we all want a man to look at us that way, as if we're the most beautiful, most desirable…" Faith sat up straight. "Just listen to me," she said, and gave a little laugh. "Sorry. I got carried away for a minute."

"I'm sorry, too. Lily's father—what'd you say his name was?"

"Ethan."

"He must have hurt you a lot."

"I hurt myself by believing in something I knew could never be." Faith looked at her watch, shoved back her chair and rose to her feet. "My goodness," she said briskly, "look at the time! I have a couple of hours of picture editing left to do."

Abby stood up, too. "You're more than welcome to stay."

"I'd love to, but really, I have to go. Let me just give Lily a hug. Lily? Baby, come give Mommy a kiss goodbye."

"We're coming," a little voice yelled.

There was the sound of giggling and shoes scuffing against the wood floor. The children burst into the kitchen hand in hand, all dressed up in Abby's clothes. Lily had a silk scarf wrapped around her like a shawl; gold drop earrings glinted against her hair. Emily wore a skirt tugged up to her armpits, and a gold and diamond bracelet clinked on her wrist. Both girls had lipstick smeared over their mouths.

Abby and Faith exchanged looks as they tried not to laugh.

"What a stunning pair of ladies," Faith said, "but where are our little girls?"

"I don't know, Faith. Ladies? Have you seen our daughters?"

Emily and Lily giggled. "We're right here!" they cried in unison.

"Really?" Abby scooped Emily from the floor. "We never would have guessed."

"We decided to dress up for our tea party."

"So I see." Abby smiled. "Complete with some of Grandma's jewelry, huh?"

"Yup." Emily leaned back and looked into Abby's face. "Did my grandma love you lots, Mommy?"

Abby felt a burn in the back of her throat. "Lots," she said softly, "and she'd have loved you the same way."

"Yeah?"

"Yeah. And she'd be thrilled that you like to play with her things."

"Lily and I both do," Emily said. Then asked, "Can Lily's mommy stay for supper?"

"Lily's mommy," Faith replied, giving Lily a big kiss, "is going on a diet as of this moment. Pizza and cookies for lunch! I can't believe it."

"We had salad, too," Emily pointed out. "That was good, right?"

"All the latest scientific journals say that salads negate the bad stuff in pizza," Abby agreed, laughing as she put Emily down.

"What's nuh-gate?"

"It's a polite way of saying your mom has a solid grasp of nutrition and a vivid imagination." Faith smiled, kissed both girls and gave Abby a quick hug. "I'll just bet Wind in his Hair could negate the effects of a lot of things, too," she whispered as they touched cheeks.

Then she grinned and said she'd come for Lily in the morning.

Abby shut the door after Faith and leaned back against it. The girls had already raced back to Emily's room; she could hear them talking, trying to figure out why grown-ups thought stuff that made you feel good also had to be good for you.

Luke's image flashed through Abby's mind. That slow, almost lazy smile. His eyes, as green as the sea.

Were the kids right? Was it okay, just once in a while, to enjoy something just because it made you feel good?

Swallowing hard, Abby strode to the sink, turned on the hot water and began to scrub the dishes.

"ONCE IN A WHILE," Dan Shayne grumbled as he took a platter from the cupboard, "just once in a while, a man should be permitted to enjoy something without it having to be good for him."

"You're having corned beef for supper, aren't you?" his wife, Molly, said, taking the lid off the big pot that held the potatoes, cabbage and beef. "Seems like that's a perfect example of having something that isn't good for you."

"You missed my point. What I said was, a man should be permitted to *enjoy* what he's having." Dan put the platter on the counter beside the stove. "I haven't taken a bite yet, and you've spent the last ten minutes telling me that what I'm supposed to sit down and eat is going to kill me."

"I never said it would kill you." Molly stabbed at the potatoes and cabbage, then lifted the corned beef from the pot and placed it on a cutting board. "I said it would probably raise your cholesterol to four digits."

"I'm healthy as a horse."

"Yes, you are, and I intend to keep you that way. Did you put everything on the tray, as I asked you to?"

Dan looked at the tray that sat on the kitchen table. It held a basket of hot rolls, a bowl of homemade coleslaw, three kinds of mustard and a dish of pickles his wife had put up during the summer.

"I did." He smiled at her and slid an arm around her waist. "Everything's perfect, as always."

"Go on with you, Daniel Shayne. There's no such thing as perfect in this life and you know it."

"Yes, there is, Molly. You are."

Molly tut-tutted. "You're such a liar!"

"I may lie about some things, but never about you." He turned his wife toward him. "How about a kiss?"

"Stop it. Luke will be here soon."

"So what? He's seen me kiss you before."

Molly smiled, tilted her face up to her husband's and met his lips with hers.

"I love you," she said softly, "but I suppose you know that."

"After twenty years, I should hope I do." With a grin, Dan linked his hands at the base of her spine and she leaned back in his embrace. "There are times I can't believe I was lucky enough to find you."

"You're sweet-talking me in hopes I won't slap your hand when you reach for a third slice of corned beef."

"Two's my limit, then?"

"Yes." A dimple winked in Molly's cheek. "All right. Three, but not a bite more." They shared another kiss and then she drew back, frowning. "Everything will be overcooked. Where is that partner of yours, anyway?"

Dan sighed and let go of Molly, then strolled into the dining room. She followed him to the window, where he twitched the drapes aside and looked out at the street. It was just getting dark; lights had come on up and down the block.

"He said he had things to do at his place when I dropped him off this afternoon."

"What things?"

"How should I know?" Dan turned toward her. "Laundry. Shopping. Bachelor stuff."

"Saturday-morning stuff, you mean. If only he'd find himself a good woman..." She saw the look on Dan's face and sighed. "Leave it alone. I know, I know."

"You mean well, sweetheart, but the time's not right. Janine—"

"Janine was a selfish, unfeeling bitch. She was never right for Luke."

"That's one of the qualities I love about you, Moll," Dan said. "Your reluctance to speak your mind."

"I'm not afraid of the truth, Daniel, and that *is* the truth." She looked at the big grandfather clock ticking away against the wall and clicked her tongue. "I'll go put everything into the microwave so we can reheat it when Luke finally arrives. I forgot he'd need the afternoon to do things at home, and all because he was off doing good deeds earlier."

"Uh-huh," Dan said, following her back into the kitchen. "Did he fix that woman's car?"

"That's what he said."

Molly took the corned beef, potatoes and cabbage from the pot and put them on a platter, which she popped into the microwave oven. "That boy has such a kind heart," she said, turning to her husband, "helping someone who's as good as a stranger... What?"

"It's not often you're wrong, Moll, but when you are..." Dan grinned. "For starters, the 'boy' is three years younger than you are."

"I've been married twenty years and I have two almost-grown sons," Molly said crisply. "Never mind chronological age, Daniel. In spirit, I'm old enough to be his mother. What else did I get wrong?"

"I'll agree he did an act of kindness, but I'm not so sure it was his heart driving him on." Dan waggled his eyebrows. "He told me that the damsel in distress is a babe."

"Yes, well, I've never been silly enough to think because Luke gave up on love, he'd give up on sex, too... What now?" she demanded.

"Nothing."

"Nothing, he says." Molly put her hands on her well-rounded hips. "You're holding something back."

Dan opened the door to the microwave, reached for the corned beef and got his fingers lightly tapped for his efforts.

"Wait until we're at the table. Now, come on. Tell me what you're thinking."

"Only that it took some effort to get Luke to admit the lady's a looker. When I referred to her as a babe the first time, just, you know, in casual conversation, he got huffy. Defensive."

Molly's eyes widened. "Protective, you mean?"

Dan shrugged. "Maybe."

"And you didn't say a word? But that's wonderful!"

"I'm not so sure of that."

"Oh, please! The man's interested!"

"Yeah, but he denies it."

"Did you expect him to admit it? Honestly, you men can be so dense."

"And the lady in question might turn out to be involved in the case we're working."

"Involved how?" Molly said incredulously. "You mean, she might be a criminal?"

Dan shrugged. "Luke says he doesn't think so. She's not that kind. He says—"

The back door swung open and Luke stepped into the kitchen holding a bouquet of flowers in the crook of his arm. He gave Dan a sharp look, but Molly got a big smile.

"What Luke says," he told her, "is that he's hungry as a bear."

Molly laughed and went into his arms for a hug.

Heaving a deep sigh, Dan met his partner's eyes over the top of his wife's head.

Dan came from a big family, lots of brothers and sisters, and even the most sensible among them did foolish things from time to time.

Advice never seemed to help.

The one lesson he'd learned over the years was that sometimes the best thing you could do for someone you loved was stand by and hope for the best.

CHAPTER NINE

IT WAS AN UNUSUALLY QUIET Thursday morning at Forrester Square Day Care, and just what Luke needed to get some work done.

Katherine was off somewhere on business, which meant that teachers and aides and parents weren't dropping by the office for quick consultations.

Kids weren't parading in and out, either. By now, a week into his assignment, the novelty of having a man on the premises seemed to have pretty much worn off. Oh, an occasional child—usually a boy—wandered in to watch Luke wield his hammer, maybe ask a couple of questions, but that was about it. Nothing to keep him from checking the camera from time to time, or looking directly through the window at the jewelry exchange across the street.

Luke stretched a yardstick across a section of wall, picked up a pencil and made two careful marks. Then he clamped the pencil between his teeth, lowered the stick and measured again.

But there were no serious distractions today. None for the last couple of days, actually. The ones that had kept him from concentrating on his job had mostly come from the Twinned Twosome, Emily and her pal, Lily. Until a few days ago, they'd visited him endlessly. Did he want juice? Milk? A cookie? Would he like an apple? A banana?

He made another couple of dots on the wall, then put down the pencil and the yardstick and reached for his drill.

All that had changed since his dinner with the Shaynes. Coming into the kitchen, hearing a few of the things Dan had been telling Molly had ticked Luke off.

Who did Dan think he was, suggesting he was getting involved with a woman who might be a suspect in a case they were working?

He'd never do that. Absolutely not.

Luke had gotten through the meal, smiling and laughing with Molly, and managing to smile, at least, with Dan. But when Molly left them alone to check on the apple pie she had in the oven for desert, Luke had leaned toward his partner and told him straight out that he didn't much like the drift of what he'd overheard.

"You think I don't know there's a line you don't cross?" he'd said tightly. "That I don't understand you can't do the job unless you remember, first and foremost, that you're a cop?"

"I didn't say that," Dan had replied.

"Yeah, you sure as hell did. I heard you, Dan. Telling Molly I was seeing Abby as a woman, not as a suspect. That I was in danger of disregarding procedure by allowing myself to get involved in a relationship with someone I might have to arrest?"

"Luke, all I said was—"

"Plus, I'm lying to her about who I really am. How could I possibly get involved with a woman with all that happening?"

"I never accused you of coming close to anything unethical. Hey, man, in some ways I know you better than I know my wife! You're a good cop. A principled cop. You'd do the right thing no matter what." Dan had paused for a steadying breath. "All I meant was that I've never seen you get drawn in this way. And yeah, maybe I should have said that to you, not to Molly, but she cares about you as much as I do."

Luke had looked at him for a long minute, the muscles in his jaw tensing as images swirled around and around in his head. Abby smiling at him when he dropped her off at her house, looking happy to see him the next morning... And then the glimpse of her working in the jewelry exchange on Monday, standing behind the very counter where the old lady and her maid claimed to have seen the stolen necklace.

Dan was right. What in hell had happened to his judgment?

He relied on his ability to view the world through eyes that saw things in black and white.

"Yeah," he'd said gruffly. "Okay." Then he'd cleared his throat, looked at Dan and taken the edge off as best he could. "So, you care for me, huh, Shayne? Have I got something to, you know, worry about here?"

He'd grinned, and Dan had grinned, and then Molly came in with the pie and a pint of Ben & Jerry's vanilla ice cream, and the rest of the evening was relaxed and easy.

Luke turned off the drill and put it on the plank of wood laid on two sawhorses that he used as a workbench. He wiped his hands on his jeans and looked out the window.

Nothing special was happening. People out for a stroll, people in a hurry. Traffic coming and going—and across the street, the jewelry store and Abby, behind that counter.

Why had it taken Dan to make him see how close he'd been to screwing things up? He'd just met the woman, for crissakes. She meant nothing to him. Neither did her kid.

That was the only thing he felt bad about.

Monday, he'd come to work knowing what he had to do— put things back on a professional track, and that meant starting with the kid. He had to make the little girl realize he wasn't Ronald McDonald or Captain Kangaroo or whoever it was kids worshipped nowadays.

So each time Emily and her sidekick showed up, he was polite. Polite, but uncommunicative. No, thank you, he didn't want juice or a cookie. No, thank you, he didn't want an apple and he really was awfully busy, so if Emily and Lily didn't mind…?

They did mind. The princess, especially. He could see it in the quick flash of hurt that shot through her eyes. But Em was a smart child, and after a couple of days, she'd stopped coming in to see him.

He'd dealt with the Abby problem, too. He knew when she dropped Em off, knew when she picked her up. It was easy not to be anywhere near the main entrance at those times, and if yesterday he'd watched, unobserved, as she collected her daughter, if she'd seemed to be glancing around as if she were looking for somebody...

Luke picked up his hammer and a nail, pounded it into the wall...

"Ah!"

Jeez.

He dropped the hammer and jammed his thumb into his mouth, hissing with pain.

"Oh. Oh, sorry."

Katherine's partner, Hannah Richards, stood just inside the door to the office with a set of ledgers under her arm. Hannah took care of the accounting and business end of things. He'd met her briefly last week.

She was the only other person at the day care who knew his real identity.

"Are you okay?" she asked.

"I'm fine," he said, shaking his hand. "A thumb has a nail, but not the kind you're supposed to pound with a hammer."

She smiled. "Shall I get a first aid kit?"

"No need. It's only a thumb. Fortunately, I have a spare."

Hannah Richards did her best to manage another polite smile, but that was about it. So much for his stand-up comedy routine.

"Katherine isn't here," Luke said. "She had some kind of meeting over in—"

"I know." Hannah hesitated. "I'd like to talk to you, if you have a minute."

Luke narrowed his gaze on her face. That one time they'd spoken before, the Richards woman had struck him as composed and efficient. She didn't look that way now. Something was on her mind, and he doubted it had anything to do with carpentry.

His pulse kicked up a notch. Wouldn't it be a bitch if it turned out she knew something about whatever was going on across the street?

"Sure. Come on in."

She not only came in, she shut the door behind her. Stranger and stranger, Luke thought as she slowly walked toward him.

"Detective Sloan…"

"Luke."

"Luke. Of course." She gave him a distracted smile. "I assume you've been a policeman for some time."

He thought about telling her he'd been a policeman and now he was a detective, then decided the finer points of the PD's hierarchy didn't mean a damn to a woman who looked as nervous as this one did. Instead he smiled in a way he hoped was reassuring.

"Yes."

"And you've dealt with all kinds of cases?"

Luke shrugged. "I've handled lots of things."

She nodded. He waited for her to say something, but she didn't.

"Mrs. Richards…"

"It's Ms. Richards." Again, that nervous smile. "Hannah."

"Right. Hannah. Look, if there's something you want to tell me…"

"What I need is advice, Detective. Um, an opinion. A professional opinion."

"On what?"

"I have—I have this friend. She wants to locate a—a person."

So much for the possible jewelry-fencing operation at the Emerald City Jewelry Exchange. The lady wanted to find a long-lost boyfriend. Her own, not a supposed friend's. People were always making cautious inquiries, asking on behalf of their friends, as if to admit they were the ones who needed help would be somehow disgraceful.

It was a little surprising, coming from a woman who seemed so coolly composed, but Luke had learned that appearances could be deceiving.

Sometimes, he was amazed at the things people thought were worth the time or even in the province of an already overworked police department.

"Did your friend tell you how long this person has been missing?"

"Uh… It's been quite a while."

"Has this person committed a crime?"

"No…"

"This is strictly personal, then?"

"Yes."

"Well, in that case, your friend's best bet would be to hire a private investigator."

Hannah nodded. "That's what my friend thought, but how would she go about finding a good one?"

"Well, that's a tough question. All private detectives are licensed, but I suppose your friend would want references. Something like that."

"Yes."

"That's not easy. Hiring a P.I. isn't the same as hiring, say, a handyman."

"Or a carpenter," Hannah said with a quick smile.

"Exactly. You want to employ someone to do work around your house, you ask him to give you the names of other customers to check him out. But private detectives generally deal in personal matters. Most of their clients wouldn't want to be used as references."

"I understand. Nobody wants to discuss personal issues with strangers." Hannah hesitated. "Or even with friends. Especially with friends. Otherwise, my friend would simply contact a private investigator she already knows…"

She fell silent. Luke waited a second, then cleared his throat.

"Your friend already knows a P.I.?"

Hannah nodded.

"A good one?"

"Oh, I'm sure—that is, my friend's sure he is."

"In that case…"

"My friend's afraid that talking with this man might change his opinion of her," Hannah told him, so softly that Luke had to strain to hear her.

"Private investigators, good ones, are like cops," he said carefully. "They don't let their personal feelings cloud their professional judgment." *Yeah, right,* a voice in his head snickered, but he ignored it. "Besides, I'd lay odds that if this guy's a true friend, his opinion of her will remain the same. And because he *is* a friend, he'll probably try twice as hard to find whoever it is she's looking for.'' He paused and decided to use straight talk. "If you need a P.I., Hannah, and you know one you can trust, by all means, confide in him.''

Luke thought she was going to correct him, remind him she was asking his advice on behalf of someone else. Instead, a smile, a real one, not the polite one she'd been holding fixed since coming into the office, lit her face.

"You're right. Thank you, Detec... Thank you, Luke. I'm glad I came to you for help.''

Luke smiled, too. "Good luck.''

Hannah opened the office door, and hurried out into the wide hall. Luke watched her zigzag through little groups of kids. She was heading straight for one of the aides, a girl named Amy Something or Other. Tidwell, that was it. Amy looked to be maybe seventeen or eighteen, a tall, gangly kid....

And Luke would have laid odds she was pregnant.

Sadly enough, one of the things you saw a lot of in his job was kids that age who'd gotten themselves knocked up and whose boyfriends booked as soon as the girls dropped the news on them.

He sighed. Time to revise the scenario he'd just written.

Hannah wasn't asking questions for herself, she was asking them for Amy. He'd noticed the two spending time together, sort of a big sister-little sister relationship. If he was right, if Amy was pregnant, then Hannah was going to help her locate the father of her unborn child.

Hannah bent over the girl and said something. The girl nodded, smiled and followed Hannah into the events room.

When the door swung shut, Luke sighed again.

Good luck, he thought. Finding a guy who didn't want to be found was never easy.

SAFELY SECLUDED BEHIND the closed door of the events room, Amy Tidwell and Hannah sat across from each other on child-size chairs.

"It won't be easy," Hannah said. "I already know that.''

Amy nodded.

"But I've made up my mind, Amy. I'm going to do it."

The teenager nodded. "Good."

Hannah chewed lightly on her lip. "I'm going to contact a private detective. In my heart, I knew that was the thing to do all along. I just didn't know how to go about finding the right one."

"And now you do?"

"I have an old friend, Dylan Garrett," Hannah told her. "I met him when I was at school in Dallas. He was a cop then, but... It's a long story. He's a private investigator now."

Amy sat back, grinning.

"Wow! So you'd really trust this guy, huh?"

"With my life. I thought about contacting Dylan almost right away, but..." She took a deep breath. "I guess I just didn't want to tell him what I'd done...."

Amy squeezed her hand. Amazing, Hannah thought, how much courage she'd gotten from knowing the teenager. At first it had been Hannah who'd supported Amy, but ever since Amy had decided to keep her baby, they'd talked endlessly, and those conversations had convinced Hannah it was time to put an end to her own torment.

For almost nine long years, she'd kept her secret from everyone, even from Katherine and Alexandra, her dearest and oldest friends. Now, in the span of a few short weeks, she'd shared it with Amy.

And she was about to share it with an old friend from the past. The same past where her secret lay.

Wheels within wheels, she thought, and blinked back the sudden pressure of tears.

"Dylan's a great guy. Now he's married, successful...he owns his own agency. Well, along with his twin sister and his half brother. We've kept in touch over the years. Christmas cards, postcards, things like that. Best of all, this is Dylan's specialty. Finding people, I mean. He'll know exactly what to do to help me."

"That's wonderful," Amy said happily.

"I admit, I hoped I could find a way to do this without involving anyone I know...."

"Hannah, just be sure you're doing what *you* want to do, that you aren't doing it because I suggested it."

"It's what I want, Amy. What I have to do." Hannah grasped Amy's hand more tightly. "You're so much braver than I was. Finding out that you were pregnant, deciding to keep your baby instead of—instead of giving it away, like I did."

"Me? Brave?" Amy snorted. "Right. I'm so brave that I kept my pregnancy a deep, dark secret until recently." She shook her head. "Just seeing how you still miss your baby after all these years, how you think about him all the time, wonder if he's happy, if he's healthy, what his adoptive parents are like... It makes me certain of my decision to keep mine." Amy flushed. "Oh, Hannah, I didn't mean..."

"No, that's okay. I did what I thought was right." Hannah gave Amy's hand one last squeeze, then got to her feet and started to pace the room. "But I can't go on without knowing what happened to my son."

"When will you speak with your friend?"

"I'll phone him tonight." Hannah took a deep breath. "The sooner I get the ball rolling, the better."

"And you're not going to say anything to Katherine?"

"No," Hannah said emphatically. "Not to her or anyone else. Not until I know something, and maybe not even then." She gave a wobbly laugh. "That's the problem with secrets, you know? They seem to take on a life of their own. I still can't believe I told you." She sighed. "Yes, I can. You're the same age I was when I got pregnant. Each time I saw you touch your belly and get that little smile on your face..." Hannah cleared her throat, then glanced at her watch. "Enough talk of the past," she said brightly. "It's juice-break time. You up for some OJ?"

Amy grinned and rose from her chair.

"Yes, thank goodness. No more morning sickness. I swear, the doctor says I had the longest bout of it in the history of the western world."

Laughing, the two women linked arms and headed out to the hall toward a table stacked with juice boxes.

They were so busy talking that they didn't see Luke directly in their path. He'd checked the time, too, and decided he was about due for a coffee break next door at Caffeine Hy's. It was easy enough to keep an eye on things from a stool at Hy's counter.

"Excuse me," he said, and stepped out of their way.

"Luke." Hannah looked up and smiled at him.

"Mr. Sloan," Amy said, and smiled, too.

Well, well, well. Everybody was smiling, Luke thought, as he headed for the front door. The Richards woman's mood had done a one-eighty and the Tidwell girl looked just as delighted.

Delighted and, absolutely, pregnant.

Obviously, he'd judged the situation right.

Hannah Richards had sought his advice on behalf of the girl, and now both of them were happy. The girl had listened to what her boss had told her and decided to find a P.I. and set him on the trail of the kid who'd made her pregnant, then taken off.

Somewhere between here and the East Coast, an irresponsible young kid was about to have his life turned upside down. That was only right. Whoever he was, he'd find out soon enough that you couldn't turn your back on a child.

"Luke?"

Luke felt a small hand tug at the tail of his shirt. He knew, even before he turned around, that it would be Emily Douglas.

It was.

Em was gazing up at him through big eyes so filled with unhappiness that he felt as if a lance had pierced his heart. Turning your back on a kid in theory was a lot different from doing it in practice.

Luke did his best to smile as if he hadn't noticed anything unusual.

"Hi, Emily."

"Hello."

He waited. Emily did, too. Was he being outplayed by a four-year-old?

"Well," he said briskly, "I see it's juice time."

"Uh-huh."

"It's coffee time for me. I think we'd both better hurry, or we're liable not to get any."

"I don't feel like juice this morning."

No. And looking at her sad, upturned face, he didn't much feel like coffee, either.

"Lily says you don't like us anymore."

Oh, hell. "Em." Luke squatted down in front of the child. "I like you and Lily just fine."

"No, you don't."

"Sure I do."

"You used to. You used to talk to us and everything."

"I'm talking to you right now, aren't I?"

"Only 'cause I talked to you first."

Luke heaved out a breath. Definitely, he was being outplayed by a munchkin.

"The thing is, Em, I've been very busy all week."

"That's what you said yesterday, when Lily and me tried to show you the dollhouse we made."

Had he said that? Probably. He'd done damn near everything but growl in his attempts to keep this exceedingly dangerous four-year-old at bay, Luke thought, muffling a groan.

"I'm sorry, princess. How about showing me that dollhouse now?"

Emily went straight for the jugular. "How come you don't like us anymore?"

A throbbing pain started up just behind Luke's eyes. Participating in dialogue with a rug rat was not part of a surveillance. All he had to do to put an end to it was stand up, tell the kid he didn't care what she thought, walk away...

And then lie awake tonight, tossing and turning, haunted by the lost-little-girl look in the eyes of the mother and the daughter.

He missed the hard-won smiles he'd brought to both their faces, especially Abby's. It had just about killed him, the way she'd seemed to be looking for him that last time at the day care.

He missed her laughter, too, silly as it was to miss something he'd only heard a few times.

Damn it, Dan was right. He'd gotten in over his head. It was a good thing he'd figured it out in time to get out while he still could.

"Here's the thing," Luke told Emily, deciding to opt for at least a part of the truth. "I have a job to do here. An important job. And I can't do it as well as I should unless I devote my full attention to it."

He could see her thinking that over, weighing it, then accepting it. Saved, he thought with relief. At least the child wouldn't write him off as a cold, cruel bastard.

"Em? You understand?"

She nodded, gave him a little smile.

"You have lots to do here, and you can't do stuff right if you're thinking about other things."

"Yes." Luke stood up. "That's it, exactly."

"So, you'd have to do those other things after work."

"Right. I'd have to do those other things after—"

He saw the trap, but too late. Emily was already smiling happily, as if he'd just told her the Meaning of Life all in caps.

"Then, you can come have supper with Mommy and me after all."

Luke blinked. "Supper?" he said, as if he'd never heard the word until this moment.

"Uh-huh. Like you were going to, remember? You drove us home, and my mommy tried to pay you, and you said—"

He knew what he'd said. What he didn't know was how he'd let this kid waltz him onto such thin ice.

"So why doesn't he like us anymore, Emily?"

Oh, Lord. The reinforcements had arrived, the other half of the Twinned Twosome. Lily Marshall grabbed Emily's hand and fixed Luke with an unblinking stare.

"I like you guys just fine," he said, and rolled his eyes at the desperation he heard in his own voice, but there was no way out, short of trampling Em's feelings into the dust. Cop or no cop, job or no job, he wasn't going to do that.

All right.

He'd check out their dollhouse and agree to dinner. Supper, just one meal. Forget about his dumb remark out there in

Abby's driveway when he'd thought himself so clever, conning her into agreeing to have dinner out with him.

Supper, one night this week. At the Douglas house. He'd bring flowers, he'd be pleasant but distant, and when the evening ended, so would his obligation to the Douglas women.

"Are you going to look at the house we made? And eat supper with Abby and Emily?" Lily demanded in the take-no-prisoners tone of a hostage negotiator.

"I am," Luke said.

Both kids beamed up at him.

Just for a minute, he felt pretty good, though the feeling faded when they grabbed his hands and dragged him off to see their cardboard-box dollhouse and he thought about how he was lying to them, letting them think everything was back to normal.

At the end of the day, he was still thinking that, trying to justify it to himself as he put on his leather jacket, shut off the lights in Katherine's office, headed out the front door and through the gate to the sidewalk…

And skidded to a stop when he found Abby and Emily in his path.

"Hello," he said, telling himself that little twist of pleasure in his gut had nothing to do with seeing Abby again.

"Emily says she persuaded you to keep your dinner appointment with us." Abby's tone was polite, but her eyes were cool.

"Well, I wouldn't exactly say…"

"That's fine. We definitely owe you a meal."

"You don't. I mean, it's not necessary if you don't want—"

"Mommy," Emily said, tugging at her mother's skirt, "Luke *does* want to come to our house. He said so!"

Abby's smile was stiff. "It's cold, Em. Why don't you get into the car while Luke and I talk?"

"But Mommy…"

"Emily, what did I just say? Go on. Get in the car and fasten your seat belt. I'll only be a minute."

Emily sighed, opened the door to the car and climbed into her booster seat. Abby closed the door behind her. Why was she so upset? Surely, it couldn't be because she hadn't heard from Luke since the weekend. It couldn't be because she suspected he regretted those tentative dinner plans, that he wouldn't have agreed to standing by them if Emily hadn't somehow badgered him into it.

"Honestly," she said, swinging toward him and smiling politely, "you don't have to do this. I know how difficult it can be to say no to a child, and Em can be very persistent, but—"

"I want to come," Luke said, and even as the words left his mouth, he knew they were true. He'd made a mess of something simple, because it *was* simple. Abby was a woman, he was a man. He was attracted to her and, damn it, she was attracted to him, and to hell with everything else. For all he knew, there was nothing going on at the jewelry exchange... and even if it turned out there was, Abby's presence at the estate jewelry counter didn't have to mean a thing. She could no more be into something illegal than he could click his heels together and wind up in Kansas.

"I want to come for dinner," he said, taking a step toward her. "Please, Abby. Say it's okay."

"Really, Luke, it's not—"

"We can go to a restaurant, if you don't have enough of whatever you're making tonight to serve three."

She blinked. "You mean, you want to have dinner with us this evening?"

"Yes," he said firmly. "Right now."

Her expression softened, the look in her eyes changing from wary politeness to pleasure, but it was gone in a heartbeat.

"Sorry," she said as she turned toward her car, "but I'd just as soon—"

Luke caught her arm. All he wanted was to stop her from walking away, but she swung toward him, her free hand upraised and balled into a fist, and her eyes filled with something more than anger, something that rocked him straight down to the bottom of his soul.

"Don't touch me!"

He let go, lifting his hand from her with exaggerated care though what he really wanted to do was far less logical, like take her in his arms and tell her that whoever had put that fear in her eyes would someday pay for it.

"Abby," he said softly, "I'm sorry. The truth is, what's happening between us took me by surprise."

"That's ridiculous." She gave a shaky laugh. "We hardly know each other. How could anything be happening?"

"I don't know, but it is. And it scares the hell out of me," he said, his voice gruff with emotion. "I'm divorced. It was a bad marriage, a painful divorce, and I guess it left me ready to back away from my own feelings, especially if I thought I felt something I wasn't ready to feel."

Even as the words poured out of him, he knew they didn't make a whole lot of sense, but making sense was for later. What mattered now was that he'd told her what he really felt. Something that had been dead for a very long time was stirring to life inside him, and he'd be damned if he'd walk away from it.

He waited, knowing he'd said all he could, that now it was up to her. She could toss everything he'd admitted in his face, tell him he was crazy, tell him to get out of her life and stay out.

She stared at him for what seemed an endless stretch of time. Then she gave a quick nod and he held his breath, waiting for her decision.

"We're having hamburgers, green beans and mashed potatoes. You can join us if you want to."

She spoke quickly, and he knew she wasn't convinced that what she was doing made sense.

Well, hell, neither was he. Doing things that made sense had never been a priority in his life.

Why would he want to change that now?

CHAPTER TEN

ABBY GLANCED IN HER REARVIEW mirror as she pulled to a stop at a traffic light.

Luke was still there, staying right behind her in his black SUV.

What in the world was she doing, taking him home?

Better still, what had he meant by those things he'd said back at the day care? That he'd felt something he wasn't ready to feel? They'd only met a week ago. They'd talked, laughed, sat in her kitchen drinking iced tea.

What could he feel for her? What could she feel for him?

Abby's hands tightened on the steering wheel.

Something. Oh, yes. Something. She knew that, even if she didn't know exactly what it was or what it meant, and now she was on her way home, with Luke right behind her, and her daughter bouncing with excitement in the back seat.

Abby looked into the mirror.

Being in the close confines of a car with a four-year-old was almost always interesting, especially if the four-year-old in question was as verbal as Emily. Em could happily chatter about the things they saw, the people they passed, the weather, the traffic lights, anything and everything throughout an entire trip.

Not tonight.

Abby took another quick look at her daughter.

Em hadn't said more than half a dozen words since they'd pulled out of the parking lot. She was too busy craning her neck so she could watch Luke's car following theirs.

Was she letting her child set herself up for disappointment? As it was, her usually happy little girl had been the very portrait of misery the last couple of days and refused to offer a reason why until finally she'd blurted out that Luke had no time for her anymore.

How much had Em heard of the conversation with Luke just now? How much had she understood? How much *could* she have understood? Abby was an adult, and *she* hadn't understood most of it, not just the things Luke had told her, but her reaction to them.

A sensible woman would have said *Yes, really, that's all fascinating, but you're wasting your time, Mr. Sloan. You don't want to get involved with me and a damned good thing, too, because I most certainly don't want to get involved with you.*

The light changed. Abby eased her foot from the brake to the gas pedal and the car moved ahead.

How could you even use a word like *involved* to describe the relationship she and Luke had? They didn't *have* a relationship. She barely knew the man. He'd given her a ride, fixed her car, made her laugh, made Emily laugh, too, and then he'd turned back into the scowling, surly stranger she'd pegged him for the first time she'd laid eyes on him.

Then why was she taking him home for dinner? Because of Em, that was why; to put a smile on Em's face.

Her daughter had handed her heart to a man who didn't know what to do with it.

Luckily, her mother wasn't anywhere near as foolish.

Abby glanced in the mirror again.

"Em?"

Emily looked around. "Yes, Mommy?"

"You don't have to keep watching Luke," Abby said gently. "His car isn't going to vanish."

"I know." Em looked back again. "Isn't it nice he's coming home with us?"

"Very nice, Em, but—but Luke's a busy man. And I'm sure he has lots of friends. We can't take up too much of his time."

"Uh-huh."

Em was staring behind her again, paying no attention to her mother at all.

"How was day care?"

"Okay."

"Did Marilyn finish telling that story you liked so much?"

"Uh-huh."

"How's Lily?"

"Fine."

"Did you two do anything special today?"

"No." Emily hesitated, then turned and met Abby's eyes in the mirror. "Mommy?"

"Yes, baby?"

"Are you mad at me?"

"No! Why would I be?"

"I don't know. Are you?"

"No, Em. Of course not. What makes you think that?"

Emily looked sheepish. "You sounded mad when you told me to get into the car before."

"I'm sorry, baby. I promise, I wasn't angry at you."

"Were you angry at Luke?"

Oh, Lord. "No. I wasn't mad at anybody."

"You sure sounded mad."

Abby expelled a short, sharp breath. What now? Was she really going to explain that she'd been upset, not angry? After all, Luke had disappointed her daughter...

And her, as well. That was the truth, wasn't it?

She'd come alive when Luke sat at her kitchen table, drinking iced tea. All they'd done was have an hour of easy conversation, but she'd smiled more during that hour than she could remember smiling, except with Emily, in years and years and years. And then he'd walked away, made it clear he didn't want any part of her or Em....

"Luke was busy. That's why he didn't have time for us, not 'cause he didn't want to."

"I know that, Emily."

"He likes you, Mommy."

Abby stared into the mirror. Her daughter was beaming.

"He likes both of us," Abby said carefully.

"He likes us enough to have dinner with us tonight."

"Well, yes. I think he wants to keep me from feeling guilty about all the work he did fixing our car."

"Is that why he asked you to go on a date?"

Abby's eyes flashed to the mirror again. "How do you know that?"

Emily blushed. "I heard. Lily and me were right in the next room, remember?"

"It wasn't a date, it was dinner."

"Sam Shulman's mom goes out to dinner with her boyfriend all the time, an' Sam says those are dates. A babysitter stays with him, and she lets Sam stay up really late an' watch horror movies. He says—"

"Here we are," Abby sang out as she pulled into the driveway. "Okay, sweetie. Let's get you out of that seat and into the house."

"I want to wait for Luke."

"Emily," Abby began, but arguing was pointless. Luke tucked his SUV in behind her car and stepped out onto the gravel.

"Luke," Emily shouted happily, racing to him as if he were an unanticipated visitor.

"Princess," Luke said, falling right into the game. He swept her into his arms and waltzed her in a big circle. "What a terrific surprise! I didn't know you were a patron of this excellent dining establishment!"

Emily giggled, which he'd expected. Abby's lips curved a little, which he hadn't. Then she got herself under control, but it gave him hope.

All the way here, he'd wondered if he'd pushed too hard, if he'd end up sitting across from an unsmiling woman who'd sacrificed herself for the night because she was too polite to send him packing.

"Silly," Em said. "This is my house."

"Then…" His face fell. "Then, this isn't the place where I'm going to dine on *boeuf américain* with *haricots vert,* and *pommes de terre parisien?*"

Emily giggled some more and bounced in his arms. "What's he saying, Mommy?"

Abby looked at her child, secure and happy in Luke Sloan's

arms. Her throat tightened; she had to clear it before she could speak.

"He's saying he loves hamburgers and green beans and mashed potatoes, and that he'll love those burgers even more if we let him make them on the grill." She fixed her eyes on Luke's. "Would that be an accurate translation, *monsieur?*"

Luke smiled, and she felt that smile shoot through her from the top of her head to the tips of her toes.

"It would be a perfect translation," he said, and Abby decided to let go of everything for a couple of hours, her doubts, her fears, her uncertainty, and simply let the evening happen.

"THAT," LUKE SAID, SIGHING with pleasure as he pushed aside his plate, "was a meal fit for royalty."

Abby smiled. "Thanks for the compliment, but I suspect Buckingham Palace isn't planning on featuring a menu like this anytime soon."

"Well, if they aren't, they're missing a good bet. Seriously, that was great."

"The hamburger patties were the best part," Emily said, swiping a furtive finger over her plate in hopes of one last bit of mashed potato. "Mommy hardly ever makes them on the grill."

"Your mom probably comes home feeling too tired to light the grill and hang around on the porch while stuff cooks." He smiled. "That's what my mom used to tell me when I complained that she didn't make something particular for our supper."

"Did your mom work, too? Like mine?"

"She sure did. She had to support both of us."

"My mommy does, too." Emily got off her chair and stood beside Luke's. "We don't have a dad," she said solemnly. "Not one who lives with us."

"Em," Abby said softly.

No, Luke thought, not just softly. The word had been meant as a reminder that the topic wasn't open to discussion.

"Yes, Mommy." Emily gave a long-suffering sigh. "I'm not s'pposed to talk about that."

"You know what, princess? If your mom doesn't want you to talk about something, you shouldn't."

Luke caught the look of surprise on Abby's face. Well, hell, he'd surprised himself, too. He wanted to know more about this past Abby was so determined to keep hidden, but only when she was ready to tell him the story herself.

Keeping secrets wasn't the greatest idea in the world, not between a man and a woman, but who was he to judge? He was walking around with some giant-size secrets himself. He was a cop, not a carpenter, and he was investigating something that might be happening at the place where Abby worked.

He didn't want to consider the other possibility. Not tonight. Luke shoved back his chair.

"Tell you what. Em, you clear the table. Abby, you dry. I'll wash."

There was no point in arguing. He'd already rolled up the sleeves of his blue denim work shirt and turned on the hot water, so Abby went along with it.

After a few minutes, she decided that doing dishes had never been as much fun as this. Em told some terrible jokes she'd picked up at day care. Luke played the perfect straight man, and after a while, they were all laughing.

Then Emily launched into a song she'd learned that morning. It was a silly thing about a puppy and a kitten and a mouse. Luke listened to a couple of verses, started to hum the chorus and finally sang along in a warm baritone.

"You, too, Mommy," Emily said.

Abby tried to beg off. She had, she insisted, the world's most atrocious singing voice, but Emily and Luke teased and cajoled until finally she gave in and, she had to admit, didn't sound all that bad. Off key, yes, and a little tentative, but nobody seemed to care.

Frank hadn't liked to hear her sing. She'd had a silly habit of warbling the latest country ballads in the shower. She knew she wasn't good at it, but that wasn't why anyone sang in the shower.

That was what she'd told Frank when he'd said she was ruining a bunch of good songs. They were on their honeymoon and she'd laughed, thinking he was teasing her, and she'd started to put her arms around him. But Frank had peeled her hands from the back of his neck and said, with cold assurance, that there was no point in doing anything unless you could do it well....

And what was she doing thinking about Frank tonight?

She glanced at Luke, who was laughing at yet another of Emily's jokes.

She couldn't recall seeing Frank laugh as much in their entire marriage as Luke Sloan had laughed tonight, but then, Luke and Frank were as different as two men could be. Not just physically, though Luke was lots bigger. Lots better-looking, too, Abby thought, and felt herself blush.

But Luke was different in ways that mattered.

For one thing, he liked kids.

Frank hadn't. He'd hardly ever glanced at Emily, except when she was fussing, and then he'd scowl and tell Abby to deal with the child. That was how he'd referred to Em, as *the* child, as if she were an intrusion in his life.

Luke would never hurt a woman, either. Abby knew that instinctively. He'd never try to dominate her, tell her where she was permitted to go and who she was permitted to see, what to buy and what to wear. He'd never raise a hand to her and inflict pain.

Frank had done all those things, and what a shock it had been. He'd seemed so kind, so generous...but then, she hadn't been thinking straight when she married him. She'd been shattered by her parents' deaths, young and vulnerable and alone for the first time in her life.

I'm here for you, Abigail, Frank had said.

Fool that she'd been, she'd believed him.

But he'd lied—lied about everything. Telling her how he'd worked for her dad, how much he'd admired him, how they'd been friends instead of just employer and employee, when the truth was that her father had fired Frank after only a couple of months because of petty theft. But how could she have known that? Her dad didn't discuss business at home.

Lies, all of it, from his feelings for her to his relationship with her father, and only so he could get his hands on the money her folks had left her.

Abby took a dish towel from the rack and began drying the pots.

No, Luke wasn't anything like that. He was a nice man. A generous man. He'd never hurt a woman, or try to control her by making her decisions for her. He wouldn't misrepresent himself and tell her lies.

And what did it matter?

Luke could be whatever he wanted. He wasn't part of her life. She didn't need a man, didn't want a man, didn't—

"Hey."

She looked up. Luke had turned off the water. He was drying his hands with a paper towel and smiling at her in a way that made her blush all over again.

"Why such a long face?"

"Me?" Abby managed a little laugh. "Oh, I was just thinking about all the work waiting for me tomorrow. My boss took inventory last weekend, and—"

"Yeah. I know."

Abby's brows lifted. "You do?"

Luke cursed himself for a fool, then backpedaled as quickly as he could.

"When I went to get your car, I bumped into your boss and your manager in the parking lot."

"Oh." She sighed, dried the last pot and hung the towel over the rack. "Well, it's been crazy at the store ever since. It always is, after inventory."

"Why's that?"

"Well, for one thing, Bettina always comes up with pieces that haven't sold for quite a while and she does markdowns on them. We have to move them into different display cases and do whatever we can to make them appealing."

"Which they haven't been all along."

"Exactly." Abby smiled. "Bettina calls it taking a creative approach."

"I worked a summer at a souvenir shop all the way up on

the peninsula. We called it trying to get rid of the junk nobody wanted.''

''Uh-huh,'' she said, laughing. ''That's pretty much what the other clerks and I call it, too.'' She batted her lashes and put on a la-di-dah expression. ''Not Bettina, of course, or Mr. Black.''

''Hey, calling it what it is is the only pleasure the peasants are likely to get.''

''And then, after inventory, Bettina adds new pieces to the stock we already have.''

''Doesn't the store acquire new pieces all the time?''

''Oh, sure. It's just that these are usually much more expensive items, and Bettina says it's easier to do it then.'' Abby sighed and reached for the coffeepot. ''Want some coffee?''

''Sure. Coffee would be fine.'' He cleared his throat. ''Is that Bettina's job? Buying new stock?''

''Pretty much. Mr. Black puts a lot of faith in her judgment.'' Abby took a canister of coffee from the cupboard and opened it. ''He's right to do it, too. Bettina picks up some wonderful things. Older pieces, especially.'' She looked up and smiled. ''I must be boring you to death.''

''No, not at all.''

On the contrary, Luke thought, and wished to God he could tell her that. He'd worried he'd feel guilty if he asked Abby any questions about Emerald City, but she had chosen to open up to him.

Instinct told him Abby had no part in any of what went on there—what supposedly went on there. He still believed that, but the more he knew about the place, the quicker he could end his surveillance and come clean about who he really was.

''So, this Bettina does all the buying, huh?''

''Most of it. I just wish she wouldn't rearrange the merchandise as often as she does.'' Abby measured coffee into the filter, then looked up and smiled at Luke ''Believe me, it can be pretty disconcerting to look into your case and suddenly discover a brooch or a ring you didn't know you had.''

''I'll bet,'' Luke said, trying to sound casual.

''And most of the time she's neglected to put a price sticker on it, so I have to turn the customer over to her and... How about cookies for dessert?''

Luke blinked at the sudden change in topic. ''Cookies? Thanks, but I'm stuffed. No dessert for me.''

''You sure?'' She glanced over her shoulder at him. ''I have a box of Mallomars.''

There was no way to get back to the subject of the jewelry store, not without making Abby suspicious. He'd played cop long enough tonight.

''Did you say Mallomars?''

''Uh-huh.'' Abby grinned. ''Oh, Sloan, how easy you are!''

''What can I tell you? Chocolate icing, that soft cookie base, the marshmallow filling...''

''Exactly.'' Standing on her toes, Abby stretched as high as she could to reach the box, but her fingertips barely brushed it.

''I'll get it.''

''No, I'm almost there.'' She reached up again as Luke rose from his chair. ''I keep stuff like this on the top shelf,'' she said, huffing a little as she strained toward the cookies, ''so I won't eat it each time I'm tempted. Got it,'' she cried triumphantly, grabbing the box and turning around...

And coming nose to chest with Luke.

She tried to step back, or maybe he tried to step forward. He wasn't sure. Whichever it was, he grasped her shoulders to steady her.

The last time he'd touched her, she'd wrenched free of his hands and looked at him with panic in her eyes.

This time, what he saw in those deep hazel depths was a reflection of what he was feeling.

Surprise. Astonishment. And, most of all, awareness.

Awareness of the scent of her, flowery and delicate and female, rising to his nostrils. Of the play of light giving her hair golden highlights. Of the feel of her bones beneath his fingers, like Abby herself, so fragile yet so strong.

His gaze dropped to her lips, which parted as if he'd stroked them. Her breath quickened; he saw the telltale leap of her pulse in her throat, the swift rise and fall of her breasts, and he knew she felt it, too.

The need to touch. To taste. To explore.

Reaching out, he stroked a dark curl back from her temple. She turned her head a fraction of an inch, brushing her face against his seeking fingers.

"Abby," he said, and she made a sound, a whispered sigh that drove the blood from his brain straight to his loins. He said her name again and she looked up, her eyes meeting his, searching his...

"Mommy?"

They sprang apart like teenagers caught saying good-night at the front door. Luke stepped back; Abby took a shaky breath and moved quickly past him.

"Yes, baby?" Tucking a stray curl behind her ear, she flashed an overly bright smile at Emily. "I was just going to call you. Luke and I are going to have dessert. Cookies. Would you like some?"

"No, thank you. I'm full."

"You sure? Because it would really be fun if you joined us."

"I want to play dress-up, Mommy. Is that okay?"

Abby had her breath back, if not her equilibrium. What had she been thinking? The truth was, she hadn't been thinking at all, she'd been feeling. Feeling things that she'd forbidden herself to feel, things she'd never expected or wanted to feel again.

Until a moment ago, Luke had been a friend. Okay. An extremely good-looking friend.

Except you didn't have dreams about a friend that woke you in the middle of the night, or get that funny little sensation in the pit of your belly when he smiled at you.

And yes, those things had been happening, even though she'd denied them to herself. Even earlier tonight, she'd pretended she'd been upset only because he'd hurt Em's feelings. The truth was, she'd been baffled and, okay, hurt. Hurt, because she'd looked forward to seeing him again, to being with him.

"May I, Mom?" Emily smiled at Luke. "I love to play dress-up. Did you play dress-up when you were a little boy?"

Luke's senses were still flooded with Abby, and he fought to bring his attention to the child.

"Uh, no. I don't think so." Somehow, he dredged up a smile. "Unless you count the time I tied a big towel around my neck and ran around pretending I was Superman."

Emily giggled. "No, silly! That's not dress-up. Dress-up is when you put on grown-up clothes and shoes and stuff, right, Mom?"

Abby forced her attention back where it belonged.

"Em, honey, it's getting late," Abby said. "Tomorrow's a weekday. We have to get up early."

That, Luke knew, was his clue to say yes, it was getting late. He would thank them for the meal, then drive home and take a cold shower for however long it took him to get the feel, the scent, the nearness of Abby out of his mind.

But of course he didn't say any of that.

What he said was that he'd stay five more minutes so he could see Em's version of dress-up, and when she smiled happily, then ran down the hall to her room, he looked around, half expecting Abby to be at the door, holding it open, with his jacket in her outstretched hand.

Instead, she was moving around the kitchen, pouring coffee, taking a small pitcher of milk from the refrigerator, clearly determined to pretend that nothing had happened.

Okay. Maybe she was right. If they both pretended nothing had happened, they could go back to where they'd been and everything would return to normal.

He took the cookies from the shelf and opened the package. "Do you want me to put some on a plate or leave them in the box?"

She furrowed her brow, giving the question almost as much consideration as if he'd asked her to do quadratic equations.

"A plate," she said, adding a quick smile. "That way, I can control how many I eat."

Luke accepted the plate as well as the conversational gambit with both hands.

"I'll have to try your method with potato chips. I'm a sucker when it comes to those things."

"A trillion calories a bite is a good reason to keep something out of reach."

"Yeah," he said. "It's hell when things that make you feel great are things you should avoid."

Their eyes met. Abby blushed, and Luke silently told himself he was an idiot.

"I was just trying to say that you don't have to worry about calories. You look just about perfect to me."

Oh, hell. Put both feet in at once next time, Sloan. Why go for only one size eleven at a clip?

"I meant," he said, "I meant…"

Her blush deepened. Her eyes darkened. And suddenly nothing mattered now except this moment, this electricity humming between him and the first woman he'd ever known who could make his heartbeat accelerate with a simple smile.

"I meant," he said softly, closing the distance between them, his gaze locked to hers, "that I need to kiss you, Abby. Right now."

She didn't move back, didn't speak, didn't do anything except watch him come toward her. And when he reached her, cupped her face in his hands, she trembled, closed her eyes and lifted her mouth to his.

His lips brushed hers as softly as silk. Lightly, coolly, and then he changed the angle of the kiss and it turned hot as the desert sun.

"Abby," Luke whispered, and when she parted her lips, he groaned, gathered her into his arms and sank into the kiss.

She sighed his name, then rose on her toes and wound her arms around Luke's neck. Years had gone by since she'd kissed a man—wanted to kiss a man, wanted the heat of him, the strength of him to utterly destroy her defenses.

And never, not once in her life, had a man's kiss made her feel like this, as if she were a creature made of light and heat and air, as if she'd been born in this moment, just for this.

Luke's hands slid down her back to cup her bottom, and he lifted her into him. He was hard, rigid with desire, and feeling him pressed against her made her tremble. Not with the remembered fear of the past, but with desire.

"Luke?"

The little voice carried from Emily's bedroom all the way down the hall to the kitchen.

Luke and Abby sprang apart.

"Luke?"

He swallowed past the dryness in his throat.

"Yes, princess."

"Close your eyes." Excitement danced in Emily's voice. "Tell me when you're ready. I want to s'prise you."

Any more surprises and his knees would buckle. Luke placed his palm against Abby's cheek and ran the ball of his thumb over her bottom lip.

"Terrific idea," he said hoarsely, watching her eyes unfocus and color climb her cheeks as he slid the tip of his thumb between her lips.

"Are you ready? Are your eyes closed?"

He looked at Abby one last time. Then he stepped back and shut his eyes.

"Ready, princess."

Footsteps clattered against the wooden floor in the hallway.

"Ta-da," Em said, and Luke opened his eyes, a smile already forming on his lips...until he saw Abby's daughter.

The child had pinned up her blond braids and smeared pink lipstick on her mouth. She was wearing a dress that had to have been Abby's, and her feet were tucked into a pair of Abby's shoes.

Just a kid playing dress-up with her mom's stuff, except for one thing.

Except for several things, Luke thought dazedly.

The pearl and diamond earrings dangling from her ears.

The silver-dollar size ruby-and-sapphire-studded pin on her dress.

And the diamond and gold bracelet catching the light as it slipped and slid on Emily's arm. Chunky bits of gold, studded with more stones, hung from the bracelet. Charms, they were called. Luke knew that because he'd taken a quick lesson in estate jewelry just yesterday.

At lunchtime, he'd made a phone call to the detective who'd

worked most of the cat burglaries and asked the guy for a quick lesson in what constituted estate jewelry. His description was the same as the lieutenant's—stuff that was old and expensive, though "old" could mean it just dated back to maybe the fifties. A lot of stuff the perp had stolen was fifties stuff.

Like what? Luke had asked.

Like a big pin that looked gaudy now but had been the rage then, the guy told him. Like big hanging earrings. Like charm bracelets with lots of flash, he said, and explained what that meant. Luke had thanked him, then gone online last night and checked out the term on the net.

Bottom line? If the stuff Emily Douglas was wearing wasn't estate jewelry, he'd eat his shirt.

The question was, was it estate jewelry stolen by a thief who'd broken into people's homes, terrorized the women, beaten those who resisted, and fenced what he stole at the Emerald City Jewelry Exchange where Abby worked? At the counter she was in charge of?

"Luke?" Emily touched the pearls and diamonds at her ears. "Isn't my jewelry pretty?"

"Yeah." Luke cleared his throat. "Very pretty."

"It belonged to my grandma. Right, Mommy?"

Luke looked at Abby, who nodded. "That's right. It was my mother's."

She said it casually, no hint of worry or concern in her voice. Well, why would she worry? She thought he was a carpenter, not a cop....

Jesus. *Slow down, man. Just slow down.*

He smiled pleasantly. "So, the stuff is real?"

"Uh-huh." Abby ruffled her daughter's hair. "It's real."

Luke nodded. Somehow, he kept his eyes off the glittering jewels, said the right things, drank his coffee, even though his throat felt as if it had closed up. Then he looked at his watch as if he'd never seen it before and announced that it was getting late and he really had to leave.

He kissed the top of Emily's head and thanked Abby for dinner. Maybe he didn't pull that off so well because the last thing he remembered seeing, before he headed out to his SUV and got behind the wheel, was Abby's face looking puzzled, even disappointed.

He damn near burned rubber, backing down the driveway. Two blocks away, he pulled to the curb, took out his cell phone and hit the button programmed with Dan's number.

"Hey," his partner said, "I was just going to call you. I just heard there was another armed robbery a couple of nights ago."

Luke closed his eyes. "What'd they get?"

"I got a list here. A big diamond ring. A ruby pendant. A star sapphire pin. Maybe half a dozen other pieces."

"No gold and diamond bracelets hung with charms? No diamond and pearl earrings? No ruby and sapphire pin the size of a hubcap?"

"Huh?"

"Just check," Luke said harshly.

Paper rustled before Dan answered.

"Nope. Nothing like that on the list. A bracelet, yeah, but it's emeralds."

Luke shut his eyes, then opened them again. "Dan? I want background checks on Bettina something-or-other, the woman who manages Emerald City. While you're at it, check out the owner, Julian Black." Luke paused. "And Abby Douglas."

He could hear the sound of Dan's breathing.

"Something happen with her?" Dan finally asked.

"Just get me the info, okay?"

"Sure. No problem. You'll have it."

"ASAP," Luke said, and hit the disconnect button.

He sat at the curb for a long time, hands clasping the wheel, eyes staring blindly ahead.

Then he put the SUV in gear and drove home to his dark and silent condo.

CHAPTER ELEVEN

AT NOON THE NEXT DAY, Luke slid into a booth at a hole-in-the-wall Thai restaurant he and Dan had discovered a couple of years before. The decor could best be described as Garage Sale Reject, and the service, if you were foolish enough to call it that, was awful.

The only draw was the food, which was terrific.

Hot, spicy, delicious—even if you were on duty and had to drink iced tea with it instead of cold beer. The place was also less than fifteen minutes from Forrester Square Day Care, which made it a perfect choice today.

Dan had said he'd meet Luke at twelve, but it was a few minutes past that before he strolled in.

"You're late," Luke said grumpily.

Dan gave him a look. "And hello to you, too."

"We said noon."

"*You* said noon. I said yeah, fine. Noon. And, by God, here it is…" Dan shot a look at his watch. "Holy hell! It's four minutes after twelve. I guess I should be marched outside and shot."

"Yeah, yeah, okay," Luke said, even more grumpily. "I already ordered for us both. Pad Thai with shrimp, all right?"

"Hey, do I look like a dummy? The mood you're in, I'm not about to say no to anything."

"Did you get that background stuff for me?"

"No."

"Is that supposed to be a joke?"

"Saying no to Pad Thai and saying it to an impossible request are two different things."

"I didn't ask for the impossible. I asked for data," Luke

said, sitting back as their waiter slapped huge bowls of fried noodles in front of them.

"And you'll get it." Dan pulled a paper napkin from the dispenser and tucked it into his collar. "In a while."

"I don't have a while to wait."

Dan stabbed a fork into his noodles. "Didn't you say you ordered shrimp in this?" he asked suspiciously.

"Damn it, Dan…"

"Because this sure as heck doesn't look like a shrimp to me."

Luke glared at the tangle of noodles impaled on Dan's fork. "This isn't the Ritz. You know better than to ask what's in the Pad Thai they serve here."

"People always say that. That a place isn't the Ritz, but I wonder, *is* there a Ritz? Someplace, maybe, but I've sure never…" He caught the look on Luke's face, quickly shoved the fork into his mouth and chewed. "I put the requests in for background info on Julian Black, Abby Douglas, and Bettina Carlton."

"And?"

"And what? It's gonna take a little time."

"How much time?"

"Two weeks, maybe more, maybe less."

"Two days. No more, preferably less."

Dan pointed his fork at Luke's plate. "You should eat while the stuff's hot."

"Yes, Mother."

"Because once it gets cold…"

"Dan." Luke leaned forward. "I told you, I need that data ASAP."

"You'll get it ASAP. I put a rush on it."

"A rush," Luke said, and snorted. "Great. That means we should have it by Christmas."

"Did I miss something? Did you see a familiar face on tape, or some perp you know walking into that jewelry store?"

"No."

"So, what's with the sudden hurry?"

"Well—" Luke hesitated. "Well, I just don't think it makes

sense for me to sit on the place Monday through Friday and you to spend Saturdays in that van without us knowing something about the people inside.''

''I thought we were going to wait until we had something.''

Luke picked up his fork and poked it at the noodles in his bowl.

''We didn't say that.''

''Not exactly, no, but we both know we don't have anything solid. Not yet. All we've got is that old lady and her maybe-it-was, maybe-it-wasn't ID of a necklace.''

Luke looked up, met his partner's eyes, flushed and looked down at his plate again.

''Luke?''

''Yeah?''

''That's still all we have, right? You just told me you haven't eyeballed anything at the store or picked something up on tape....'' The men's eyes met. Dan put down his fork. ''What have you got? And don't bother telling me you haven't got anything, because I know you do.''

''I had dinner at Abby's last night.''

Dan thought about questioning the wisdom of what his partner had done, decided against it and simply nodded.

''She's got this kid...''

''Emily. So you mentioned. And?''

''And...'' Luke lifted his iced tea to his lips and took a drink. ''And the kid played dress-up after we ate.''

''Dress up? Yeah. It's a little girl thing. My nieces used to do it all the time.''

''Some of what she dressed up in was gold and pearls and diamonds.''

''And? I don't see—''

''That necklace, the one the old lady thought she saw.. It dated back to the fifties.''

''You're going to have to say something I can understand, partner.''

''The stuff Abby's kid was playing with dates back to that same period. Estate jewelry, it's called.''

"I thought estate jewelry meant stuff owned by the Vanderbilts."

Luke nodded. "Sometimes." His mouth twisted. "I've spent two nights now surfing the Internet, learning more about jewelry than I ever wanted to know." He took a deep breath, then expelled it. "Anything old—actually, anything that dates back a couple of decades or more—anything you buy used, assuming it's the real stuff and expensive—pretty much qualifies as estate jewelry."

"I still don't see—"

"The old lady's necklace appeared, then disappeared in a case filled with estate jewelry at Emerald City. Abby is the salesclerk who works the estate jewelry counter. And now it turns out she's got a stash of stuff that a jeweler would call estate jewelry at home."

"Could be costume stuff."

"Could be, but isn't." Luke shrugged his shoulders. "It's real," he said quietly. "I asked."

"And you think that Abby…"

"No!" The word exploded into the silence of the all-but-empty restaurant. Luke looked around, hunched his shoulders and leaned across the table. "Abby couldn't be fencing jewels. She couldn't do anything illegal. She's a good, decent woman."

"And you," Dan said calmly, "are in so deep you're close to drowning."

"Don't be an ass, Shayne. The only thing I'm in, as you so deftly put it, is a surveillance assignment in the middle of a bunch of rug rats."

"The hell you are! You've gone from surveilling to investigating, and you know why?" Dan leaned in, his normally ruddy face a beet red. "You've seen something the cop in you knows should be checked out. Meanwhile, the man in you is involved with this woman."

"I told you before, I'm not—"

"She's a suspect, Luke! Everybody in that effing store's a suspect, especially her, if she's got a cache of jewelry tucked away."

"It's not a cache of anything, it's just a bunch of old jewelry!"

"Yeah?"

"Yeah."

"Then why am I breaking my ass to get you background on Abigail Douglas?"

The men, breathing hard, glared at each other. They had been partners for a long time, friends for almost as long. Each trusted the other with his life, yet now they faced each other in anger.

No, Luke thought, not anger. Worry and concern, and it was all his fault.

"All right," he said quietly. "It's more than a bunch of old jewelry."

A muscle twitched in Dan's jaw. "I'm glad to hear you admit it."

"It's incriminating." Luke ran the tip of his finger around the rim of the glass of iced tea. "It *looks* incriminating. That doesn't mean that it is."

Dan sat back. "I agree with you. It could be nothing."

"It probably *is* nothing."

"But we don't know that," Dan said. "And until we do—"

"I know what you're going to say. Until we check this out, I've got to remember I'm a cop."

"Exactly."

"That Abby's a suspect."

"Uh-huh."

"That every person who works at the jewelry exchange is a suspect." Luke looked up and met Dan's eyes. "The cop in me knows all that, but the man knows something more. Abby's innocent. She could no more do something illegal or immoral than I could fly to the moon."

"That Soyuz spaceship, the one somebody's always paying a zillion-trillion bucks to get a ride on, could probably get you there and back," Dan said, and offered a quick smile.

"I'm serious, Dan. If you knew her,.."

"Are you sleeping with her?"

Luke's eyes darkened. "That's none of your business."

"It damned well is, and you haven't answered the question. Are you sleeping with Abby Douglas?"

"No." Luke ground the word out through his teeth.

"But you want to."

"You know what, Shayne?" Luke shot to his feet. "I'm not about to discuss my sex life with you."

Dan put his hand on Luke's arm. "So, she's more than some babe you've got the hots for."

"I just said…" Luke glowered at Dan. Then, slowly, he eased back into the booth. "I don't know. That's the problem. I don't know what I feel for her, and even when I think I do, it doesn't make sense because I hardly know her."

Dan sighed. "You're in trouble, my man."

"You know me, Dan. I'll do my job no matter what happens."

"Oh, right. You're falling in love with a woman you've just met, and if you have to arrest her, you will."

"You're jumping ahead, partner. Liking Abby is a long way from loving her, and I'm no place near busting anybody."

Dan nodded. "Yeah." He picked up his fork and dug into the Pad Thai. "I was wrong."

"Damned right, you were wrong."

"About the Pad Thai, I mean. It's pretty good cold."

Dan devoured a few more forkfuls. Luke pushed his bowl aside and longed for the good old days when he'd have reached into his pocket for a pack of cigarettes. He hadn't smoked in a decade, but if he were going to start again, now would be the perfect time.

"Okay." Dan shoved his lunch aside and folded his hands on the table. "I'll see if I can shake those background reports loose faster than usual."

"How?"

"You remember Silicone Sally?"

Luke grinned. Dan was referring to Sally Hoffman, the department's primary computer whiz. Sally was reputed to sleep with a computer next to her bed so she could hear its loving hum all night long.

"Sure. What about her?"

Dan shrugged, then wagged his hand toward the two waiters hovering near what passed for a bar and mimed signing the check.

"She owes me one."

"Sally?" Luke said skeptically. As far as he could tell, Sally never had enough interaction with another human being to owe anybody anything.

"Yup."

The waiter dropped the check on the table. Dan began to reach for it but Luke got there first.

"My turn, remember?"

"Damn," Dan said affably, "I forgot. Otherwise, I'd have ordered the Ptomaine Special."

Luke looked at the check, dug out some bills and dropped them alongside it.

"So, how come Silicone Sally owes you a favor?"

Dan grinned as the men slid from the booth.

"A couple of years ago, that child pornography bust over near Pioneer Square, remember? The perp had a computer in his apartment, and we got a search warrant to take a look inside. I put in a hurry-up call to Sally before All Thumbs Tuckerman got the chance to sit himself down in front of it." Dan's grin broadened. "Give a woman like Sal a shot at a code-protected hard drive, she's your buddy for life."

"And she can get what we need?"

"More than what we need. Sally's got access to every police department data base in the States and some places we probably don't even want to know about."

The men stepped out of the restaurant into the midday sunshine. Luke held out his hand.

"Thanks, partner."

Dan clasped Luke's hand and gripped it hard.

"Yeah, well, thank Sally after she delivers. Send her a new floppy disk. That ought to get her all worked up."

Both men chuckled. Then Luke's smile faded.

"Thank you for everything, not just the connection to Sally. I know you're worried about me."

"No way. I'm worried about you screwing up and me having

to go into that day care center in your place. What I know about carpentry could fill a matchbook.''

The men grinned at each other. This time, Dan sobered first.

''Just do us both a favor, okay? Take things slow. And take them logically. You do that, you'll be fine.''

''You're right.''

''I know I am.''

The men exchanged light jabs in the arm. Then Dan drove back to the station house. Luke got in his SUV and headed for the day care center.

The afternoon went quickly. The babies and toddlers were napping upstairs, and the older children had gone on some kind of field trip with their teachers and the aides, meaning the center was unusually quiet. Katherine and her partners, Hannah and Alexandra, were holding a meeting elsewhere in the building, so Luke had the office all to himself. A couple of kids popped in—Emily first, then Lily—but since few children were around, he had hardly any interruptions.

That was fine. Better than fine. Working—hammering, sawing, measuring—cleared his mind. So had his conversation with Dan.

His partner was right.

He had to slow down. Be logical. He'd only just met Abby; he knew virtually nothing about her. Wouldn't he be crazy to form an opinion about her guilt or innocence?

People who were guilty and trying to hide it gave themselves away, talking too much, being too helpful, working overtime at coming on like good-natured Boy Scouts.

It took skill and chutzpah to be an effective liar.

Luke frowned as he glued two pieces of rabbeted wood and clamped them together.

But those who were innocent often behaved the same way as those who were guilty.

He was a trained investigator. He'd gather all the facts he could, look at the evidence and decide on a plan of action, starting with whether or not there was anything out of line going on at the jewelry exchange in the first place.

So far, both on tape and to the naked eye, the place was as

quiet as a tomb. BMW and Lexus sedans pulled in and out of the parking lot; well-dressed customers went in and out the front door. Not a one of them even vaguely resembled someone who'd break into houses, shove a gun in people's faces, terrorize them, maybe beat them up and walk off with a small fortune in jewelry.

That didn't mean something wasn't going on at Emerald City. Jewelry was a commodity a thief could turn into cash, but thieves didn't generally walk into jewelry stores every day.

It would hurry things along if they did.

Luke looked up from the cabinet he was finishing and stared out the window. That damned jewelry exchange seemed to loom like a mountain, cutting off his view of everything else. It was turning into his own private Mount Rainier.

Since it was impossible to predict when and where a robbery would occur, the only way to catch the guy was when he tried to sell the loot. And if he tried to sell it at the exchange, that was when Luke would know that somebody at Emerald City was involved.

He could only pray it wouldn't be Abby, but if it was… If it was…

His cell phone rang. Luke plucked it from his shirt pocket and put it to his ear.

"Yeah?"

"It's me," Dan said.

"What's up? Did you hear from Sally?"

"She's a computer geek, not a miracle worker. But I've got some news you might like."

"What?"

"Somebody finally sat down and put together a master list of everything taken in those robberies the last few months."

"And?"

"And, I took a look. No big charm bracelets on it. Actually, no charm bracelets at all."

Luke closed his eyes. "How about pearls?"

"A string, twelve millimeter black pearls, eighteen inches long."

"No. These were earrings. White pearls and diamonds. The kind that dangle."

He heard paper rustling. "Nope, nothing like that on this list. No pin with rubies and sapphires, either."

A weight lifted from around Luke's heart. "I owe you one."

"Luke. Just because the particular pieces you saw aren't on here doesn't mean—"

"I know. But it's a good start. Thanks, man."

"Yeah. Just remember—"

"Slow and logical. You've got it."

Once he'd disconnected, Luke took a deep breath and looked out the window again in time to see the door to Emerald City open. The clerks, all of whom he recognized by now, came hurrying out.

He glanced at his watch. It was six o'clock and the day was over.

The door opened again, and this time it was Abby.

She was wearing a buttercup-yellow wool coat. It had started drizzling, and her hair was beginning to curl, tendrils of it pulling loose and lying against her temples.

Damn, she was beautiful.

He felt his throat tighten. Swallowing suddenly took effort.

Go slow, Dan had said, be logical. But how could you do either thing when just looking at a woman made you feel good, better than you'd felt in a long, long time?

Abby looked both ways, checking for traffic, then started across the road. Luke knew he had to put away his tools, clean up, wash up. Instead, he hurried from the office and got out the front door just as she reached the bottom of the steps.

When she saw him, a smile lit her face.

"Hi."

"Hi," she said, and her smile turned wary. He didn't much blame her. Though he'd tried to disguise it, he suspected she'd been aware of his rushed exit from her apartment the previous night.

"Here to call for Emily?" *Brilliant gambit, Sloan. What else would she be doing?* "I mean, I didn't realize it was six already."

"Yes. The day went quickly for me, too."

Abby started past him. He stepped in front of her.

"I spent some time with Em this afternoon."

"Oh?"

"She came by to tell me she and Lily were building a house out of Lincoln Logs." Luke grinned. "She wanted to know if I'd lend them a hammer and some nails so they could make furniture."

This time Abby smiled for real. God, what a great smile it was. Open, honest, warm. No way could a woman who bought and sold stolen jewelry smile like that.

"Let me guess. You turned down her request."

"I did. But I told her to get Lily while I collected some wood scraps, and then I helped the two of them put together a table and chair for their house."

"That was nice of you."

"It was fun. Besides, I figured if I didn't do something to keep the hellions occupied, they'd get into serious trouble. They had that look about them, you know?"

"I definitely know," Abby said, laughing.

There was a little tick of silence.

"Thanks again for supper last night."

"Oh, it was nothing."

"Hey, it didn't come out of the freezer, and it wasn't wrapped in plastic."

Abby laughed again. She had a great laugh. Nice, easy, un-affected.

"Besides, it was delicious. If I, uh, if I seemed to run off..."

She waved her hand as if to tell him it didn't matter, but he knew that it did.

"It was getting late. And today was a workday for you, and..."

His words trickled away. He'd lied enough, telling her he was a carpenter. And yet, for all he knew, she was lying, too, letting him think she was nothing but a salesclerk when in reality she was...she could be...she might be...

"Anyway," he said, blocking the thought, "I had a great time."

She nodded. "I did, too—I mean, Em and I enjoyed the evening."

Another tick of silence. *Go slow,* Luke could hear Dan saying, *be logical.*

It was fine advice.

How come he couldn't accept it?

So," he said, clearing his throat, "we're almost even."

Abby's brows rose. "Sorry?"

"You and me. The dinner thing. You did the buying last night. Next time, it's my turn."

"Oh. Oh, that. No, don't be silly. That was just—"

"How about tonight?"

She was staring at him as if he'd lost his mind. Hell, if it were physiologically possible, he'd have stared at himself.

What he'd meant to say was, *How about some night in the next century?* Surely by then Sally would have tapped into every criminal, personnel and all-around, all-purpose database between here and Tahiti, and he'd know, as much as he could know, who Abby Douglas really was.

But the words had been there, waiting to come out, and now that he'd said them, he found himself holding his breath, waiting for her to say yes.

"Tonight?"

"Sure. Unless you and Em have other plans..."

"No other plans, no, but—"

"We can get to know each other. You know, talk a little. Right now, I know more about your car than I know about you."

She smiled, as he'd hoped, though the smile was stiff.

"What's that old saying? What you see is what you get. I'm just me, Abby Douglas, single mother, age twenty-six, works in a jewelry store."

"Luke Sloan," Luke said solemnly, "divorced, no kids, age thirty-five—"

"Works at Forrester Square," Abby said.

The twinge of guilt was so sharp it cut like a knife.

"Only for a while. Until my job is completed."

"How long will that take?"

"I don't know," he said, and wished he could tell her everything, ask her everything, say to her, *Abby, I'm not a carpenter, I'm a cop. Is there something going on where you work? Are you part of it? Because if you are—even if you are...*

"I guess not knowing is part of what you do."

"What do you mean?"

"Well, you can never really be sure when you're going to finish a job, can you? I mean, estimations are one thing, but there are always unforeseen delays."

"So true," Luke said softly. He stepped closer and spoke the words he'd been thinking since last night. "I can still taste you on my lips."

Color flew into her face. "Don't talk like that."

"Why? It's the truth. The memory of that kiss kept me awake."

"Luke, please—"

"I'm rushing you."

"Yes."

"I know I am, but..." He took a breath. "Let me take you to dinner tonight. You and Emily."

Abby shook her head. "Thank you, but––"

"But," he said, getting right to the heart of it, "I'm scaring the hell out of you. Would it make it easier if I told you I'm scaring myself, too? That I've never felt...that all of this is..." He drew himself together. "Dinner," he said, lying to her, lying to himself. "That's all I'm asking."

"Luke." She drew her bottom lip between her teeth. "I don't—I don't date."

He was tempted to make light of it, say, Hey, this isn't a date, It's just a meal. But how many lies could a man tell before he despised himself?

"Not at all?"

"That's right. Not at all."

His heart sank. "You're still in love with your husband?"

"No!"

She said it so emphatically that the small part of him that

was still functioning as a cop told him that he was right—somebody had put fear in Abby's soul.

Whoever it was would pay for it, someday.

But now was not the right time to ask questions about her past. Instead, he had to concentrate on the present.

"If it means anything," she added, her eyes flashing to his, then away, "until now, I've never even been tempted."

It meant everything, male chauvinist pig that he was. Instead of feeling compassion for what was surely a lonely life, he felt a hot surge of pleasure at knowing he was the only man who'd broken through the wall that enclosed her.

"I don't understand. You're young. You're beautiful. Why don't you date?"

"For a thousand different reasons. Em, for one. It's tough enough for a four-year-old to have a divorced mom. I don't want to make things more complicated for her."

"I'd risk a paycheck that half the kids at the day care come from divorced parents."

Abby nodded. "Maybe, but not all divorces are the same. Mine was—it was rough."

"Yeah, mine was spent in lawyer hell, too," he said, even though his gut told him that wasn't what she meant.

"It was…unpleasant. And Emily never sees—"

She stopped in the middle of the sentence and clamped her mouth shut, as if she knew she was saying too much. She hadn't said enough, as far as Luke was concerned, but he knew better than to push.

"Her father," he said.

Abby nodded.

"Well, in that case, Em might benefit from having a positive male role model hanging around."

Abby gave a little laugh. "You sound like Dr. Phil."

He reached out and cupped his hand along the side of her face. Her skin felt cool against his fingers; a soft scent of rain and night rose to his nostrils.

"We're quite a pair," he said. "You don't date, and I don't move this fast." He gave a choked laugh. "I don't move at all, according to my best friend's wife. She says I'm as wary of commitment as a canary is of a cat.''

"A woman who speaks her mind," Abby observed. "I like her already."

"She's right, too. That's why what I'm doing now, what I'm feeling…" He drew a steadying breath. "Okay. I *am* rushing you. Let's go back to square one. Dinner. That's all. Just dinner.''

Abby hesitated. It was, he knew, a good sign. A step up from an outright turn-down.

A better sign would be if the floor opened up and swallowed him whole for violating everything he knew about not mixing private life and police work, about the importance of keeping your emotions turned off when you were on the job.

"Perhaps—perhaps another time."

Luke tucked his hands in the back pockets of his jeans.

"Did you ever see those T-shirts that read, Maybe the Hokey Pokey *Is* What It's All About?'' he said, smiling, and she laughed. "It's just a catchy way of saying that life's short."

"You're right. I know you're right, but…" She gestured to the door of the day care center. "I have to go in. Em's waiting for me.''

"There's this little Chinese place near the Pike Place Market. High-backed booths. Beaded curtains. They cook sizzling rice in a wok right at your table. Em'll be impressed, even if you won't." His voice softened. "Come on, Abby. Take a chance and say yes."

How could she say yes, Abby wondered, when ''no'' was the only safe response, the response she'd given any man who'd shown interest in her since her divorce.

She didn't want to get involved with anybody ever again. It was too painful to open your heart to a man and then discover that everything you'd believed him to be was a lie.

And there was always the possibility that she'd have to take Emily and run. She could never explain that. It was her terrible secret, that she'd let Frank fool her, that she'd stayed with him, even after he'd begun abusing her, because she was too weak, too frightened, too accustomed to having someone else make her decisions for her.

"Abby?"

Luke was still waiting for her answer. He was so big, so masculine, and yet he was kind and gentle, too. And what he'd said, about their kiss keeping him awake most of the night, was true for her, too. She'd never tasted such sweetness or such passion.

She looked up, met his eyes, felt herself tumble into them, and gave him the only answer she could.

She said yes.

CHAPTER TWELVE

EMILY LOVED THE LITTLE Chinese restaurant.

Actually, what she'd loved most was finding out that Luke was taking her and her mom out to supper. The beaded curtains, the high-backed booths, the flaming pots Luke said were called woks were just extras.

There wasn't dessert, though. Not at a Chinese restaurant. They had chocolate fortune cookies and some kind of banana that was cooked in the wok, and when Em bit into it, it tasted like sugary syrup.

It was a wonderful time, and Luke took them out again and again.

They went to a place where a man in a funny black suit stopped beside their table and played a violin while she ate her spaghetti, and another place where you tucked little pieces of chicken and steak inside a skinny pancake along with a sauce that tasted yummy even though it made your mouth burn.

And then Luke started coming to their house. Mommy sang in the kitchen, and so did Luke, and she got to help. Like the night they made chicken fricassee—her favorite—and Mommy said, Em, you can help Luke make the dumplings.

It was so much fun, especially when Luke dabbed flour on her nose and she dabbed it on his, and then he dabbed it on her mom's nose, too, and when they both thought she wasn't looking, he held her mom and kissed her, and even though it was just a little kiss, not one of those yucky wet-looking things they did on TV sometimes, her mom's face turned all pink and happy.

On Saturday they went to Discovery Park, which was pretty near where she and her mom lived, except they'd never been there before. It was a chilly day, but the sun was out and there was only a little breeze, so Luke said he figured it would be okay.

Oh, it was a beautiful place. They walked along the beach. Well, Luke and her mom walked, holding hands. She just raced over the sand, loving the way her braids slapped her shoulders. She found a piece of driftwood that looked like a tiny tree, and an empty shell in a tidal pool, and she even saw a bunny rabbit.

"Luke," she yelled, "Mommy, look!"

She ran after the rabbit, but it was faster than she was. That was okay because she didn't really want to catch it.

"Happy, princess?" Luke asked, and she smiled and said yes, she was, but the truth was bigger than that, because she couldn't remember ever being this happy before.

At the playground, Luke put her on a swing and sent her flying high into the air, and she laughed with delight. He caught her when she came down the slide, lifted her high in his arms and swung her around. She looked at her mom, but she wasn't laughing. Her mom was smiling in a funny way, a way that made Emily's throat feel all tight.

When Luke trotted off to buy them hot chocolate, she and her mom sat down at a picnic table. Her mom smiled at her.

"Are you having fun, Emily?" her mom said, and Emily decided to skip all that and say exactly what she was thinking.

"Mom? Do you think maybe Luke wants to marry us?"

Her mom made a little sound, kind of like she had something stuck in her throat.

"Honey, Luke's a very nice man. He's our friend. But that doesn't mean... Getting married is... Baby, if that's what you think is happening here..."

"I know what's happening, Mommy. You and Luke are dating."

"No, we're not. We're just—we're spending time together, that's all."

"What's the difference between spending time together and dating?"

"Well, it's complicated, but there's a difference, Em, believe me."

Her mom always told the truth, but this time it was hard to believe her. How come you couldn't call these dates? Lots of kids at day care had moms who were divorced and they went out on dates.

Well, not everybody. Lily's mom never did, Lily said. But the other kids told Emily and Lily what it was like.

A man came to the house to call for your mom and he was really, really nice to you. He talked to you, smiled at you, and sometimes he even brought you presents.

Luke talked to her all the time and he smiled at her a lot. He brought her presents, too. A rag doll she slept with every night and a little dump truck. He was right, too. He'd helped her dig a hole right by the porch steps this morning, so she could fill the truck with dirt and haul it away.

The kids said that when a mom went on dates, the man took her out to a restaurant or to the movies. Luke did that. He'd taken both of them to lots of restaurants, and last night, he'd taken them to the movies.

It was one of her favorite movies, the one about the little mermaid, and even though she'd seen it at least six times, Luke had never seen it. Well, that was because he didn't have kids of his own, but he had her now, and she kept thinking about that while they'd sat in the dark, all three of them, her in the middle between Luke and her mom.

Suddenly she knew why her mother said she and Luke weren't going on dates.

A date was for two people. Two grown-ups—a man and a woman. Luke was a man, her mom was a woman, and she—

That was it! A date wasn't for kids.

She bit her lip.

Luke and her mom had to go out on dates alone. *Then* Luke could marry them and become her daddy.

Oh, it was all so simple! She bounced with delight.

Her mom laughed. "Happy?"

"I'm very happy, Mommy."

And she was, now that she'd figured it out. All she needed was some help from her best friend, Lily.

MAKING THE CALL WAS EASY.

Emily picked up the cordless phone from the night table in

her mom's room, took it into the bathroom and closed the door.

She knew Lily's number by heart. They called each other almost every day to check on important stuff like what color tops they'd wear to day care, or if they'd ask their moms to put their hair in braids.

But this was the most important call ever, Emily thought, and her heart beat just a little faster.

"Hello?"

She heaved out a breath. "Lily?" she whispered.

"Emily?" Lily whispered back.

"Yes. Is your mom right there?"

There was a tiny pause.

"She's in the shower," Lily whispered. "We was cleaning some leaves from the garden and we got all dirty." Another pause. "Em? Why are we whispering?"

Emily hunched over the telephone.

"Are you and your mom going anywhere tonight?"

"Nope. Mom's gonna make some popcorn and we're gonna watch videos."

"Well, can I come and stay over?"

"Did your mom say you could?"

"I haven't asked her yet," Emily said impatiently. "How about your mom? You think she'll say yes?"

"Of course," Lily said. "Em? Bring your Tina Teen doll. I got a new outfit for mine today."

"Can I stay tomorrow, the whole day?"

"Oh, yeah! Maybe you can sleep over tomorrow night, too. Mommy can take us both to school Monday morning!"

Lily's voice was really loud and Emily looked at the bathroom door.

"Shh!"

"Okay," Lily said. "But you still didn't tell me how come we're whispering."

Em took a breath. "Because it's a secret."

"But I have to tell my mom, and you have to tell yours."

"I know. But we'll pretend we already told them about this."

"But that would be lying," Lily said.

"Yeah," Emily agreed in a small voice.

That was the part that bothered her, too. You were never, ever supposed to tell a lie. She knew that. She also knew that there were lies, and then there were fibs. A fib was a lie you told when you wanted to do the right thing.

Well, that was exactly what she was doing. She wanted to do the right thing again, and make her and her mom and Luke happy.

How could that be bad?

"It's a fib," she told Lily with authority, "not a lie. My mom and Luke have to go on a date without me. Two dates, if I stay at your house tonight *and* tomorrow night."

"How come?"

"So one day they can get married."

"That would be nice. Would you be a flower girl at their wedding?"

Emily smiled. She hadn't thought about that.

"Hmm. I could wear a pink dress and pink ribbons in my—"

"Em? What are you doing, baby?"

Emily felt her heart hammer. She spun toward the door.

"I'm in the bathroom, Mommy. I'll be right out."

"Luke's going to start the grill soon, honey. Finish up, wash your hands well, then come join us in the kitchen, okay?"

"Okay." She waited until she heard her mother's footsteps go away. Then she clutched the phone tighter and turned her back to the door. "Lily?" she whispered.

"Uh-huh?"

"Tell your mother you invited me to sleep over for two nights. I'll tell my mom I said yes. It won't be a big fib, right?"

"I think this is a big fib, Emily," Lily said, sounding worried.

"Me, too. But I really want Luke to be my daddy."

There was a long silence. Then Lily sighed.

"Okay. I'll do it. Can Luke be my uncle?"

Emily agreed, then said goodbye.

She flushed the toilet, scrubbed her hands and face, then returned the phone to her mom's bedroom. Her tummy felt all quivery, but she headed for the kitchen.

To her amazement, her mom believed her. At first she seemed puzzled, but then she looked at Luke and blushed and said, "Well, I have been a little preoccupied lately, but if Faith says it's okay, you can go."

Then her mom called Lily's mom and looked all puzzled again.

But her mom laughed and said, hey, maybe they were *both* suffering from early Alzheimer's. Em didn't know what that meant, but her mother hung up the phone and said, "Okay, Em. Go pack your duffel bag and I'll drive you to Lily's."

Luke drove her to Lily's. Em sat in the back, her mom sat in front, and when they got to Lily's, Luke and her mom both walked her to the door.

"You be a good girl," her mom said, giving her a big hug.

"Have fun, princess," Luke said, and swung her up in his arms the way he always did.

"I will." She looped her arms around his neck. "You have to take my mom out on a date," she whispered.

Luke jerked back and stared at her.

"What?"

"A special date," she hissed, then wiggled. He put her down just as Lily and Lily's mother opened the door.

"Hi," she said, and ran into the house.

From now on, Luke and her mother were just going to have to figure things out on their own.

LUKE DROVE BACK TOWARD Abby's place, both of them stiff and silent inside the SUV.

They'd never been this quiet, not during the entire past week. They talked, almost nonstop, about everything and anything. Abby was easy to talk to. She listened, really listened. That was a rare quality in anyone, male or female.

And they had a lot of things to talk about, all the way from football—she was a Seahawks fan, which figured; he was a

New York Jets fan, which didn't—to music, even when he got started on Chicago and Buffalo Springfield and groups that had been around before she was born.

Abby listened and smiled and said she'd heard of them, and what did he think about Beethoven?

He didn't think anything about Beethoven, he'd admitted, so she'd put on a CD for him. The music was filled with power and emotion and reached right down inside him. The next night he'd brought over some Chicago, and she said she loved the vitality of the music and the tenderness of some of the lyrics.

Oh, yeah, they talked about everything.

Luke's hands tightened on the wheel. Everything except what mattered.

Like who he really was. Like her marriage, and why she got that dark look in her eyes if he mentioned it.

Okay. He had his secrets, she had hers, but soon—soon, he'd be able to tell her the truth about himself because nothing, absolutely nothing was happening at the jewelry store. The old lady who'd told them something was going down at Emerald City had clearly been imagining things. Another week, he'd turn over his tapes and notes and tell the lieutenant they were barking up the wrong tree.

And then he'd tell Abby about his real job, that he was a cop, that he'd lied to her from Day One—

That he had a list of suspects and she was on it.

He reached out, punched a key and let music fill the SUV. He didn't want to think about that now, not when he was alone with Abby for the very first time. Oh, they'd had some time alone together after Emily went to bed, but the child's presence resonated through the house.

He'd kissed Abby, really kissed her, only that one time. Since then, knowing Em was around and that Abby was skittish about getting involved, he'd kept things light and easy, stealing a quick kiss as they washed up after dinner, or when he brought her to her door and Em went inside, but he'd been careful not to scare her off.

Now, without expecting it to happen, they were alone. Just the two of them, alone in his car on a Saturday night.

Abby was sitting beside him, her hands folded tightly in her lap, facing straight ahead. In the faint light of the dashboard, he could see her jaw clamped tight with tension.

It had hit her, too, that they were alone. They were two adults on what he supposed you could call their very first date.

Luke frowned. Could Em have set this up? Impossible. The kid was only four years old.

However it had happened, they were alone, and what were they doing? He was tongue-tied and Abby looked as if she were going to the dentist. Two people, both wondering what in hell to say next.

It was so reminiscent of the very first date he'd ever had that he burst out laughing.

Abby swung toward him, eyebrows raised.

"I'm sorry," he said, choking out the words, "but I looked over at you and it made me think back to my very first date. Mary Lou Brightband. I was sixteen, she was fifteen, and when it was over, I remember thinking that at least I'd never have to suffer through all that agony again."

"Your first date was agony?"

"You know what I mean. Should I wear jeans or chinos? What do I say to her parents? What do I say to Mary Lou? What if we ride to town in silence? Do I try and hold her hand in the movie theater? Do I try and kiss her good-night? Do I ask her out again right then and there, or do I wait?" Luke snorted with suppressed laughter. "The only good thing to come out of that date was knowing I'd survived it and could put the whole first-date nightmare behind me. But I was wrong. It's nineteen years later, and here I am, my gut in a knot, my brain in a whirl, flop sweat breaking out on my forehead...."

"Flop sweat?" Abby asked.

"You know, when there's an audience and you're terrified you're going to make an ass of yourself."

"If I'm the audience, you can relax. I'm a nervous wreck, too."

Luke looked at her. "You are?"

"We're alone, no Emily in the back seat. Of course I'm nervous." She glanced at him, looked away and decided to go for the truth. "All this time we've spent together, I've been able to tell myself that's all it was. Time spent together. Now, all of a sudden, it's as if—as if—"

"We're doing more than spending time together, Abby. We can't keep pretending that's all it is."

She nodded but didn't look at him. "You're right."

Luke reached for her hand. Her fingers were cold, trembling. He wondered what she'd think if she knew he was trembling, too, inside, where nobody could see it.

How many times had he promised himself nothing like this would happen? It was wrong, dead wrong to get involved with someone who might turn out to be a suspect.

The thing was, sometimes your heart just took over from your head.

Abby couldn't be a criminal. But if fate were truly cruel, if his judgment of her was wrong... Luke brought Abby's hand to his lips. If that's how things went, he'd stand by her, anyway. Do whatever it took to help her, because nothing would change what he felt for this woman he'd waited for all his life.

He kissed her knuckles, then lowered their joined hands to his thigh.

"What are we going to do about it?" he said softly.

She looked at him again, her eyes glittering with unshed tears.

"Nothing," she said in a small voice. "I told you right at the beginning, I don't—"

She gasped as he swung the car to the curb, undid his seat belt and reached for her. He kissed her, not gently as he had the few times he'd stolen kisses over the past week, not tenderly as the brush of his hand so often had promised, but with a hunger that she knew could only be assuaged one way.

She held back for a heartbeat, made a little noise, and then she wound her arms around him and opened her mouth to the dark sweetness of his, returning the kiss.

After a long, long time, Luke drew back. Abby started to speak, but he placed his fingers lightly over her parted lips. Then he lifted her hands to his mouth, pressed kisses into the soft flesh, fastened her belt and his, and pulled into traffic without saying a word.

Stunned, Abby stared directly ahead, watching the street lamps flash by. The flare of headlights from oncoming cars illuminated the private world in which she and Luke sat side by side.

She was trembling.

What now?

In Emily's absence, the rules of the game had changed.

Until tonight, she'd managed to get through the week without letting herself dissect what was happening.

She worked all day, spent evenings with Em and Luke. He took them to dinner some nights; others, she made dinner at home.

Luke was fun. He was nice. He made her smile. And Emily was wild about him. Why wouldn't she be? He'd shown her more affection, more concern than her own father had in all the months after she was born.

And she'd kept telling herself that was all there was to their relationship—if you wanted to call it a relationship. Except, really, it wasn't. They were just friends.

Then, this afternoon, Em had turned a hopeful look on her, raising questions Abby had avoided. And now Luke had asked another question, one she hadn't dared ask herself except in the dark of night, alone in her bed, when it was safe to dream.

Abby drew a shuddering breath.

She didn't want to go on "spending time" with Luke Sloan. He was her friend, yes. They laughed together, and talked together, and played together.

But she wanted more.

She wanted his arms around her, the way they'd been that night in her kitchen an eternity ago. And in this car a little while ago.

She wanted him to touch her. Not just her face or her hair. She wanted his hands everywhere, his mouth…

"Abby?" Luke's voice was a husky whisper.

They'd reached her place. Luke had pulled into the driveway

and killed the lights but not the engine. The air hummed with tension, their silence with expectation.

"If I come inside," he said roughly, "I'm not going to pretend anymore. If that's not what you want, say so. All you have to do is tell me to go, and I will."

She let the answer come, savoring the joy of it before she turned toward him.

"No," she said, "oh, no, don't go. Stay with me. Stay..."

And then, oh then, she was in his arms.

CHAPTER THIRTEEN

THE KISS WAS ALL LUXURIANT sensation, the silken glide of tongue against tongue, the sexy nip of male teeth against soft female flesh.

Desire, pent up for what felt like an eternity, could no longer be denied. Cocooned in their own small universe, Luke left the ethical code of his profession behind and Abby abandoned the safe harbor of a heart kept locked away.

Everything was forgotten in the sweet fire of their kiss.

Luke cupped Abby's face and angled his lips over hers, drinking in the richness of her taste. Abby moaned as she surrendered to him. Catching his jacket in her hands, she struggled to get closer.

The seat belts. The console. The restrictions of clothing…

Luke pulled back and undid his belt and hers, then sprang from the car. He reached Abby just as she opened her door and lifted her in his arms, his mouth claiming hers again as she clung to him and kissed him back.

She was trembling…or was it him? The only certainty was knowing that he'd never felt this way in his life.

He set her on her feet but kept one arm around her, holding her close against him.

"Key," he said thickly.

She opened her purse, dug inside it. Metal rattled against wood as the keys dropped from her nerveless fingers. Luke bent down and retrieved them, but it took two tries before he could get the key into the lock.

The door swung open.

A small lamp on the hall table cast a soft golden pool on the floor.

Luke elbowed the door shut and Abby turned toward him without hesitation, lifting her face for his kiss, sighing his name when his arms went around her and drew her, hard, against him.

"Abby. Oh, Abby…"

Everything she needed to hear—his passion, his need—was in his low, rough voice.

He wanted her, and she wanted him.

How could that be? She'd vowed never to want a man again. No. She hadn't had to vow it, she'd *known* she'd never want to lie in a man's arms, feel his hands on her, let him take possession of her.

"Abby." Luke framed her face with his hands and speared his fingers into her hair. It came loose from its clasp, falling to her shoulders in a tumble of rain-misted curls. "Sweetheart, don't be afraid. I won't hurt you. I'll never hurt you."

"I haven't…" Her voice was a thready whisper. "I haven't been with anyone in a very long time."

"I'll be gentle."

"I know you will, but—but there was only my husband, and he…" A tremor went through her. "I'm not much good at—"

Luke stopped the flow of words with a kiss. He didn't want to hear any more. Not now, or the rage that had been growing inside him might overpower his urgent need to show this woman, this incredible woman, what he felt for her.

"Let me show you, sweetheart. This won't be anything like what you knew in the past. Trust me."

She hesitated, then gave him her answer in a kiss.

He swung her into his arms and started down the hall to her bedroom.

The room he stepped into was so Spartan it would have suited a convent. A plain double bed. A night table and lamp. A dresser. That was all. No satin or silk, no carpet underfoot.

He felt his throat constrict. This was Abby. His Abby. A woman who lived simply, cautiously, and who was about to give herself to him because he'd told her she could trust him.

Except, she couldn't.

Don't think about that. Not now.

When he lowered her to stand beside the bed, she was trembling, and he tilted her face up and brushed his lips over hers.

"Sweetheart," he whispered, "if you want to stop—"

"No," she said fiercely. "Don't stop. Keep kissing me, and touching me, and don't let me think about how insane this is."

A muscle jumped in Luke's jaw. A better man than he would have told her that she was right, this *was* insane, maybe even wrong.

But he wasn't that man.

He'd spent too many days pretending he didn't want her, too many nights dreaming about having her. He was wild to taste her, touch her...

Make her his.

So he did what she asked. Kissed her. Caressed her. Skimmed his hands over her sweater, then under it, cupping her breasts and filling his palms with their exquisite weight.

He needed more. The feel of her skin. Her hot flesh. He reached behind her to unclasp her bra, and when he cupped her breasts this time, she moaned with pleasure.

His knees almost buckled.

How could stroking the satin of Abby's breasts fill him with such joy?

He'd promised to be gentle. He wanted to be gentle. To take her slowly and watch her face as he raised her up and up and up, but the truth was that he was only human, and the need for her thundered through his body with each beat of his heart.

He stepped back and took a shuddering breath. She reached out to him and he caught her hands in his and stilled them against his chest.

"I can't," he murmured. "I can't go slow, be gentle—all those things I know you need, sweetheart. I'm trying, but you have to know I might not succeed. I'm crazy with wanting you, Abby."

Sobbing his name, she leaned in and caught his bottom lip between her teeth, then bit him with the elegant delicacy of a cat.

Luke was lost.

His fingers flew over buttons, down zippers, and all the time he was undressing her and tearing off his own clothes, her hands were moving in conjunction with his until at last they were both naked.

She was beautiful.

She was the essence of everything female.

And she was his.

Her breasts were high, small, rounded like apples ripe for the tasting. Her waist flared into gently curved hips that might have been shaped for his hands. Her legs were long, topped by a patch of soft-looking, coffee-colored curls.

Luke could feel his frantic heart slow its pace. For the moment, seeing her like this, so vulnerable, so feminine, eased his hunger if not his need.

"You're beautiful," he said in wonderment.

Her smile was slow and tremulous, and he sensed that it took all her effort not to shield herself from him, now that those hot moments in which they'd undressed each other had been supplanted by reality.

"Don't be afraid," he whispered, and drew her to him, kissing her mouth, licking the taut centers of her breasts. He slid his hand over her warm belly and stroked the soft curls, a lightning bolt of pure delight shooting through him when she shuddered with pleasure.

His touch grew more intimate as his fingers tangled in the soft curls, seeking confirmation of the blurring he saw in her eyes. Yes. She was hot and tight, wet with desire for him, and when she moaned his name and grabbed his biceps for support, his hard-won composure flew away.

Just touching her was driving him toward the brink. If he wasn't careful, it was going to be all over before they made it to the bed.

He bent down, groped for his jeans, and found the foil-wrapped condom he carried in his wallet. After fumbling it on, he lifted Abby in his arms and brought her to the bed, easing down on the mattress beside her.

Too fast, he told himself, way too fast, but now she was urging him on, clasping his shoulders, arching toward him and offering him everything he'd ever longed for.

"Abby," he said, because it was all he could say, all he needed to say.

With a groan, he entered her, and she sobbed his name. He drove deep, drew back, then surged forward again, and her cry of fulfillment rang out like a bell in the silence.

"Luke," she said, "oh, Luke…"

The sound of his name on her lips was a hope, a promise, an affirmation that he felt in his heart.

"Yes," he said fiercely, and he let go of everything, threw back his head and claimed Abby Douglas as his.

THEY LAY TANGLED TOGETHER in the sweet afterglow of passion, Abby's head on Luke's shoulder.

Luke pressed a tender kiss to her hair.

"Are you all right, sweetheart?"

"Mmm."

He smiled. "Can I take that as a yes?"

"A definite yes," Abby said, gazing up at him.

He kissed her eyes, her nose, her mouth, then drew her tightly into the curve of his arm.

"Tell me about yourself."

Did she stiffen just a little? Or was it his imagination?

"There's not much to tell that you don't already know."

"Sure there is." He rolled onto his side so that they were face-to-face and propped his head on his hand. "Where were you born? What were you like as a little girl? Did you love to play dress-up, like Em, or were you a tomboy?"

"Dress up," she said promptly. "With all the same jewelry."

Luke felt himself being dragged back to reality.

"What do you mean?"

"My mom had some beautiful jewelry. It's the stuff Em had on the other night. I played with it, too, when I was little." Her smile turned wistful. "It's all I have left of her, except for memories."

Abby's mother's jewelry. Luke wanted to shout for joy. Instead, he drew her close against him.

"You see how much I don't know about you, Abby Douglas? Important stuff, like, what's your favorite ice cream flavor? Do you like old movies? How many times have you seen *Young Frankenstein?*" He grinned. "And if it's less than five, explain how come?"

"Five's the magic number, huh?"

"Well, considering it's the funniest movie of all time—"

"I guess."

"You guess?" he said, his voice filled with mock indignation. "What did you ever see that was funnier?"

She cocked her head and pursed her lips, and it was all he could do to keep from kissing her. Okay. What was she going to come up with? Something schmaltzy. A chick flick like…

"Monty Python and the Holy Grail."

Luke blinked. "Not *When Harry Met Sally…?*"

"Bleep," Abby said, doing her best imitation of a buzzer. "You're a male chauvinist pig, Sloan. You expected me to pick something totally female."

"Well, yeah."

"Well, you were right." She smiled and snuggled closer, then lifted her head just a little to kiss him. "The truth is, I loved *When Harry Met Sally….*"

"Mmm."

Luke shifted his weight and rolled above her. Abby caught her breath.

"You're not listening to me."

"Of course I am." He ducked his head and kissed the slope of her breast. "You said you loved *When Harry Met Sally….*"

"I did. I do. I've seen it…." She caught her breath again and moved a little beneath him. "Luke."

"I like the sound of my name on your lips," he whispered, and he reached over the side of the bed, dug another—hell, his next to last—little foil packet from his wallet, and for a long, long time, they spoke only in sighs and moans.

THEY SLEPT FOR A LITTLE while, wrapped in each other's arms. Luke awoke first, then watched Abby surface.

"Hello," he said softly, and kissed her.

Smiling, she linked her hands behind his neck. Sometime

during the hours they'd been in bed, the rawhide thong had fallen from his hair, and she ran her hands through its black, silky weight.

"I like your hair," she murmured.

Luke grinned. "I like yours, too."

"No, I'm serious. I like the way it falls around your face when you make love to me, and encloses us in our own little world."

He kissed her again, long and sweet.

"When I was a kid, my mother used to keep after me to cut it."

"Why?"

"She said I'd make my way faster in the world if I looked more like my father than like her."

"Your father was Anglo?"

"Yeah." Luke nuzzled Abby's throat. "But I wouldn't cut it and I wouldn't pretend to be Anglo. I was Indian and Anglo, one foot in each world." He grinned. "Of course, when I became a marine, a barber came at me with an electric razor my first day at Parris Island and, whap, my hair was gone."

Abby touched the tip of her finger to his cheekbone, tracing the high, proud arch.

"So, after you got out of the corps, you became a carpenter?"

Luke felt his smile slipping. "Yes."

It wasn't a lie. Not exactly. He'd done carpentry work, construction work, before becoming a cop.

"And you like your work. Em says you're always engrossed in it when she goes into Katherine Kinard's office."

Hell.

"I've always liked working with wood."

That wasn't a lie, either.

"And you were married."

He nodded, glad to be on safer ground.

"Did you meet your wife when you were in the corps or after?" The corner of Abby's mouth rose. "I'll bet you were a heartbreaker in that marine uniform."

"Hey," he said, with what he hoped was a lazy smile, "let's not waste time talking about me."

"Come on, Sloan. Don't be modest. You probably looked like a recruiting poster."

"Well," he said, "I have to admit…"

"And here I was worried you'd be modest," Abby laughed, framing his face with her hands. "So, you got out of the corps and decided to become a carpenter?"

Back to square one.

Two questions, and only lies to give as answers. He'd married Janine after he joined the force. That's what he was. A cop. He'd been one for almost a decade. It wasn't just what he did, it was who he was. It was why he had no choice but to lie to this woman.

Lie to her, even as he fell in love with her.

The realization rocketed through him and he sat up suddenly, swinging his legs to the floor.

"Luke?"

Abby shifted back against the pillows, holding the covers to her chin, her body language telling him that his withdrawal had made her uncomfortably aware of their new intimacy.

"Yeah." He cleared his throat. "I have to, uh…"

He tossed back the blanket, shot her a quick smile and walked down the hall to the bathroom. Then he closed the door and leaned back against it. How much longer could this go on?

All he wanted to do right now was go back to that bed, take Abby in his arms, tell her everything was okay, and make love to her until the only truth that mattered was what was happening between them.

But he couldn't. He was out of condoms and out of lies.

Condoms were easy to come by. The truth wasn't. He'd already violated the rules he lived by just by being here with her, but there had to be a way he could show her who he *really* was, deep down inside where it mattered. That he'd grown up poor, missing his mom, unsure of what world he belonged in, that for years he'd buried himself in his work and avoided anything that resembled real emotional involvement.

It was one of the reasons he'd married Janine. She'd been

just like him, perfectly willing to maintain a relationship that never once delved below the surface. But he wanted more than that from Abby, wanted her to understand who he was, why he was...

Luke opened the bathroom door. Abby was standing at the window, looking out into the night, wrapped from her throat to her toes in an old-fashioned terry-cloth robe.

"Abby."

She turned toward him. The look on her face, the pucker of uncertainty etched between her eyes tore at his heart. Cursing himself for a fool, he went to her and pulled her into his arms.

It took a minute, but finally she relaxed against him.

"I'm sorry," she said. "If you don't want to talk about the past and your marriage, that's okay. It's none of my business."

"Everything about me is your business. I just..." He clasped her shoulders and kissed away the frown. "I'm just not much for talking about myself, you know?"

She managed a little smile.

"I know. Women talk about themselves. Men talk about baseball."

She was letting him off easy. Unfair, but he had no choice but to be grateful.

"An astute observation, Dr. Douglas."

"An old joke, Mr. Sloan." She pulled back a little, leaning against the cradle of his arms. "I'm starved. How about you?" She blushed at the smile that curved his lips. "Don't let it go to your head. I just thought you might want a sandwich or maybe some scrambled eggs."

"I have a better idea. How about we go out for something?"

"Well, sure, if you'd rather."

"What I'd rather do is take you back to bed." Luke dropped a light kiss on the tip of her nose. "But I'm out of condoms."

Another blush. "Oh."

"Oh, is right." He drew her closer, loving the pink that rose in her cheeks as much as he loved the way she fit against him. "So, we go out, grab a bite to eat, stop at a drugstore or a supermarket while I pick up a couple of cases of condoms...."

Abby laughed.

"Okay. One case." Luke bent his head and rested his forehead against hers. "Em's going to be at Faith's tonight and tomorrow night, right?"

"Uh-huh. Faith will drop her off at the day care Monday morning."

"Good."

"Mmm," Abby said, and kissed his chin.

"If Em's all taken care of, you can come with me."

She slid her arms around his waist and smiled up at him.

"To pick up a pizza?"

"No. To Neah Bay."

He'd spoken impulsively, but once he'd asked her to go with him to the place where his life had begun, he knew it was right. He could be himself there—Luke Sloan, a man who'd found the missing piece of himself, not Luke Sloan, undercover cop.

Undercover liar.

And in Neah Bay, away from everything that stood between them in the real world, he would put his trust in Abby and tell her the truth. What he felt for her was more important than anything in the world.

"Neah Bay?"

He saw the puzzlement in her eyes and remembered that she'd moved to Washington State from San Francisco. The name wouldn't mean anything to her.

"It's a little town all the way up at the tip of the Olympic Peninsula. It's on Makah land. My people's land."

"But why would you want to go there now? It's far from here, isn't it?"

"A four-hour drive." Luke slid his hands to her wrists, brought them to his mouth and pressed his lips to each of her pulse points. "I want you to know me. The real me."

"I already know the real you," she said, leaning into him, savoring the warmth of his skin against hers. "You're Luke Sloan, and you're wonderful."

His lips curved under the soft pressure of hers, but it was hard to maintain the smile. Would she still think he was so wonderful once she knew he'd been lying to her?

"Abby." He kissed her hair, nuzzling it back from her ear. "Come with me. Please."

Drawing back, Abby looked at Luke. His eyes were filled with pleading, and guilt rose up inside her, burning the back of her throat with bile.

He was offering to share everything about himself with her, while she'd kept everything that mattered from him.

That she hadn't just divorced a man, she'd run for her life.

That she lived her days listening for Frank's footsteps, terrified he'd find a way to get her back.

She dropped her gaze to her hands, still clasping the edges of her robe together.

Life had taught her to trust no one. That was the maxim she lived by and it kept her safe. But the man she'd just made love with wasn't just any man. He was Luke. And she was in love with him.

She didn't want to believe it.

Lying in his arms, she'd tried telling herself that what she felt was infatuation. Luke was the kind of man women dreamed of. Strong, generous, tender, funny…and gorgeous. He was an incredible lover, taking her to heights she'd never dreamed existed.

Maybe, she'd thought, she was simply seeing everything through a haze of sexual pleasure.

"Abby?"

He put his hand under her chin and gently lifted her head until their eyes met. His were the deep, dark green of the ocean and, like the ocean, they drew her in. She knew she could drown in the depths of those eyes, tumble into them and stay there forever.

"Sweetheart." He kissed her lips, slowly, tenderly, until she murmured his name and opened her mouth to his kiss. His hands cupped her face, and she sighed, giving herself up to his touch, to his taste, to the love for him brimming in her heart.

It was like taking a step off the edge of the earth. Abby jerked back, gasping for breath.

This wasn't supposed to happen. Her life was complicated enough. She hadn't wanted to fall in love again, hadn't even believed she could—though now that it had happened, she knew she'd never really been in love before.

Not like this.

She made a little sound, half laugh, half sob. Luke whispered her name and drew her against him, one hand making soothing circles between her shoulder blades, the other urging her to snuggle into his protective warmth. She rested her cheek against his chest, shut her eyes as she listened to the slow, steady beat of his heart.

"It's all right," he said quietly. "If you don't want to go to Neah Bay, that's okay. I was crazy to suggest it. You're right. It's a long drive, and there's nothing much up there except my cabin."

Abby clasped Luke's face and looked deep into his eyes.

"Thank you for asking me."

"Hey, we'll do it another time."

His smile was quick, meant to be casual, but it wasn't. He'd offered something special and her refusal had hurt him.

"No," she said softly, "we'll do it right now."

His smile tilted. "Abby. You don't have to do this."

"You're right." She took a breath. "I *want* to do this. I want to see your town, your cabin...." She shook back her hair and lowered his face to hers. "I want to know the real Luke Sloan," she said, kissing him. "Please. Take me with you to Neah Bay."

CHAPTER FOURTEEN

THEY SHOWERED, DRIVING themselves a little bit crazy by soaping each other's bodies and then toweling off together, Luke keeping his sanity by thinking about the next shower he'd take with Abby, when he'd be better prepared.

Abby put on jeans, a T-shirt and an old pair of hiking boots, then began figuring out what she'd need to take with her on their trip.

Luke dressed quickly, impatient to get on the road.

"Come on, lazy bones. We've got a long drive ahead of us, remember?"

"I have to phone Faith."

"Sure."

She sat down on the edge of the bed and reached for the phone. He took a look at her face, went to her and kissed her.

"Sweetheart," he said gently, "Em will be fine."

"Am I that transparent?"

"You love her," he said simply. "But she's in good hands."

Abby sighed. "You're right. It's just that…" Her cheeks pinkened. "What do I tell Faith?"

"You tell her," Luke said calmly, "that you're going away with me and you'll be back, bright and early, Monday morning."

"You're right. I know you're right. It's just that I've never…" She laughed. "I need a number where Faith can reach me, if she has to."

Luke nodded. "Give her my cell phone number." He looked around, saw a notepad and pencil on the night table. "Here. I'll write it down."

"It's not as if I've never left Em at Faith's before. I mean, the kids have done sleepovers. But—'' Abby groaned. ''I'm being impossible, aren't I?''

''You're being Em's mom.'' Luke squatted down in front of her. ''You're a terrific mother, Abby. I saw that right away.''

''And you're terrific with Emily.'' Abby smiled. ''She's crazy about you.''

He grinned. ''Of course she is. The princess has excellent taste.'' His expression grew serious. ''She's a great kid. What more could a man want than to have two wonderful females in his life, and be crazy about them both?''

Abby's eyes met his. What she saw there made her heart start to race.

''That's nice to hear,'' she said softly.

''It's the truth.'' They fell silent. Then Luke cleared his throat. ''About my cabin…I should warn you, it's not anything special.''

''I have the feeling it is.''

''Actually, it's pretty rustic.''

She smiled. ''So am I.''

''A San Francisco lady, rustic?'' Luke teased. ''I don't think so.''

''But I'm not…'' Abby stopped in the middle of the sentence. She'd waited this long, she'd wait a little longer to tell him the truth. ''I'm not a city girl at heart.''

''Hang on to that thought.'' He took her hand and drew her to her feet. ''Remember the first time I came here?''

''How could I forget? You walked into my kitchen and my heart rose right into my throat.''

''It did?''

''Yes, and stop fishing for compliments. What about the first time you came here?''

''You were wearing a T-shirt that read Save the Rain Forest. And I asked if you wanted to save any particular rain forest.''

''I remember.''

''My cabin is tucked into a rain forest, in a stand of big old hemlocks and spruce.'' His expression was suddenly grave. ''It's a small cabin, Abby.''

''Smaller than this apartment? Hard to believe.''

"I'm serious."

Abby cocked her head. "I see that. Honestly, small is fine."

"The thing is…" Luke tunneled his fingers into her hair then tilted her face to his. "I want you to understand that it's not some weekend bachelor pad." A soft laugh rumbled in his throat. "Actually, when you see it, you're liable to say, 'Luke, that was a beautiful drive. Now, could we turn around and head back to civilization?'" His eyes darkened. "The only woman I've ever taken there was my wife. She hated it."

"Ah." Abby touched her finger to his mouth, sucking in a breath when he drew the tip between his teeth. "Not a fan of the rain forest, huh?" she said, trying to lighten things.

"She wasn't a fan of us being alone. The truth is, neither was I. Janine and I weren't very good at this."

"At what?"

"This. Talking. Opening up to each other. Not doing anything special, just being together."

"Just being together is wonderful," Abby said. "You make me feel things I've never felt before."

It was an admission that she hadn't intended to make, but it had come from the heart. With Luke, denying what was in her heart was close to impossible.

"Yeah. You have that same effect on me." He hesitated. "Abby? I don't know how to say this. I mean, I don't know if you want to hear it. I…" He took a deep breath. "I think I'm falling in love with you."

Luke's admission stunned her. It was everything she'd longed to hear—and everything she was afraid to hear. Tears scalded her eyes, and he took a quick step back.

"Hell," he said, "I'm rushing things again."

"No. Oh, no, you're not. Because I—because I—" Abby took a deep breath of her own. "I'm falling in love with you too."

The sweetness of those words seemed to penetrate his soul. Luke gathered Abby in his arms and kissed her mouth, tasted her tears…

And knew that he'd just added one more lie to the list.

He wasn't falling in love with Abby.

He was in love with her already.

THEY DECIDED TO SAVE TIME. Abby would phone Faith while Luke drove a couple of blocks to gas up the SUV and pick up sandwiches.

"And coffee," he added, and then a sexy grin tilted at the corner of his mouth. "And something for dessert," he said, kissing her in a way that left no doubt about what he meant.

She was still smiling when she dialed Faith's number.

"Hi," she said. "It's Abby. How're things going?"

Faith assured her everything was fine. The girls were having such fun and being such angels that she'd decided to let them stay up a little longer. Right now, they were in the living room, sitting on the sofa in their pj's with a bowl of popcorn, watching *Beauty and the Beast.*

"For the zillionth time," Abby said.

"Zillion and one," Faith corrected, "but who's counting? Hang on and I'll get Emily."

"No need," Abby said quickly, and took the plunge. "Actually, I called to speak to you. I want to give you a number where you can reach me. I'm—I'm not going to be home until late tomorrow night. Um, actually, it'll probably be more like very early Monday morning."

"Oh."

The "oh" was ripe with meaning. Abby felt her face turn hot.

"It's the number for Luke's cell phone."

"Ah."

An "oh," and now an "ah." Abby's face went from hot to blazing.

"Faith, Luke and I…"

"Hey," Faith said, "I think it's wonderful. Just let me take down that number."

Abby read it to her.

"If you need me—"

"I'll call."

"Or if Em wants to talk to me—"

"Honey, you just go away with that gorgeous man and have a good time."

"I'm in love with him," Abby blurted.

"And he's in love with you. No big surprise there, Ms. Douglas. The two of you might as well wear signs. You guys were made for each other."

"I didn't expect... I mean, I didn't plan..."

"Nobody plans love," Faith said gently, "but if you're lucky enough to stumble across it, grab hold with both hands."

After choking out a goodbye, Abby hung up the phone. She checked that the windows were all closed, turned on a couple of lights in the living room and finally ran out of things to keep her busy while she waited for Luke.

Was Faith right? Should she grab hold and hang on to this miracle? Life didn't come with guarantees, but it *did* come with hope.

And Abby, who had long thought herself safe from such a foreign emotion, felt her heart fill with it now.

THEY ATE THE SANDWICHES, drank the coffee and settled in for the drive north.

"Why don't you put your seat back and take a nap?" Luke said.

Abby assured him that she wasn't sleepy, but she dozed off almost as soon as they left the city. She had a little smile on her face. Luke wondered if she was dreaming of him, playing out the moments of their lovemaking in her sleep as he was playing them in his thoughts.

When Abby murmured in her sleep, Luke glanced at her again and wished he were driving the old truck he'd had in his teens, with its bench seat. She could have snuggled up against him, her head on his shoulder, the warmth of her body pressed against his.

God, how he loved Abby! He hadn't meant to tell her, not until after he'd unburdened himself of the lie that had brought them together. The admission had just slipped past his lips.

Now that it had, he was glad.

Maybe it would make the moment of truth a little easier on both of them.

The car's headlights picked out an eighteen-wheeler laboring up the long hill ahead. Luke flashed his lights to signal that he was about to pass, stepped down on the gas pedal and swung into the passing lane.

Time to think. Time to plan how best to tell Abby he was a cop and explain why he'd been lying to her.

His jaw tightened.

In other words, time to say, Listen, I love you…and I'll move heaven and earth for you, even if you've done something wrong.

How in hell could a man tell a woman something like that? Bad enough he'd lied about what he was, but how could he tell her that if—that if—

Luke put on his signal and eased back into the right-hand lane.

He'd present the thing logically. The old lady thinking she'd spotted her stolen necklace at the Emerald City Jewelry Exchange. Luke working undercover surveillance in an attempt to nail down what was going on in the jewelry store, then discovering Abby worked there, at the same counter where the old woman had supposedly spotted the necklace.

His mouth thinned.

I'm a cop, Abby, and we have this report that makes us think something crooked is happening in your store, at your counter, and if it is, and if you're part of it, even though we have feelings for each other, I'll have no choice but to…

Oh, yeah. That would go over really well.

Okay. Start again.

Abby, sweetheart, I'm a cop. I don't really know if anything's going on in that store, but if it is, I don't believe you're part of it. Or if you are—which I'm certain you're not, but, you know, just in case, if you should be mixed up in it and I have to do my thing, I want you to know that I'll stand by you….

Crap.

From the top, for the last time.

Abby, I'm a cop. I couldn't tell you that before. I shouldn't really tell it to you now, but I'm crazy in love with you. And no matter what's going on in Emerald City, I'll always believe you're innocent.

Yeah.

He could feel the tension easing from his muscles. That was exactly what he'd tell her. She'd understand, because she loved him. Trust. Faith. That was what love was all about. He'd never understood it until now.

The other thing he'd never understood, not down deep where it mattered, was that being a good cop didn't mean forgetting he was, first and foremost, a man.

Was that part of what had gone wrong in his marriage? That he'd put his job ahead of everything else? Janine had never complained. Now that he considered it, he was pretty sure she'd preferred it that way. She'd had her life. He'd had his. The only place they'd really come together was in bed.

Luke glanced at Abby, still asleep in the seat beside him.

And being in bed with Janine was nothing like it was with Abby.

He wasn't into comparing women that way. Sex was pleasurable and each experience was different…but he'd learned something during the past few hours.

Sex that involved the body was exciting, but sex that involved the heart was, it was—

There was no way to describe it.

Holding Abby in his arms. Feeling the warmth of her breath against his throat. Inhaling her scent, looking deep into her eyes as she moved beneath him…

"Mmm."

He glanced at her. She was yawning, stretching like a cat. She would feel as soft and warm as a cat, too, if he pulled over to the side of the road and gathered her close.

Luke cleared his throat. "Hello, sleepyhead."

She yawned again, gave him a little smile and sat up straight. "Hi."

"Good nap?"

"Wonderful. How long was I asleep?"

"Just a little while." He reached for her hand, kissed it, then laid their joined hands on the armrest above the center console. "We'll be at the ferry soon."

"Oh, that's nice. I've never been on the water at night."

"Never? Well, you're in for a treat. A clear night, stars shining, moon looking down, no wind… It's like you're sailing right up into the sky."

"It sounds perfect. Just like this day. This night." Abby smiled. "Don't let it go to your head, Mr. Sloan, but I'm very happy."

"Are you?"

"Uh-huh. Happier than I've ever been. Well, except maybe the day Em was born, but that's a different kind of happiness."

"I'll bet it is. My cousin Sara had her third kid at home. One of those rush jobs nobody was prepared for. I was fifteen, sixteen, something like that, at Sara and Bill's house, helping him build a storage shed.

"Anyway, Sara yelled the baby was coming. Bill went running and got up to the house just in time. Fifteen minutes later, there was a baby wailing its lungs out. And the look on Bill's face when he came outside and told me he was a father was…" Luke shook his head. "I've never forgotten it."

Abby squeezed his hand.

"Didn't you and Janine…? Sorry. That's none of my business."

"Didn't we want kids?" Luke shifted his weight to ease his shoulder muscles. "We talked about it, but we kept putting it off. Considering the marriage didn't last, I'm glad we…" He shot a look at Abby. "Oh, hell. I said that before, didn't I? And I didn't mean —"

"No, that's okay. Divorce is lousy for kids most of the time. Sometimes, though, it's the only answer."

He waited for her to say more, but she didn't. After a few seconds, he squeezed her hand.

"You've done a fine job raising Em all by yourself. She's one terrific little girl."

Abby smiled and leaned her head back. "You won't get any argument from me." She turned toward him. "You've made a wonderful impression on her. That means a lot to the both of us. Em really didn't know anything good about men until now.''

Luke tightened his grip on Abby's hand. She still wasn't going to say more than that. Well, he was going to ask. He didn't want to pry, but the haunted look she got on her face whenever she mentioned her marriage just about killed him.

''What happened between you and your husband?''

''I told you.'' She stared straight ahead, watching the black road unwind before them. ''We had a difficult divorce.''

''And a difficult marriage,'' Luke said, making it a statement instead of a question.

Suddenly, Abby wanted to tell him everything, that it had been worse than that, much worse, but how could she tell him the truth and risk seeing his eyes fill with pity? It was humiliating. Even the lawyer who'd handled her divorce had looked at her with pity after she'd told him what Frank was like.

She didn't want to see that same look in Luke's face.

Besides, what good would it do? Knowing Frank had hurt her, that he might still be looking for her wouldn't change things. Luke could no more stop Frank from coming after her than she could.

And yet, he deserved the truth. Some of it, anyway.

''Yes,'' Abby said in a low voice, ''it was difficult. I didn't know Frank very well when we got married. My folks died in an accident just before my eighteenth birthday, and he came to the funeral. He was much older than I was, almost my father's age. He said he'd worked for my dad and that they'd been friends.'' She drew a breath. ''A few months later, he proposed. He said he loved me....''

Luke waited, giving her time, telling himself to stay calm. He could hear the strain in her words, feel it in the air.

''It didn't take me long to realize he'd lied. He never loved me. He married me for the money my folks left. It wasn't a fortune, but it was more than he'd ever had. He spent everything except the few dollars I'd managed to stash away...and then he—he started telling me I wasn't the right kind of wife.''

''He hurt you,'' Luke said coldly.

Abby let out a long breath. Denying it was useless. Luke had read between the lines of her story. He knew.

"Yes."

Luke said nothing. Then he slammed the heels of his hands against the steering wheel and said something ugly and guttural. Abby put a hand on his arm.

"It was a long time ago," she said quickly. "It doesn't matter anymore."

"Son of bitch like that needs a taste of his own medicine."

"Luke." She could feel his muscles coiled like steel under her fingers. "I got Emily away before any of it touched her. And I've made a new life for her and for me. That's what counts."

A long moment passed. Then Luke nodded. What was the sense in arguing? But if he ever stumbled across Frank Douglas...

"How about you?" Abby asked. "How long did it take your marriage to fall apart?"

He swallowed hard and let her lead him to a safer subject.

"How does two minutes and ten seconds sound?" he said with a bitter laugh. "The truth is, it was a mistake from day one. We had different friends, different tastes in almost everything, especially in what kind of life would make us happy. She said I was a loner, and I guess she was right."

Abby smiled. "A loner who let a woman and a child into his life, you mean."

"You and Em...that was different. You didn't intrude in my space, you enhanced it." He signaled and passed another truck, but this time he stayed in the faster lane and goosed the speed a little. "Hell, I sound like I took one of those those Feel-Good Courses," he said, wincing at how close he'd come to saying he'd sounded like a graduate of the courses the PD's top brass were taking. "Janine ran with a crowd. They did things as a group. Nothing wrong with that, except it isn't what I do. She'd want to go to a resort with them for a weekend, I'd want to go kayaking." He flashed Abby an enticing grin. "Am I scaring you off?"

He was terrifying her, Abby admitted, but not the way he

thought. Luke was talking about a life she'd have sold her soul to share. Suddenly, she wanted to tell him that. To tell him everything about herself.

No. Not yet. It was too soon to risk spoiling things.

"Well, you're talking kayaking to a woman who thinks the height of watery danger is climbing into a hot bath and leaving a book and a box of Godiva on the rim."

Luke flashed her a sexy grin. "The bath and the chocolate sound fine, but I can think of a substitute for that book."

"Yes." She put her hand on his thigh, amazed at her own boldness. "So can I."

He made a sound deep in his throat and caught hold of her hand.

"Keep that up, woman, and I'm just liable to pull into the next motel."

"In which case, my virtue is safe, because I haven't seen so much as a sign of civilization for hours."

"You think this is uncivilized?" He smiled. "Wait until we get to Neah Bay. There's nothing but the sea, the forest…and me."

Abby sighed.

"Sounds wonderful," she said softly, and moved as close to him as her seat belt would permit, her hand still in his, where it remained for the rest of the trip.

IT WAS ALMOST FOUR IN the morning when they reached Neah Bay. They drove through the silent village and headed deep into the forest on a dirt road.

Abby was asleep again, breathing softly beside him.

Luke let down the windows of the SUV and drew in the perfume of sea and salt, cedar and hemlock as he turned onto the rutted track that led to his cabin. Though he'd never lived in it for more than a couple of weeks at a time, he'd always thought of it as home.

The house he'd grown up in had been filled with people—his mother, until her death, and his grandfather, and a never-ending stream of aunts and uncles and cousins who'd traipsed in and out throughout his childhood. They'd all been kind to him, but they'd never stayed around long.

He'd been a lonely kid in a houseful of people. Here, at the cabin, he'd never felt lonely, only alone.

There was a big difference between the two.

The cabin was warm with memories.

His grandfather had been a tribal elder, and it was in the cabin that he'd told Luke stories of the days when the Makah had been a powerful, fierce people. He'd taught Luke to hunt and fish and carve harpoons in ways passed from generation to generation, and though Luke rarely fished, never hunted and had no desire to honor the spirit of the gray whales in the old ways, he was grateful his grandfather had taught him all those things.

The old man had imbued him with the importance of tradition and honor long before the corps and the cops.

Was that why he'd brought Abby here? Had he hoped that sharing the past with her might somehow guarantee she'd accept the future, once she understood who he was, and why he'd had no choice but to live by the code he'd chosen?

Luke slowed down as the car's headlights picked out the cabin. He took a hard look at the place—a one-room cabin on a fieldstone foundation, sided by his grandfather with hand-hewn cedar logs. Two years ago, Luke had added a small bathroom and a generator to provide electricity.

The cabin looked squat and gloomy. Maybe Janine was right. She'd called it desolate and uncomfortable.

Tension put a knot in Luke's belly.

He brought the SUV to a slow stop and took a flashlight from the glove compartment. Then he went around to Abby's door, undid her seat belt, lifted her into his arms…

And stopped.

All he had to do was turn around, drive down the peninsula to Port Angeles and stop at a motel for the night. He could tell Abby he'd decided against staying at the cabin, that he'd been dead wrong to have brought a city girl into the woods.

Why would he want to show her this part of himself? He'd done that once, with Janine, and look how that had gone.

Abby stirred. "Are we there?" she asked sleepily, winding her arms around his neck.

It was too late to run. Luke switched on the flashlight and turned the beam on the cabin.

"Yeah," he said, trying to sound casual, "we are."

She sucked in her breath. "You said it was in the forest, but I didn't realize…"

"I know."

"And you said it was a cabin, but—"

"I know that, too. Look, we'll get a night's sleep. Then, in the morning—"

"But you didn't say how beautiful it was!"

His voice crawled up the scale. "You think it's beautiful?"

"I wish I could come up with a better word. Did your grandfather build it?"

He felt his heart swell. "Yeah," he said as he carried her up the old steps, "he sure did."

"I can hardly wait to see the inside."

When he got nowhere fumbling with the key, he set Abby on her feet and handed her the flashlight.

"Just let me get this lock…"

The door swung open. The old hinges were silent. For some dumb reason, that pleased him, because he'd oiled them the last visit.

"There are lights. Well, there will be, as soon as I get the generator going."

Abby brushed past him, checking the cabin in the beam of the flashlight, touching the old iron headboard on the big bed, stroking the cherry-wood dresser that listed ever so slightly to the left. All the time she was making the kind of little oohs and aahs he'd heard women make over babies and puppies.

The light illuminated the patchwork quilts heaped high on the bed. Abby stroked her hand over them.

"Someone put a lot of love into these blankets."

"Yeah. My grandmother. I never knew her. She died before I was born."

"And that rocking chair… Did your grandfather make it?"

"Well," Luke said cautiously, "yeah, he did."

Abby turned in a slow circle, taking in the old stone sink in the corner, the ancient harpoon above the fireplace and the fireplace itself, which was almost the height of the cabin.

"You said it was just an old cabin."

"That's what it is," he answered, still wary.

"It's a *wonderful* old cabin!"

The simple words sent a rush of happiness zinging through his blood.

"Yeah." He cleared his throat. "Well, it's okay. I mean, it'll be comfortable once I build a fire, then get the generator going and turn on the space heater."

Abby put her hands on his chest.

"A fire would be perfect. But can't the generator wait until morning?"

"It'll be cold in here without the heater."

"I bet."

"I'm serious, sweetheart. Your teeth will chatter."

"Even if we're in that big bed, under all those quilts?"

She smiled and tipped back her head. Luke felt his body leap to attention.

"Well," he said slowly, putting his hands under her jacket and around her waist, "there might be a way to keep warm in that bed."

She laughed. "You think so?"

"In fact," he said huskily, "I'm sure of it."

"Me, too," Abby whispered shamelessly as he swept her up in his arms, kicked the cabin door closed and crossed to the bed.

CHAPTER FIFTEEN

ABBY AWOKE IN LUKE'S ARMS.

Sunlight, a rare and precious commodity in the northwest at that time of year, streamed through the cabin window, burnishing Luke's naked shoulder and the powerful arm that held her close.

Rising from sleep, Abby had thought she was dreaming. Now, hearing Luke's heartbeat beneath her ear, feeling the warmth of his body, seeing his strong, beautifully sculpted face so close to hers, she knew that it was all true.

She was here, held safe in Luke Sloan's arms. They'd been friends and now they were lovers, too.

"You belong to me now," he'd murmured the last time they'd made love.

Abby snuggled closer.

Amazing, how such possessive words could stir the heart of a woman who would once have assumed they were a statement of domination. But Luke had spoken them softly and tenderly, and added that he belonged to her, and would for the rest of his life.

Frank had destroyed her belief in love and trust. Luke had restored it, and she knew that she would love him forever.

"Forever," she whispered, and he stirred in his sleep, then threw his leg across hers as if holding her in the curve of his arm wasn't enough.

Abby closed her eyes.

She would never tire of lying here with him, or of the way he had of looking at her and telling her without words that he wanted her. She thought about kissing him awake, about putting her mouth on him and watching his eyes darken with pleasure.

Then she thought about what he'd see.

Tangled hair, smeared lipstick and mascara. For the first time ever, she hadn't taken off her makeup or done anything she normally did to get ready for bed. Instead, she'd tumbled into bed, wrapped in Luke's arms.

They'd made love again, and she had a foggy memory of Luke building a fire on the hearth, then returning to her and taking her in his arms again.

That was when he'd whispered those words about her belonging to him and him belonging to her that had stirred her so. She'd kissed him, he'd drawn her head to his shoulder, and she'd fallen into the deepest sleep of her life.

And now it was morning, and none of it—oh, none of it—had been a dream.

Luke sighed and rolled onto his back. He still had his arm around her, but if she wiggled just a little she could ease away from him, sneak from the bed and make herself look human.

Women in movies always looked sexy and gorgeous in the morning. Maybe some women looked like that in real life, too, but Abby knew she wasn't one of them. Early morning meant slits for eyes, snakes for hair and sleep creases in her cheek.

No way was Luke going to see her like that.

She slipped from the covers and got to her feet. Her teeth banged together like castanets in the hands of a flamenco dancer.

Omigod, it was cold!

Weren't temperatures supposed to stay above freezing in the rain forest?

The fire was out. Goose bumps the size of golf balls were rising on her arms and her nose was rapidly turning into a chunk of ice. Her clothes were—well, they were somewhere in the tangled mess on the floor.

She spotted Luke's shirt and put it on. His socks, too. They were huge, flopping like clown shoes when she tugged them over her feet, but who cared? They were made of wool and they were warm.

Better. Much better.

Her tote bag was on the chair where she'd left it. Everything she needed was inside, from some basic toiletries to lipstick, mascara and a change of clothes. Abby picked up the bag, went into the tiny bathroom and quietly shut the door. She turned on the water in the shower stall, put her hand under it and sucked in her breath.

Pure ice. Okay. She'd just wait for it to heat. Meanwhile she used the john, brushed her teeth and tissued off the raccoon rings around her eyes. Then she checked the water again.

Still ice cold.

How long could water take to heat? It felt as if it were coming straight from the spring....

"Idiot," she muttered.

The water *was* coming straight from the spring. No electricity, Luke had said, except what was produced by a generator. All she knew about generators was what he'd explained to her the day he'd fixed her car, but one thing was certain.

You had to turn one on to make it work, and Luke hadn't turned anything on.

Well, nothing except her.

Abby giggled.

She was becoming one wicked woman, and wasn't it lovely? Actually, an icy shower might do her some good. One quick duck under the water, just long enough to soap up and rinse off...

Somewhere outside the cabin, an engine rumbled to life.

The generator.

"Oh, yes," Abby whispered.

Okay. She'd just wait in here for however long it took for the water to heat, then shower, get dressed, find the coffee and put on a pot...

The bathroom door swung open.

"Good morning."

Luke smiled at her, naked except for his white boxer briefs. He looked incredibly beautiful, incredibly sexy, incredibly everything.

"Good morning," Abby said, and before she could tell him

it wasn't fair that he was so wake-up gorgeous and she was such a mess, she was in his arms for a long, sweet kiss.

When it ended, Luke knotted his hands low on her spine and nodded at the shower stall.

"Forgot your basic science, huh? No power, no hot water."

"If that water could come out of that showerhead in little cubes, it would," she assured him, leaning back in his arms.

"Uh-huh. And aren't you lucky I was around to perform some magic?"

"Otherwise known as cranking up the generator."

"And here I was all prepared to tell you how I'm descended from a long line of shamans." When she lifted her eyebrows, he explained, "Magicians."

"Ah. That's nice. I like having my own personal magician."

Luke held her face in his hands and looked down at her wide, lovely eyes and tangled hair.

"What I like," he said softly, "is having my very own *ishcuss.*"

"Me?"

He laughed. "You."

"And is that good? For me to be your—"

"*Ishcuss,*" he said, and kissed the tip of her nose. "It's more than good. It's wonderful. It means you're my wild woman. My *sasquatch.* How else could you have stolen my heart so quickly?"

Abby put her arms around his neck.

"Magic," she whispered.

LUKE HAD PICKED UP SOME groceries along with the sandwiches back in Seattle. He'd bought eggs, bacon, bread, butter, coffee, even steaks and a bottle of wine for dinner tonight.

He was amazed he'd had enough presence of mind to think of such a mundane thing as food. And a good thing, too, because he was hungry enough to eat an elk.

So was his Abby. She said she would just have some toast and coffee… Okay, maybe an egg… Well, maybe a couple of slices of bacon…

He said yes, right, uh-huh—and went on cracking eggs and

turning over the browning slices of bacon on the old woodstove while Abby toasted bread over the fire he'd rekindled.

He put the food on the table as Abby buttered the toast, tut-tutting that he'd made enough food for an army. She took what he thought of as typical weight-conscious female helpings of everything and began eating…and then took seconds and thirds, just as he'd figured she would.

After the night they'd spent in each other's arms, she had to be as hungry as he was.

Watching her mop up the last of her eggs with a piece of toast, Luke was hungry all over again.

Hungry for Abby in his arms.

He'd been right to bring her here. She was at home in this place. She saw the beauty of it, fit into the settings of simple cabin and lush forest as if she'd been born to it.

As they ate, she'd asked him questions. What sort of animals lived in these woods? What was the name of that fern she could see through the window? How old were these immense trees?

His grandfather would have liked her.

"I bet I'd have liked him, too," Abby said, and Luke realized he'd spoken aloud.

"You would have. You guys would have gotten along just fine." He grinned. "For one thing, Grandpa always liked a lady with an appetite."

Abby grinned back at him. "Okay, Sloan. You were right and I was wrong, but don't let it go to your head."

"You go to my head," Luke said softly. He leaned toward her over the table and took her hand in his. "I love you, Abby."

Those words, those amazing words. They'd been said to her before but never like this, never from a man like this. Abby lifted their joined hands to her lips and brushed a kiss over Luke's work-roughened knuckles.

"I love you, too," she whispered, and thought how inadequate the words were.

How did you tell someone he'd fulfilled the dreams you'd long abandoned? That feeling what she felt now—loved, and safe, and happy—was all she'd ever wanted from life, and all she'd thought she'd never find?

Happy. It had been one of Em's favorite words when she was a toddler. *Emily happy, Mommy,* she'd said, but back then happiness had been an illusion for them.

This was real. It would endure. This was happiness, and that smile in Luke's eyes was love, and his arms were her safe haven.

All through the morning, while she'd watched him make breakfast, she'd thought about how much she loved him and what she had to do next.

It was time for the final giving of herself, and that meant telling him the truth about the marriage she'd escaped. There'd be no more lies between them, not after he'd opened himself to her so completely.

Abby swallowed hard.

"Luke?"

"Yes, sweetheart?"

"We have to talk."

The expression on his face turned grave and his hand tightened on hers.

"You're right. We do. Abby—"

"No." She shook her head. "Don't stop me, please. This isn't easy." She looked down into her cup, then raised her eyes to his. "I'm not proud of what I'm going to tell you. Try to understand. I did what I thought I had to do to survive."

Luke felt his heart plummet. Sweet God in heaven, it was true. Abby, his Abby, was involved in something criminal at the Emerald City Jewelry Exchange.

Okay. The thing was not to get worked up. He'd listen, then he'd tell her...tell her what? That he'd help her? Stand by her? Get her a good lawyer? Yes, of course he would, but what good would such help do? She'd have to stand trial, face a jury. Maybe even go to prison.

He felt his blood turn cold.

Why hadn't he realized all this sooner?

Maybe he could help her more by turning his back on everything he believed in, take her across to Canada. No. She'd never leave Emily. Okay. He'd get Em, slip into Canada with the kid...

And do what after that? Be fugitives for the rest of their lives? Yes, if they had to. If it was the only way they could be together.

God, oh God, oh God!

"Abby." Luke shot to his feet and pulled her up beside him. "Sweetheart, listen to me—"

His cell phone rang.

Jesus, not now! He wanted to let the damned thing ring itself into the ground, but Abby turned white.

"Emily," she said, digging her fingers into his arm.

Luke plucked the phone from his back pocket and flipped it open.

"Faith?"

"Who the hell is Faith?" Dan snarled, "and where the hell have you been, Sloan?"

"It's okay," he told Abby, covering the phone. "It's not Faith."

Abby shut her eyes and drew a deep breath, then let it out.

"It's—it's business. I'll take the call outside."

She looked at him strangely. Why wouldn't she? Why would a carpenter get a business call early Sunday morning when he was in the middle of nowhere?

He walked a few feet away from the cabin and put the phone to his ear again.

"What do you want, Dan?"

"Hell, I've been calling you every hour for the last—"

"I'm on the peninsula. At my cabin. Sometimes the phone works up here, sometimes it doesn't."

"Yeah, well in the future—"

"If this call is so goddamned important, get to it. What do you want?"

"Hey, man, I'm calling you with news. You don't want it, just say the word."

Luke rubbed a hand over his face. "Sorry. It's just—I'm in the middle of something. What's the news?"

"Well, for openers, guess who slinks into the Emerald City

Jewelry Exchange Saturday, carrying what looks to be a four-hundred buck attaché case. Forget the guessing game, I'll tell you who it is. Jack Rotter.''

''Who?''

''Luke, you paying attention here? Jack Rotter. We took him down for robbery and assault a few years ago. Little guy, quick fuse, looks like—''

''A weasel,'' Luke said, his pulse quickening. ''Yeah, I remember.''

''He still looks like a weasel, even when he goes into a place like Emerald City on a Saturday afternoon wearing a suit and tie.''

''And?''

''And, he comes out five minutes later, looking pissed. So I got out of the van, took myself on a stroll and caught up to old Jack. I hassled him a little, asked him what he was up to, how things were going…all nice and legal, I promise you.''

''Dan, for crissakes, get to it.''

''Jack gets nervous, thinks I know more than I do and hotfoots it up the street like he was wearing felony flyers, straight into the arms of the pair of uniforms that had just turned the corner. When we finally wrestle him down to the ground, the attaché case pops open.'' Dan chuckled. ''Man, it was like Christmas morning at the Rockefellers'. Half a million bucks worth of jewelry, all of it from that last robbery.''

For a moment, Luke forgot everything else and shared Dan's elation.

''Don't tell me,'' he said dryly. ''Jack said hey, he was just carrying the case for a friend and he didn't have any idea what was in it.''

''Wrong. Remember I said Jack seemed royally ticked off at something? Well, he was. Seems the lady he does business with at Emerald City —''

''Wasn't there,'' Luke said softly, certain he knew what was coming next.

''Exactly. Said the lady had made an appointment with him, that she'd pissed him off one time too many and he'd had it.''

Luke nodded. There was a sharp pain building in his temple, one he knew no amount of aspirin would relieve.

"Dan, listen—"

"The background checks you'd wanted had come in maybe an hour before. They were, like, the icing on the cake. Black's clean as a whistle. Comes from money. Private schools, Ivy League degree in art history. Travels in fancy circles. The odds on his fencing stolen property are zero to none."

"Yeah. Okay."

"Bettina Carlton. Not quite so clean. A couple of arrests for shoplifting in her early twenties, but that's it. After that, she's a model citizen. Odds on her being the fence…"

"Zero to none," Luke said quietly.

"Based on that, absolutely. So then I read the data on Abby Douglas." Dan hesitated. "You're not going to like this."

"Just tell me."

"Abby Douglas, born Abigail Chaplin in Eugene, Oregon."

"Oregon?"

"Yup. Married to Frank Douglas. Divorced him almost three years ago." Dan cleared his throat. "Here comes the bad part."

"Just tell me, okay? I can handle it. And, Dan, before you say anything else, you need to know I'm in love with her."

"Aw, man—"

"I love her." Luke's tone hardened. "Nothing you tell me will change that. Whatever she's done—"

"She didn't do anything."

"I'm going to stand by her, no matter— What do you mean she didn't do anything? You said you were going to tell me the bad part."

"More than bad, especially if you love the lady. See, her husband—he used to get pissed off, drunk, whatever, and he'd beat her up."

Luke sagged back against a tree.

"Neighbors called the cops. She did, too—the whole works." Dan paused. "Luke? You still there?"

Luke nodded, as if Dan could see him. "Yeah," he finally said. "Yeah, I'm here."

"I'm sorry, partner. I hate being the one to give you this kind of news."

"Was he arrested? Did the arresting officers put the fear of God into him?" Luke knotted his free hand into a fist. "Did Abby press charges?"

"Yeah, but it was the usual Saturday-night, booze-it-up and then-bash-the-old-lady crap we used to see when we were in patrol. He was going to change, yadda yadda yadda. She dropped the charges. Surprise, surprise, it started up again. She took her kid and ran. Ended up in a women's shelter and filed for divorce."

"And there's nothing else? No criminal history?"

"No."

Luke wanted to pump his fist into the air. Abby wasn't selling stolen jewels. She was on the run from a brute of a husband. That was the big secret she'd been so reluctant to tell him.

He turned and stared at the cabin, at Abby, standing in the open doorway, her arms wrapped around herself, her eyes on him.

"I'll call you later, Dan."

"Hey, show a little patience, okay? I didn't tell you the best part yet. Jack gave up the name of the fence. It's the Carlton woman. Would you believe it? Bettina Carlton, pulling deals right under Julian Black's nose. She buys the stuff, takes the stones out of the original settings, resets them, then sneaks them into stock right after inventory. Smart, huh?"

Luke thought back to what Abby had told him, that new pieces she'd never seen before were always turning up after inventory. Smart was right. What better way for Bettina to hide a rose than in a bouquet of roses?

For a moment, he felt the excitement of the breaking case leap in his blood. Then he looked at the cabin, saw Abby again, and knew that nothing mattered half as much as what he felt for her.

"Rotter's singing his heart out, doing a deal with the D.A. to get a reduced sentence. We'll arrest Carlton tomorrow, but I'm sure she's gonna play dumb. Smart lawyer will say all we

have is the word of a felon. If we only had somebody to cor-
roborate his story, we'd be home free.''

"I have to go, Dan."

"Like, maybe Abby, if she could think of something she
might have seen—"

Luke snapped the phone shut and turned it off. Abby was
watching him with apprehension as he headed for her.

"Something's wrong. I can tell. The look on your face…"

Hauling her into his arms, he stopped her words with a kiss.
She held back for a second. Then she kissed him, too.

"Abby." Luke rested his chin on the top of her head.
"Sweetheart, why didn't you tell me?"

"Tell you what?"

"You're not from San Francisco, you're from Oregon. Your
divorce wasn't just difficult, it must have been hell." A muscle
flickered in his jaw. "You should have told me."

Abby pulled free of his arms. She looked stunned. "You
know?"

"About your husband? That you ran away from him with
Em? Yeah, I know."

"*How* do you know?" Abby took a step back. Her face was
pale. "I was just going to tell you about my husband. How
could you know without me telling you?"

"The son of a bitch! If he ever gives me an excuse to lay
my hands on him…"

"But—but how do you know these things? Did you hire
someone? Did you go behind my back?"

"I know because I'm a cop, god damn it," Luke growled,
"and I could have helped keep you safe if you'd only…"

He fell silent, mercilessly pinned by the shock in Abby's
eyes.

"You're a cop?" She shook her head and gave a little laugh.
"No, you're not. You're a carpenter."

"I'm a detective with the Seattle Police Department," he
said, watching her face, glad the subterfuge was over but re-
gretting the way he'd blurted out the truth. "I'm working undercover at the day care center."

"Working undercover…?"

"Yes."

"You're not a carp—"

"No."

Luke reached for her, but she shook him off.

"You lied to me."

"Yes." He fought against grabbing her, holding her as he explained. "I lied," he said steadily, "but I had to."

"You had to."

Her voice was toneless. She wrapped her arms around herself again; she was trembling and he knew it wasn't with cold.

"Sweetheart—"

"All that stuff about wanting to bring me here so I'd know who you were, and meanwhile, you were living a lie."

"Just listen, okay? Don't say anything until you've heard me out."

She stared at him for what seemed an eternity. Then she nodded.

"I'm listening."

Luke took a steadying breath. "When a cop works undercover, nobody can know who he is or what he's doing, or he can compromise the investigation."

"You should have told me," she said, and he could tell from the set of her jaw that she was hearing what he said but not absorbing it.

"Abby." He gave in to his instincts and caught hold of her shoulders, holding on when she tried to jerk free. "I'm a cop, I have an obligation to the citizens of Seattle to catch the criminals who harm them. What do you think would happen if I went up to somebody when I'm doing my job, stuck out my hand and said, 'Hi, nice to meet you. I know you think I'm a ballet dancer, but the truth is—'"

"A ballet dancer?"

He could tell that she was trying not to smile. The knot in his gut began to ease. Maybe this would work out okay after all.

"You don't think I could pass myself off as a ballet dancer?"

She didn't answer, but he could see the color coming back to her face.

"Abby," he said softly, "when you came into my life, everything changed. I took one look at you and my world turned upside down." He slid his hands from her shoulders to her face. "I wanted to tell you the truth so badly, sweetheart, almost from the beginning. It's one of the reasons I brought you here, because it seemed like the right place to tell you who I really am."

"People should be honest with each other," Abby said stubbornly, but she didn't feel as rigid under his hands as she had a moment ago.

"You're a fine one to talk. Why didn't you tell me about your son-of-a-bitch husband?"

"So you could have done what? Looked at me with pity in your eyes?"

"Not pity, sweetheart. You're a strong, brave woman." Luke's eyes darkened. "You're still afraid of him."

Abby nodded. "He said things. About never letting me go…"

"Well, I damned well can change his mind," Luke said in a hard voice. "Abby…" His voice turned gentle. "I love you. And I respect the courage it took for you to build a new life for you and for Emily."

"Oh, Luke," Abby whispered. "Luke, I love you so much."

He lifted her to her toes and kissed her, holding her close and rocking her against him. It was going to be okay. Everything was out in the open. No more lies, no more anything to keep them apart.

"So, tell me!"

Luke drew back and smiled into Abby's eyes. "Tell you what?"

"What's going on at the day care that's got the police department interested?" The little smile that had begun forming on her lips faded. "It's not something dangerous to the kids, is it?"

"No, no. Nothing like that."

"Well, what is it? I can't imagine Hannah or Alexandra or Katherine involved in anything shady."

"They're not. It's—"

Luke hesitated. It was wrong to tell her any more than he already had, but he knew he'd trust this woman with anything, even his life. Besides, the investigation was pretty much over. They'd caught the crook, he'd ratted on Bettina. A corroborating witness would nail the case, but they didn't have one yet so they'd just have to rely on playing good cop, bad cop with Bettina.

But they did have a witness. Dan knew it. So did he. They had Abby. She could testify to what Rotter had said, that Bettina always moved pieces she fenced into stock after inventory.

No. God damn it, no! He'd never involve Abby. Never.

"Come on, Officer." Abby fluttered her lashes. "Tell me the juicy details."

"I'm surveilling the Emerald City Jewelry Exchange."

She stared at him, her expression blank. "The Emerald City... You mean, my store?"

"Yes."

"But why?"

"We had a report that somebody there might be buying and selling stolen jewelry." He smiled, thinking what a relief it was to get all this out in the open. "That was my partner on the phone just now. He called to say he knows who the fence is."

"This is impossible, Luke. Nobody at the store could possibly—"

"Well, we thought that way, too. See, what tipped us off was that one of your customers—"

"One of *my* customers?"

"Uh-huh. We've had a spate of robberies in some of the tonier areas of the city, some guy doing strong arm stuff and stealing only estate jewelry. Sweetheart? What's the matter?"

"I'm just trying to get this straight, that's all. How do you do your surveillance? Do you watch the store from the window in Katherine's office?"

"Right. And I have a camera set up. Two, actually, because I can get a clear view of the door to the jewelry exchange."

"And of my counter."

"Yes."

"And of me."

"Well, yeah, of you. But…"

Luke fell silent. He saw the way Abby was looking at him, heard his words echoing in his head.

"No. Abby, it's not what you're thinking."

"Were we all under suspicion?"

"Everyone's under suspicion in a situation like that."

Abby pulled away from him. "Everyone, including me."

Oh, shit. That look on her face. That ice in her voice.

"Sweetheart—"

"Answer the question," she said coldly. "Was I a suspect?"

"I told you, everyone was under—"

"And now I'm not. Because your partner just called and told you he caught the crook."

"Well, not yet. Not exactly. He knows who it is, but…"

Luke winced. What in hell did that matter right now? He could see what was happening, what Abby was thinking. "Sweetheart…"

Abby slapped at his hands as he reached for her. "Don't call me that!"

"Abby. You're getting this wrong."

"You came into my home, played with my child, befriended me." Her voice trembled. "Made *love* to me, and all the time you thought I was a criminal?"

"No! Yes!" Luke threw his arms wide. "Damn it, you're making it sound simple and it wasn't. I had no way of knowing who was doing what, don't you understand?" He swung around and paced a few feet, then turned and glared at her. "You think this was easy for me? Damn, when I think of how crazy I went when I saw Em wearing all that old jewelry—"

"It was my mother's jewelry," Abby said, her voice trembling. "I told you that."

"Yeah, but right then… Abby, don't look like that. A couple

of hours ago I looked at you and thought, okay, I can't believe she has any part in this, but if she does—''

''Oh, don't stop now. If she does, what? You'd have baked me a cake with a file in it once I was behind bars? Smuggled me over the border to Canada?''

She'd hit so close to the truth that he felt his face heat.

Abby's eyes narrowed. ''You lying bastard!''

''I never lied to you about anything that mattered!''

''You used me! You were so nice to me, to Emily. You pretended we meant something to you, and all the time—all the time...''

Her voice broke. Tears filled her eyes and she swung away from him, shoulders shaking, head bowed. He went to her and turned her toward him, but she drew back her arm and struck him hard in the face.

''Don't touch me,'' she said hoarsely. ''You hear me, Luke? Don't touch me, or talk to me, or come near me ever again.''

''Abby...''

She stormed away from him and into the cabin, and while he was still standing there, trying to come up with a way to make her see that he'd only been doing his job, she came marching out again, her duffel bag in her hand, and got into his SUV. She tossed the bag in the back, fastened her seat belt and waited.

Luke waited, too. Surely she'd change her mind, realize that he'd done what he had to do....

But it was as if she were made of stone. She didn't move, didn't even turn her face toward him.

Slowly Luke headed into the cabin. Once he'd killed the fire and turned off the generator, he came back out and got behind the wheel of the car.

So much for thinking he'd found the right woman, one who was interested in understanding him and his life. So much for thinking she'd understand the code by which he lived, the ethics of his profession.

So much for being dumb enough to think Abby loved him, or that he loved her, when all it had been was sex.

They drove all the way back to Seattle without either of them saying a word.

It was all over, Luke thought, watching Abby walk stiffly to the door of her house, and a damned good thing, too. Why in hell had he ever thought he needed a woman in his life?

Luke floored the gas and sped out of Abby's driveway, headed for the Nine-Thirty-One Tavern. At least there, Lacey would greet him with a smile....

But when he got to the tavern, he didn't pull into the lot behind it. Instead, he floored the gas again, drove to his condo and slammed the door shut on the world.

CHAPTER SIXTEEN

MONDAY MORNING, BRIGHT AND early, Katherine Kinard sat on the edge of her desk, arms folded, and watched Luke pack up the last of his surveillance equipment.

He'd already swept the area, boxed his carpentry tools and taken them out to his car. Another minute and the only sign that Forrester Square Day Care had been home to a surveillance operation would be the shelves and cabinets he'd built.

Katherine thought back to that first day Luke had turned up at the door. What had Daniel Adler told her then? Something about having been assured Sloan was a good cop who'd stay out of her way. Neither she nor Daniel had anticipated that he'd turn out to be an excellent craftsman, or that he'd make friends with so many of the children, especially after he'd grumbled about having to deal with them.

The kids would miss Luke Sloan, especially little Emily Douglas, who had become the detective's special pal.

Katherine tapped her index finger against her mouth.

Strange that Emily hadn't stopped in to say goodbye. Katherine had made a point of going from group to group first thing that morning, telling the children that their friend was leaving. They'd trooped in and out while he packed, giving him hugs, some of them handing over crayon drawings they'd made in his honor.

Not Emily, though Katherine had caught her peering into the office with a sad look on her face. Did that have some special meaning? Was the little girl more upset than she'd let on? Hannah had mentioned something about seeing the detective and Abby Douglas together

Was that part of the problem?

Katherine made a mental note to ask Marilyn Albee to keep an eye on Emily. If the girl's mother and the detective had forged some kind of relationship and it had gone bad, that was their business. If Emily was an innocent bystander caught up in the turbulence, it would be Forrester Square's business to help her through a bad time.

Nice man though he'd turned out to be, Luke Sloan's departure was welcome news. Hannah and Alexandra could move back into the office. And besides, the last thing a day care center needed was to be involved with the police.

As if on cue, Luke taped up the last carton and hoisted it under one arm.

"Well," he said, "that should do it."

Katherine stood up. "Goodbye, then, Detective Sloan. Thanks for that terrific storage area."

"Hey," he said lightly, "the Seattle PD lives to serve."

They smiled at each other.

"I'll remember that. Luke? Now that it's over, any chance you can tell me what's been going on?"

She hoped for a real answer, though she expected something humorous. *Sure, but if I did, I'd have to kill you.* That kind of thing. Instead, the detective got a grave look on his face.

"Sorry, I can't. We're still tying up loose ends."

"Ah, well. Can't blame me for trying."

"Goodbye, Katherine. Take care."

She stuck out her hand. Luke shook it, tossed her a quick salute and strolled out of her office for the last time.

Thank God, Luke thought. No more day care center. No more kids in his space. No more heartfelt offers of juice and milk and apples, no more quick hugs.

Damned if he wasn't going to miss all that.

The kids had come to say goodbye. They'd brought him drawings and cookies, given him sticky kisses.

Not Emily. She hadn't come near him.

He'd gone looking for her first thing this morning, wanting to tell her goodbye without an audience, but when she'd spotted him coming, she'd ignored him. Later, when the kids were having juice, he'd sought her out again.

"Em," he'd said, "princess..."

"I'm not your princess," she'd said, two huge tears rolling down her cheeks, and she'd turned away from him with a finality that had damn near broken his heart.

Whatever Abby had told the kid had turned her against him.

He'd dropped Abby off at her place Sunday afternoon, which meant she'd had plenty of time to go to Faith's, collect Em and tell her that Luke Sloan was the rotten human being they'd thought he was when he'd first come into their lives.

Well, so what?

Luke squared his shoulders as he loaded the last box into his car.

This had never been about winning a popularity contest. Abby, the kid, the silly weeks playing good guy at Forrester Square... An interlude, all of it, and now it was over. Yeah, he was sorry the kid's feelings were hurt, but that was part of growing up.

On the way to the station house, Luke stopped to buy two coffees, an espresso and a latte. When he reached the squad room, he deposited the latte on the edge of Dan's desk. His partner looked up, gave him a long once-over, then nodded.

"Thanks."

Luke slumped down behind his own desk. "No problem."

They sipped their coffee in silence for a few minutes.

"Guess you were right about bad cell phone connections up at your cabin," Dan said casually. "I must have tried to call you back half a dozen times before I gave up."

"Bad luck," Luke said, just as casually. "So, where are we? You get anything more out of Jack Rotter?"

"Details, nothing major." Dan shook his head. "Man, you look—"

"Spare me the eyewitness commentary, okay? I know how I look. We ready to arrest the Carlton woman?"

"Got a warrant, all nice and legal. I've just been waiting for you to show up."

Luke stood up. "Then let's do it."

"Well, there's one thing."

"Make up your mind, okay? Are we ready to roll or not?"

Dan put down his coffee. "Listen," he said quietly, "do us both a favor. You're in a bad mood, go punch the wall a couple of times. It's Monday morning, I spent yesterday trying to convince Molly now's not the time to redo the kitchen, and then I watched the Seahawks lose. I don't need this from you."

Luke stared at his partner, then sighed and scrubbed his hands over his face. "You're right. I'm sorry. I have—I have some personal stuff going on, but I shouldn't be taking it out on you."

"Anything you want to talk about?"

"No. I just want to make the arrest and close this damned file."

"Okay, fine." Dan started to get up. "In that case—"

"I told Abby I'm a cop."

Dan sat back down. He looked as surprised by the admission as Luke felt for having made it.

"I get the feeling the news didn't go over so well."

"It was okay until I told her that I've been observing the place where she works."

"Observing her."

"Yeah. That's what she said, too."

"She didn't like that, huh?"

"That's the understatement of the century. I even explained I'd have stuck by her, should it have turned out she'd been involved... What?"

"Nothing. Okay, look, I'm probably nuts. God knows, nobody's ever accused me of being the sensitive type, but even I can see how that wouldn't exactly make a woman feel a whole hell of a lot better."

"It was the truth, but that's the trouble. Women don't want to know the truth!"

"You got that right. Well, she'll get over it."

"I don't think so." Luke's mouth thinned. "Besides, what about me? I'm a cop. This is the sort of work I do. She's supposed to be smart enough to understand that. Was I supposed to put aside my professional obligations because I fell in—because I imagined that I felt something for her?"

Dan thought about pointing out that Luke had done just that

by getting involved with Abby in the first place, but he knew better than to go there.

"You know," he said carefully, "there's no reason for you to go over to that jewelry store with me. I can take a uniform with me while you do some paperwork."

"We started this together, we're ending it the same way. We're going to arrest Bettina Carlton for receiving stolen property."

"For selling it, too. Who'd have believed she takes the stolen pieces apart, has them reset and then mixes them into the regular stock and sells them right under the nose of the guy who owns Emerald City?"

"You think Black's in on it?"

"No. But we'll ask him nicely, to make sure." Dan grinned. "Just like we always do."

Luke grinned back. He felt better, being on the job again. "Anything else I need to know?"

Dan handed him a couple of four-by-six photos.

"These are some of the stolen pieces. The owners had the pictures filed with their insurance companies. Forget the settings, just look at the stones. A blood-red ruby, weighed in at ten carats. A perfect star sapphire. An emerald-cut diamond, 12.5 carats."

Luke whistled softly through his teeth.

"The Carlton woman had a good thing going, all right." Dan hesitated. "It would be a real stroke of luck if Abby had ever noticed stones as distinctive as these, or if she knew anything specific about how Bettina worked her scam."

"We agreed Abby wasn't involved in this," Luke said sharply.

"Yeah, but she might have seen something useful without knowing what it was."

Dan was right. Witnesses to criminal acts often thought they'd seen nothing important, but under questioning revealed that they had.

Abby had already told him that Bettina rarely remembered to put price stickers on new pieces she added after inventory, and that when Abby asked her for the prices, Bettina said she would handle those sales herself.

The odds were there were no records of those sales. Bettina would have simply pocketed the money. That, coupled with Abby's testimony about how those sales were handled, would be damning evidence against Bettina. And if Abby recalled any of the more unusual stones, it would be icing on the cake.

Somebody would have to question Abby, and he was the one to do it. He knew her; Dan didn't. He didn't want to, but hell, what did it matter? She already believed he'd used her, that he hadn't trusted her, that he'd imagined her capable of being a criminal.

What were a few questions on top of all that? He could hardly do more to make her despise him.

He was a cop. This was his job. Whose fault was it that women didn't understand the world could be a crappy place?

"You're right," Luke said grimly. "Abby Douglas might know something that will help us." He got to his feet and put on his jacket. "Where's that arrest warrant?"

"Right in my pocket."

"Then let's go execute it."

"I AM APPALLED," JULIAN BLACK said, "utterly appalled to think my manager would be involved in such a nefarious scheme. Are you sure of the facts, gentlemen?"

Luke nodded. "I'm afraid we are."

"Incredible." Black paced his office, his hands folded behind his back, a look of bewilderment on his face. "Bettina, of all people. When I think how I've trusted her..." He paused suddenly and peered at Luke. "Haven't we met before, Detective?"

"Yes, sir. Early on a Saturday morning, a couple of weeks ago. My partner and I—"

"Of course." Black nodded. "I'd asked Ms. Carlton to come in early and help me get a head start on inventory that day. To think she was selling stolen jewelry right under my nose..." He frowned. "Detective Shayne identified himself as a police officer that morning, but you said you worked across the street.''

Luke shrugged. ''I was working undercover.''

''On this case?'' Black gave a little laugh. ''Amazing! If only the authorities had let me in on things, I might have been of help. But I suppose I was kept in the dark because I was under suspicion, too. Am I right?''

Luke acknowledged Black's supposition with a smile.

''Everyone's always a suspect until we identify the perpetrator, Mr. Black.''

Emerald City's owner settled into the black Eames chair opposite the small white leather sofa on which Luke and Dan were sitting.

''I suppose I can't be offended by that. Your business is catching criminals. Mine is dealing in fine jewelry. We each know how to do our jobs. But Bettina Carlton...'' He shook his head. ''I want her arrested quickly, gentlemen, before she has the chance to do any more damage. Not on the selling floor, though. The good name of my store... Perhaps you'd let me get her by myself? I won't let on what's happening, of course....''

''That's fine,'' Luke said. ''Bring her here. My partner will arrest her, read her her rights and take her out as quietly as possible.''

''Excellent.''

''While you do that...'' Luke cleared his throat. ''I'd like to speak with Abby Douglas. Is there someplace where we won't be disturbed?''

''Don't tell me that sweet young woman is involved in this, too!''

''She's not. But we think she might have inadvertently witnessed some things that will help our case.''

''How interesting.''

Luke knew Black was waiting for him to explain, but until he questioned Abby, he wasn't about to say anything more. Instead, he got to his feet. Dan and Julian Black took his cue and rose, too.

''Very well, gentlemen. I'll get Ms. Carlton. And you can

use the employees' locker room in the back for your chat with Ms. Douglas.''

Black and Luke went down the short flight of steps that led to the selling floor. Then they went in different directions, Black to the discreetly placed alcove where Bettina had a desk and computer, Luke to the estate jewelry counter.

Abby hadn't seen him enter the store. She'd been on a coffee break. Now she was working, showing necklaces to a customer.

Luke paused a few feet away, wanting to fill his eyes with her…wanting to purge his heart of what it still felt.

What if he said to hell with everything, took Abby in his arms and kissed her? What if he went on kissing her until she kissed him back, admitted she loved him so that he could admit he loved her, that he'd always love her?

The customer moved off. Abby opened the glass case and put away the tray of necklaces as Luke went toward her. She looked up, smiled pleasantly—and her expression changed. He saw the shock in her face, and then the anger.

''What are you doing here?'' she demanded.

''I have to talk to you.''

''I don't have anything to say to you, Detective Sloan.''

''Damn it, Abby—''

''Is there a problem here, Ms. Douglas?''

A guy in a security guard's uniform stepped up to the counter, his eyes steely under bushy gray eyebrows as he glared at Luke.

Great. Just what this scene needed. An old man who wanted to play Dirty Harry.

''I didn't notice you come in, mister.'' The guard's hand hovered just above his holstered gun.

''Easy, Pop,'' Luke said softly. ''I'm a cop.''

''Prove it. Take out your shield, nice and slow.''

Luke took his badge from his pocket, his eyes never leaving the old man's.

''See? Detective Sloan, Robbery and Homicide. I'm here to question Ms. Douglas.''

The guard looked startled. ''Our Abby?''

"It's all right, Bill. I know the detective." Abby's eyes flashed to Luke's. "Am I under arrest?"

"You know better than that."

"I don't know anything," she said, her words heavy with sarcasm. "Not where you're concerned. Where do you want to question me?"

The back room, he began to say. Instead, he jerked his head toward the street and Caffeine Hy's, right across the way.

"How about coffee?"

"With a touch of hemlock?" Abby said sweetly.

Luke gritted his teeth as he tucked his shield into his pocket and reached for her arm.

It was drizzling outside and neither of them had a coat, but he didn't care. He checked traffic, hurried her across the street and into the warm interior of the coffee shop.

"Grab a table. I'll get the coffee."

"Get your own. I don't want any."

He bought two coffees, anyway, and plunked one in front of Abby, who looked at it disdainfully and pushed it aside.

"What do you want?"

"We're arresting Bettina Carlton for receiving and selling stolen property."

Her mouth dropped open. "Bettina? No way! Bettina's not a crook."

"That's for a jury to decide. What I need is your help in corroborating some information."

"I have no interest in helping you, Detective Sloan."

Luke leaned forward. "Listen," he said in a clipped voice, "we can do this here or down at the station. Your choice."

The look she gave him would have frozen seawater.

"What do you want to know?"

"Does Bettina always work the estate counter alone on Saturdays?"

"As far as I know, yes, she works the counter alone on Saturdays. Is that it?"

"Not yet. How come? Isn't it unusual that a manager would take a Saturday shift?"

"Bettina was kind enough to understand I needed Saturdays

off so I could be with Emily. But that's only been for the last couple of weeks. Now, if that's all…''

Luke grabbed Abby's hand before she could slide from the booth.

''Those pieces you said she added after inventory, the ones she didn't put prices on.''

''How nice,'' Abby said, her eyes hot with rage. ''I was making conversation. *You* were taking notes.''

''You said you'd turn the customers interested in those pieces over to Bettina,'' Luke said, refusing to be drawn into defending himself for doing his job. ''Did she make the sales at the counter, or did she make them in that private office of hers?''

Abby hesitated. He could see the beginning of doubt in her eyes.

''She'd take those customers to the alcove.''

''So, you never saw a sales slip?''

''No. But that doesn't mean—''

''Can you recall what the stones in some of those pieces looked like? Would you remember them if you saw them again?''

''I might,'' she said reluctantly. ''Some were unusual.''

Luke took the photos from his inside jacket pocket and put them in front of Abby. She examined them, frowned and looked up.

''Never mind the settings. Do you recognize any of the stones?''

''It's hard to say without more information, but…the ruby. And the sapphire. Maybe that diamond. They look familiar. So what?''

Luke put the pictures away. ''Would you have any problem telling a judge and jury what you've just told me?''

''I still don't think…''

''Bettina's a crook,'' Luke said flatly. ''And the D.A. can subpoena you, if you don't agree to cooperate.''

Abby flushed. ''You have a way with words, Detective. Is there anything else?''

"No. Yes. Goddamn it, didn't this past weekend mean anything to you?"

"You mean, the weekend you lied to me?"

"Why didn't you tell me you'd run from the son of a bitch that hurt you?" Luke said, ignoring the taunt.

"I didn't see that it was any of your business, just like you didn't see that telling me you were a cop was any of mine."

"Abby." Luke leaned over the table. "I could have helped you. Protected you. Kept you from having to live in fear."

"You mean, because you're a policeman? Maybe you've forgotten I had no idea that's what you were."

"I'm talking as a man, damn it, not as a cop."

"You lied to me. Used me. Even suspected me of being a crook." Her mouth trembled. "I'm glad I didn't confide in you."

"I did my job."

"I know." Her eyes glittered, not with anger but with tears. "The thing is, you did it too well."

"Abby—"

Luke reached for her hand. She pulled it away and rose from the table.

"Goodbye, Luke," Abby said, and all he could do was watch her walk out of the coffee shop and out of his life.

CHAPTER SEVENTEEN

MOLLY SHAYNE OPENED THE OVEN, pulled the bottom tray out halfway and regarded the enormous turkey browning in its pan.

"Beautiful," she murmured, and dipped a pastry brush into a bowl of melted butter.

"Beautiful, indeed," Dan said, coming up behind her and kissing the back of her neck.

Molly dimpled as she basted the bird. "I was talking about the turkey."

"He's beautiful, too."

Once she'd shoved the tray back inside the oven, Molly closed the door and turned in her husband's arms.

"I like you in that dress," he said.

"I'm glad, because it set you back a pretty penny." She smiled and kissed him. "I can hardly believe it's Thanksgiving. Where has the month gone?"

"Where has the day gone, you mean," Dan said plaintively. "My stomach's asking when we're going to eat."

"Tell it to be patient, and make do with the shrimps and the dip." Molly pressed another kiss to her husband's mouth, then gently disentangled herself from his arms so she could drain the water from the potatoes that had been boiling on the back burner. "Where are the boys?"

Dan smiled. "In the den, forgetting they're almost all grown up as they kill the monsters on their GameBoys."

"Where'd you find those old things?"

"I think Dan Junior dredged them out of his closet. I've told them to hurry and finish their game, because we're eating soon."

Molly smiled at the wistful tone in her husband's voice.

"And we will," she said, "just as soon as Luke gets here."

Dan sighed, plucked a sugar snap pea from another pan and crunched down on it before his wife could slap his fingers.

"Luke isn't coming," he said. "I told you that already."

"He always comes here for Thanksgiving."

"Well, not this year."

"No. He'd rather sit home and brood over what an ass he's been."

"Molly—"

"Oh, it's the truth, Daniel Shayne, and you know it!" Molly swung around, her hands on her hips. "Blaming that poor girl for not telling him she'd run away from her husband. For goodness' sake, why *would* she have told him?"

"Well, because—"

"Did she know anything about Luke? No. Was he honest with her? No."

"He couldn't tell her he was a cop, Moll. Surely you understand that."

"Oh, I understand, all right." Molly picked up a long wooden spoon and started to stir the turkey broth simmering in a pan, then changed her mind and poked the spoon at Dan instead. "He broke her heart. A man has no right to sleep with a woman without being honest with her."

"Now, Molly, we don't know that—"

"Of course he slept with her! They made love, Daniel, otherwise neither of them would be so upset."

"You never even met Abby. How can you know she's—"

"I'm a woman, aren't I? She's upset. She's more than upset, she's heartsick. Didn't that marriage of his teach the man anything? Either you open yourself up to someone you love or you lose them." Molly stabbed the spoon into the broth. "Not that his ex-wife was worth keeping."

"Be reasonable, Molly. If Luke had told Abby the truth about himself—"

"And then, trying to make her feel better by telling her if she had been a crook, he'd have stood by her."

"Mother of God," Daniel said, rolling his eyes. "I shouldn't have told you any of this."

"Of course he'd have stood by her. Of course he wouldn't have abandoned her. We all know that." Molly turned the spoon toward Daniel again and he danced back a step. "But could a man be thick enough to expect a woman to throw herself into his arms with joy at such a declaration?"

"He shouldn't have said it?"

"Are you dense, Daniel? Yes. He should have said it, but there are ways to tell a woman things...." Molly sighed and shook her head, turning back to the stove. "Luke still loves her."

"He says he doesn't," Dan said carefully.

"Who cares what he says? He loves her. One look at his face and any fool can tell that."

Dan nodded. He was male and he was often a fool, but even he could see what was in his partner's eyes.

"Luke went to Oregon," he said in a low voice. "Paid a visit to Abby's ex."

Molly's eyes widened. "And?"

"And...Luke told him to stay away from Abby and the child, or he'd be happy to have him try to resist when he arranges for his arrest for violating the restraining order." Dan gave a quick smile. "I'm sure the gentleman got the message."

"You see? I *told* you Luke loves her!"

"Maybe so, but it's too late to do anything about it. Abby won't see him."

"Has he actually *tried* to see her?"

"I told you, Moll, when we arrested that woman—"

"Great God almighty, I don't believe it! Luke told Abby he was a cop on Sunday, went to question her as a cop on Monday, and she said she never wanted to see him again. And he's willing to let it go at that?"

"Don't you two have anything better to do than talk about me?"

Daniel and Molly looked toward the front of the kitchen. Luke stood in the arched entryway, a bottle of wine in each hand.

"The boys let me in the front door. I thought I'd come in that way, seeing as it's a holiday." No one smiled. No one laughed. Luke sighed. "You two really need to find a hobby," he said. "Seems as if every time I step in here, I find myself the topic of conversation."

"It's Molly," Dan said. "She worries about you."

Luke put the wine on the counter.

"One red, one white, because I never can remember which goes best with turkey." His expression softened as he came toward Molly. "I'm fine. Honestly, I am. I'll be even better after I've had some of that food that smells so good."

Molly let Luke kiss her cheek, but she kept her hands planted on her hips.

"Daniel didn't think you were coming."

"Ah. Well, I changed my mind. Somehow, the prospect of a frozen turkey dinner just didn't—"

"Is Dan right? That you've not tried to see this woman since you interrogated her?"

"Aw, hell." Dan pulled out a chair at the kitchen table and sank into it. "Luke," he muttered, putting his head in his hands, "I'm sorry."

"Answer the question, Luke Sloan. Is he right?"

"Molly. I know you mean well, but you don't understand. You're making much more out of this than—"

"Do you love her?"

"Hey. Listen, I appreciate your concern, but you've no right—"

"It's a simple question. Even a cop should be able to answer it."

"And what's that supposed to mean?" Luke said, his voice hardening.

"Oh, you know. Simple questions deserve simple answers. Yes or no, black or white, no in-between. Men who wear badges usually can't deal with anything more complicated than that."

Dan gave a soft groan. Molly ignored him.

"Do you love this Abigail Douglas woman?"

"Molly, I adore you, but this really isn't any of your business."

"It is my business. I want to see you happy."

"If you do, you'll drop this conversation right now."

"You're in love with her, and you're afraid to admit it."

"Damn it to hell," Luke growled, "you're spouting nonsense. Afraid? Me?" He paced the length of the big room, swung around and glared at Molly. "I told Abby I was in love with her. Okay? Are you satisfied? And she said she loved me, but she loved the man she thought I was, not the man I really am."

"And how do you know that?"

"Because she turned away from me when I told her I was a cop."

"You told her more than that. You said you'd thought she might be guilty of fencing stolen jewels."

"Damn it, Shayne, do you tell your wife everything?" Luke demanded hotly.

"I put a red-hot poker to his privates," Molly said, before her husband could open his mouth. "First you told her you'd considered her a suspect in a criminal case. Then you told her you'd have stood by her if it turned out you were right."

"And you know what she did with that? With me saying I'd have defied the department, defied my bosses—hell, that I'd have quit my job, if it came to that, to stand by her?" Luke stalked to within an inch of Molly and glared at her. "She tossed it in my face, that's what. I said I'd give up everything I had, everything I was, and she said, thank you very much and now get the hell out of my life."

"Did you really tell her those things?"

"What, that I'd have done anything to help her? That I love her more than I ever imagined you could love someone?"

"Yes," Molly said, her tone gentling. "All that. Every bit of what you just told me."

"Of course." Luke's mouth thinned. "Not in those exact words, maybe."

"Why not?"

"Because she understood. She knew." He paused, cocked his head as if he were listening to a voice only he could hear. "She must have known, Moll," he said. "How could she not?"

"She had a husband who abused her. A life spent listening for footsteps. And suddenly a man comes along and sweeps her off her feet. He says he loves her, and then she finds out that what was happening wasn't about her, it was about something else entirely."

"No. It *was* about her. About loving her."

"Yes, but is that how it seemed to Abby? Be honest with yourself, Luke. Look at things from her vantage point and then see if you can still say, well, she must know what I feel without me telling her.

"Luke," Molly continued gently, "I know you. I know you'd never use anyone, the same as I know you love Abby Douglas with all your heart. But sometimes—sometimes, a woman needs to hear it all, you know? To have her man tell her he'd sacrifice the earth for her, that given a choice between her and his world, he'd choose her."

The kitchen filled with silence. Then Luke hauled Molly into his arms and hugged her tight. He held out his hand to Dan, but when his partner got to his feet, Luke muttered something instead and caught him in a bear hug.

"Don't hold dinner for me," he said, and before either Molly or Dan could say a word, he raced out the back door.

ABBY OPENED THE OVEN DOOR, took out the pan that held the turkey and put it on the top of the stove.

The turkey was a sad-looking thing, hardly bigger than a chicken, but how much could she and Emily eat? As it was, they'd be eating turkey sandwiches, turkey casserole and turkey à la king for a week. She'd invited Faith and Lily to join them for dinner, but Faith had taken possession of the house she'd recently bought and was eager to celebrate the holiday in her new home.

"Why don't you guys come to us?" she'd said.

Abby had thanked her and mumbled something about staying home and having a quiet holiday. Faith, reading the pain in her friend's eyes, had hugged her and said the invitation was open, should Abby change her mind.

Now as she looked at the turkey again, Abby sighed.

Maybe she should have accepted Faith's invitation. It was unfair to Emily, all this moping around, especially since Em was doing her own share. Her little girl missed Luke, but moping wasn't permitted today.

This was Thanksgiving, a day that was supposed to be all smiles and thankfulness. And she had a lot to be thankful for. This apartment. Her job. Faith's friendship. A sweet, wonderful daughter...

What was Luke thankful for today?

Abby cleared her throat.

"Em?" she called. "Dinner's almost ready."

No answer. Abby checked the candied sweet potatoes, the mashed white potatoes, the peas cooked with mint—Emily's absolute favorite—and tried again.

"Honey? Do you want milk or apple juice with your meal?"

"I don't care."

The voice came from right behind her. Her daughter had slipped into the kitchen and was sitting at the table. The expression on her face made Abby's heart constrict.

"There you are," Abby said brightly. "Oh, I almost forgot to take the cranberries from the—"

"Mommy?"

"Yes, baby?"

"You think Luke is all alone today?"

"I don't know, Em."

"It's not nice to be alone on a holiday."

"Well, we're not alone," Abby said briskly. "I have you and you have me."

"I wish Luke was here, too."

"Just look at that! I folded those napkins wrong. Would you redo them, please?"

Emily moved the forks aside and smoothed out the special napkins with pilgrims on them that Abby had bought.

"Why did Luke stop loving us, Mommy?"

Abby swung toward her daughter.

"Em. Please, let's not—"

"Did I do something he didn't like?"

"No!" Abby squatted down and clasped Emily's hands. "I

told you, baby. It was a grown-up thing between Luke and me. It had nothing to do with you."

"Lily said, 'I told you so.'" Emily's eyes filled with tears. "She says we're never going to have a daddy."

"Come here," Abby said fiercely, and drew her child into her arms. She rocked her gently and kissed her face, tasting salty tears. She didn't know if they were hers or Em's.

"I loved Luke," her daughter sobbed, and Abby couldn't hold back the truth.

"I loved him, too," she said brokenly, "but—but it just went wrong, baby, it just went wrong."

"Can't you fix it, Mommy? Can't you make everything okay again?"

Abby buried her face in her little girl's neck. "I wish I could," she whispered. "But this is something nobody can fix."

"I can," a deep voice said, "if only you'll let me."

Abby shot to her feet and spun around. Luke stood in the open doorway, an enormous bouquet of roses in one arm and a huge pink elephant in the other.

"Abby?"

She could see his Adam's apple lift, then drop as he swallowed.

"The door was open, so I just—"

"Luke!" Emily shrieked, and ran to him.

Luke dropped the roses and the elephant on the table and caught the little girl in his arms, hugging her tight. His princess was weeping, but how could her tears be streaming down his cheeks? Unless they were his tears...

"Princess," he whispered. "I've missed you."

"I missed you, too. Oh, I missed you a whole lot!"

Luke hugged Emily again and looked over her head at Abby. She hadn't moved, hadn't smiled, hadn't done anything except stare at him.

Slowly, his eyes never leaving Abby's, he put Em on her feet.

"Is that elephant for me?" she said breathlessly.

Luke nodded. "Yes, honey. He's for you."

Em grabbed the elephant, which was almost as big as she was, and hugged it to her.

"I'm gonna call him Babar. Is that okay? He doesn't have a crown or anything, but he reminds me of Babar. Do you know who Babar is, Luke?"

"Babar's a wise old king," Luke said. "He knows how to say the right words when he needs to." A little smile curved his mouth. "Maybe that's why he's an elephant instead of a man."

Did that draw the faintest of answering smiles from Abby? It was hard to tell. She was so far away from him, not only in physical distance but in all the ways that mattered. How was he going to make her understand that she was his heart? His soul? That she was his life?

For the first time since he was a little boy, Luke Sloan felt the coppery taste of fear.

"Abby," he said. "I have to talk to you."

Abby's heart felt as if it were lodged in her throat. She wanted to fly across the room the way Emily had, throw herself into Luke's arms…

But he'd hurt her once. Why would she be foolish enough to leave herself open to more hurt? Why would she drag Emily through all this pain again?

"I love you," Luke said clearly.

Abby shook her head. What did love really mean? To her husband, it had meant the right to control her. To Luke, it had meant the right to lie to her.

"Emily?" Luke said. "Princess, how about taking Babar to your room and introducing him to your dolls?"

Abby started to countermand the suggestion, but Emily was already beside her, tugging on her apron.

"Mommy?" she whispered.

"Yes, baby?" Abby said, bending down.

Emily put her lips to Abby's ear. "I know you don't think so, but Luke loves us."

"Oh, Em."

"He does, Mommy. I know he does."

Abby looked from her little girl to the man she loved. The

man she would always love, from now until the end of time. His eyes were dark with anguish, and bright with something else.

With tears.

She rose to her feet. Emily scampered away, her elephant in her arms. Abby took a hesitant step forward.

"You hurt me," she said.

He nodded. "I know."

"But—but I was wrong, too. You had a job to do, and you did it."

"My job didn't mean a damn after I fell in love with you."

Abby's lips curved in a smile. "Your job means the world to you, Detective Sloan. And it should. You're a fine police officer."

Luke started toward her, eyes locked to hers.

"I love you with all my heart, Abby. With my soul, my mind, my spirit, with everything that I am or ever hope to be." He stopped inches from her, breathing in her scent, remembering the taste of her lips, the silkiness of her hair. "I want to marry you, sweetheart. To share my life with you. To raise Emily as my own, to have more kids and a dog and a house and to know that you're waiting for me each night—"

Abby sobbed Luke's name and flung herself into his open arms.

"I love you," she said. "I'll love you forever."

He drew her close. Their lips met in the most tender of kisses as she wound her arms around his neck.

They held each other tight, knowing how close they'd come to losing the joy they'd found. And when, moments later, they felt the sweet warmth of a child's arms wind around their legs, Abby and Luke laughed, bent down as one and brought Emily into the warmth of their embrace, where she would always belong.

EPILOGUE

NIGHT HAD FALLEN ACROSS Seattle, and windows glowed with light.

Candles flickered brightly on dining room tables topped with linen napery, fine china and sterling. Ceiling fixtures illuminated kitchen tables gaily outfitted with paper turkeys and cardboard pilgrims.

Thanksgiving, that most American of holidays, was almost over. People were prolonging its end, still eating and laughing together as they shared old memories and created new ones.

But not everyone was celebrating.

In an elegant house on a hill overlooking the bay, a man sat alone in a high-ceilinged room lit only by the flames blazing on the hearth of a stone fireplace. Shadows lay like mist in the corners of the room, but it didn't matter.

The man knew the room as well as he knew the beat of his heart.

The room, like the house, was filled with the fruits of his wealth. An eclectic mix of elegant furniture that spanned two centuries. Paintings by Degas, de Kooning and Johns. An antique Aubusson carpet. Even the brandy snifter on the table beside him was priceless, as was the liquid in it.

The man cradled the snifter in his hands, swirling it to warm the Napoleon brandy, then lifting it to his nostrils so he could draw the rich aroma deep into his lungs.

This was his kingdom. His father had left him a fortune, but what was money without beauty? He had created that beauty, designed the lifestyle that was his.

And all of it was about to end.

How stupid he'd been to rely on Bettina Carlton. He'd found

her, seen the possibilities in her, molded her into the woman he'd wanted, but the old saying was true.

You couldn't make a silk purse out of a sow's ear, no matter how you tried.

He lifted the snifter to his lips and drank.

Because of her stupidity, two people—two small, insignificant human beings who had never dined with senators or spent a weekend on a king's yacht—were going to destroy him.

It was almost impossible to believe.

A policeman who spent his days dealing with common criminals and a woman fit to do nothing more than sell baubles were going to ruin his life.

The man sipped at the brandy as he stared into the flames.

They would pay. All of them. He'd see to that. Bettina, for failing him. The cop, for setting the trap that caught her. The woman, for providing the incontrovertible proof.

His hands tightened on the glass.

The woman was the worst. Without her testimony, the case against Bettina would collapse.

But she could be dealt with. If he was to lose everything, so would she. He'd make sure of it.

For the first time in days, the man smiled. He raised his glass and saluted the darkness.

"To Abby Douglas," he said softly, "and to the pain she'll suffer."

He drained the last drops of brandy from the snifter, then hurled it into the fireplace. His smile turned to laughter as the glass shattered into dozens of bright shards.

Let the fools outside these walls celebrate a meaningless holiday.

He would celebrate the only thing that mattered.

The taking of revenge.

FORRESTER SQUARE,
a new Harlequin series,
continues in December 2003
with KEEPING FAITH
by Day Leclaire...

Even after learning Ethan Dunn was a merce-
nary, Faith Marshall had dreamed of a "white
picket" life together. Then she was told he had died.
But Faith's memory had kept the captive Ethan
alive. Now his search for her lead to Seattle, where
headlines blared Local Girl Abducted. Faith's little
girl...and he was the father. Ethan would do every-
thing in his power to rescue their child. But was it
in his power to make them a family?

Here's a preview!

CHAPTER ONE

FOR THE FIRST TIME in five and a half long, lonely years, Ethan felt hope stir.

The minute they came up for air, Faith's words flowed, singing in his ear like the sweetest jazz, tumbling over themselves in a rhythmic staccato. "You have no idea. It's been awful. Awful! I needed you. Badly. Elizabeth helped, but it wasn't the same. It took years before I came to terms with—" The singing ended as abruptly as it had begun, the jazz fading from the air on a jarring note. "I hurt for years and years, Ethan. But you…you said you were only imprisoned for—"

She broke off, struggling free of his arms. She took a quick step backward, then another. He stood silently, waiting. He knew what she was thinking.

"Say it," he ordered.

She'd gone from joy to fury in the space of a heartbeat. "You son of a bitch," she whispered. "You said six months. You said they imprisoned you for six months. What about the rest of that time? What about all those years I thought you were dead? Where the *hell* have you been?"

"Staying out of your life."

"No sh—"

Lily. She shook her head, her thoughts muddled and confused. Too much was happening too fast. First Lily was taken. Then, Ethan arrived. Lily, then Ethan, Lily, Ethan. Her brain made the connection, two pieces of a jigsaw puzzle locking together even though the colors looked wrong and the fit was slightly off. It didn't matter. She'd found a possible passageway through the chaos and she seized on it, desperately following it to its irrational conclusion. It was something she

could focus on, a possibility she could grab hold of, an avenu
of hope. It was a road to Lily, no matter how skewed a road

The timing of Ethan's return struck her as too convenien
too orchestrated. The minute Lily disappeared, her fathe
showed up on her doorstep. What were the chances that th
two were unrelated? Somewhere between zero and none. Sh
faced him down, half crazed, exhaustion vying with a disori
enting combination of fear and suspicion.

"Where's my daughter?" The question exploded from hei

"That's what I'm here to find out."

"No. *No!*" She wouldn't let him get away with it. "Where'
Lily? Did you take her? Do you have my daughter?"

"Is that what you think?" he asked. He stared at her wit
the sort of impassive expression she remembered from old. I
meant that he'd stuffed his emotions into an unreadable pit. I
meant he was hurting. Not that she cared. She was hurting, too
"You think I'd snatch her like some sort of lowlife thug?"

No. Yes. She pressed her hands against her temples. Sh
didn't know anything anymore. The one fact she could stat
with any certainty was that her daughter had been taken. "Ho
should I know what you might do? You've lied to me before
You claimed you were a businessman, when in truth you wer
a mercenary. You promised you were through with all that
then went back the minute they called. Even your death was a
lie." Her arms dropped to her sides, her hands balling into fists
"Now answer me, damn you! Did you take Lily?"

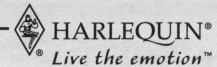

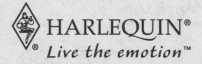

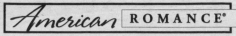
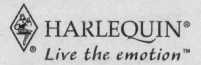

HARLEQUIN®
INTRIGUE®

BREATHTAKING ROMANTIC SUSPENSE

Shared dangers and passions lead to electrifying
romance and heart-stopping suspense!

Every month, you'll meet six new heroes
who are guaranteed to make your spine tingle
and your pulse pound. With them you'll enter
into the exciting world of Harlequin Intrigue—
where your life is on the line
and so is your heart!

THAT'S INTRIGUE—
ROMANTIC SUSPENSE
AT ITS BEST!

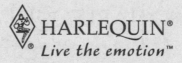

HARLEQUIN®
Live the emotion™

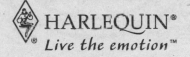

Harlequin® Historical
Historical Romantic Adventure!

Imagine a time of chivalrous knights and unconventional ladies, roguish rakes and impetuous heiresses, rugged cowboys and spirited frontierswomen— these rich and vivid tales will capture your imagination!

Harlequin Historical . . . they're too good to miss!